SPQR V

SATURNALIA

Also by
JOHN MADDOX ROBERTS

Other Books in the SPQR Series

SPQR V

SATURNALIA

JOHN MADDOX ROBERTS

THOMAS DUNNE BOOKS
ST. MARTIN'S MINOTAUR
NEW YORK

THOMAS DUNNE BOOKS.

An imprint of St. Martin's Press.

Production editor: David Stanford Burr

Design by Heidi Eriksen

Map by Mark Stein

Library of Congress Cataloging-in-Publication Data

Roberts, John Maddox.

SPQR V : Saturnalia / John Maddox Roberts.—1st St. Martin's
Minotaur ed.

p.   cm.

ISBN 0-312-20582-1

I. Title.   II. Title: Saturnalia.

PS3568.O23874S66   1999

813'.—dc21   99–22250

CIP

First Edition: October 1999

10   9   8   7   6   5   4   3   2   1

For Priscilla Ridgeway

who wouldn't give up,

eternal thanks for years of support

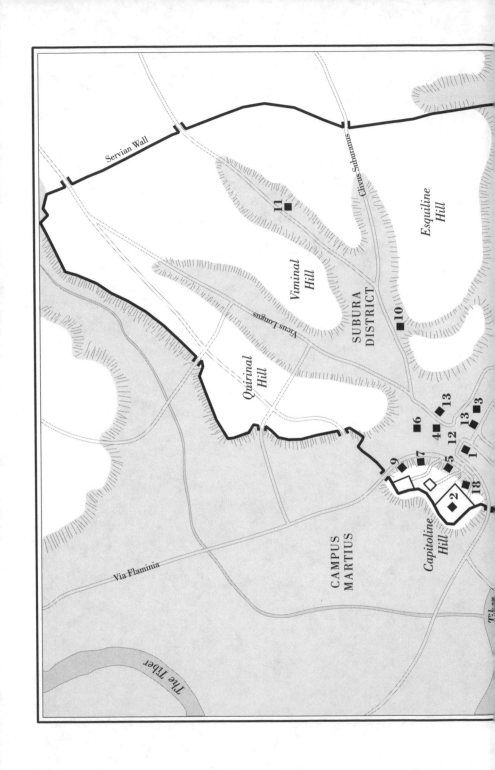

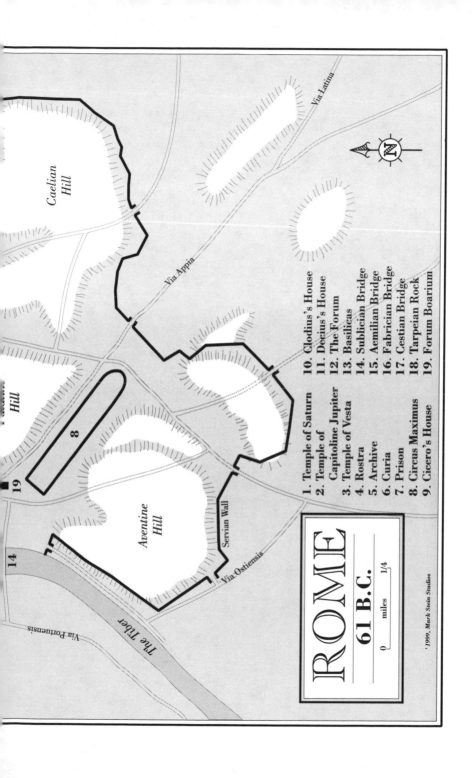

ROME
61 B.C.

0   miles   1/4

© 1999, Mark Stein Studios

The Tiber

Via Portuensis

Via Ostiensis

Servian Wall

Via Appia

Via Latina

Caelian Hill

Aventine Hill

Palatine Hill

1. Temple of Saturn
2. Temple of Capitoline Jupiter
3. Temple of Vesta
4. Rostra
5. Archive
6. Curia
7. Prison
8. Circus Maximus
9. Cicero's House
10. Clodius's House
11. Decius's House
12. The Forum
13. Basilicas
14. Sublician Bridge
15. Aemilian Bridge
16. Fabrician Bridge
17. Cestian Bridge
18. Tarpeian Rock
19. Forum Boarium

N

SPQR V

SATURNALIA

SPQR

Senatus PopulusQue Romanus

The Senate and People of Rome

1

I SET FOOT IN ITALY ONCE MORE on a filthy day in December. The wind blew cold rain in my face as the little naval cutter pulled up under oars to the dock at Tarentum. It was an evil time of year to be at sea, months past the good sailing season. Of course, as far as I am concerned, there is no such thing as a good sailing season. We had left Rhodes in similarly foul weather and hopped among the tedious string of islands, then up the ragged coast of Greece. From there we hopped across the strait that separates Greece from Italy, then around the southern cape and into the relatively sheltered waters of the Tarentine Gulf.

I went up the gangplank and stepped ashore with my usual sense of profound relief. I didn't quite get down on my knees and kiss the ground, but only from a sense of decorum. Immediately, my stomach began to settle. But it was still raining.

"Land!" Hermes cried with intense, heartfelt relief. He

was carrying the bundles of our belongings beneath both arms. He hated the sea even more than I did.

"Enjoy it while you can," I advised him. "You're about to exchange a heaving stomach for sores on your backside."

"You mean we have to *ride?*" He disliked horses almost as much as he hated the sea.

"Did you think we were going to walk to Rome?"

"I think I could stand it. How far is it?"

"Almost three hundred miles. Luckily, all of it is over first-class roads. We'll take the Via Appia at least as far as Capua, then we'll either continue on the Appia to Rome or take the Via Latina, depending on the conditions. About the same distance either way. The Latina may be a little drier this time of year."

"That far?" Hermes asked. As my slave he had traveled a good deal farther than most boys his age, but he was still a little hazy about geography. "But we're in Italy!"

"There's more of Italy than you would think. Now go get the rest of our luggage."

He went back to the ship grumbling to fetch my chest and a few other belongings. As he did this, an official-looking man came down the pier, accompanied by a secretary.

"Quintus Silanus," he said, "Master of the Port. And you would be . . . ?"

"Decius Caecilius Metellus the Younger," I told him.

"The Censor's son, eh? We were told you might be landing here or at Brundisium. Welcome back to Italy, Senator. We've made provision to get you back to Rome as quickly as possible."

I was impressed. I had never before been considered that important. "Really? What sort of provision?"

2

"Let's get in out of this rain," Silanus said. I followed him to an office just past the naval dock, where we ducked beneath the portico and shook the rain from our clothes. Then we went inside his office, a cramped cubicle, its walls honeycombed with cubbyholes for documents.

"Here, have something to settle your stomach," Silanus said. A slave poured me a cup of pale wine. It was a decent Bruttian, not excessively watered.

"I have horses waiting for you at the municipal stable near the Appian Gate, and somewhere here I have requisition chits for you, so you can get stabling and fodder for them between here and Rome. Fresh horses, too, if you need them." He rummaged around in the cubbyholes for a minute until the secretary smoothly brushed him aside and reached into one of them and came out with a leather sack full of little scrolls.

"Who arranged for all this?" I asked.

"The Censor," Silanus said. "Weren't you expecting it?"

"Well, no," I admitted. "I got his summons on Rhodes and jumped on the first ship headed for Italy, but I thought I'd have to make my own way to Rome. Ordinarily, when I come home my father doesn't come running out the gate to greet me, arms open and toga flapping, if you know what I mean."

"Well, fathers are like that," Silanus said, pouring himself a cup. "You can't really expect them to behave like your old Sabine nurse."

"I suppose not. What's the countryside like these days?"

"Uncommonly quiet. You can leave your arms in your baggage for a change."

"What about the city?" I asked.

"That I couldn't say. I hear it's been rough lately."

"Clodius?" This was the year Clodius was standing for

tribune. In most ways it was the most powerful office in Rome at the time: and if Clodius was elected, he would for a year be both immensely powerful and sacrosanct, untouchable by the law or his fellow citizens. The very thought gave me stomach twinges. It was generally agreed that he would win his election easily. The Claudians were patricians, barred from the office, and Clodius had campaigned hard to get transferred to the plebs. Finally, with the influence of Caesar and Pompey, he had achieved his wish through adoption by an obscure plebeian relative named Fonteius. Everyone who had fought against his transfer had much unpleasantness to look forward to in the coming year.

"He's Caesar's dog," Silanus said, "but word has it that the Consul doesn't keep him on a tight leash." Silanus, like everyone else, spoke of Caesar as if he were the only consul. His colleague in office, Bibulus, was such a nonentity that Romans ever since have referred to that year as "the consulship of Julius and Caesar." I took my chits and gathered up my slave and my belongings, and I trudged through the rain to the Appian Hate.

By general agreement, I wasn't supposed to return to Rome until Clodius was safely out of office and, by preference, out of Rome. But then, Metellus Celer wasn't supposed to die, either. My father's summons had been peremptory, to say the least.

Our kinsman, Quintus Caecilius Metellus Celer is dead: it is believed by poison. The family is convening for his obsequies. You are to return to Rome immediately.

It seemed a bit extreme. Granted, Celer was the most distinguished Caecilian of the time, but ordinarily only his immediate family and any members of the gens who happened to be in Rome at the time of his death would attend his funeral

4

and see to the other observances surrounding the passing of a prominent man. To call in Caecilians from as far away as Rhodes suggested that a political crisis was in the offing.

We Metelli were political creatures down to our bones, but I was the one member of the whole family whose presence in Rome was considered to be a political liability. My knack for making enemies was remarkable in a man devoid of political ambition. People with things to hide were nervous around me.

At the city gate Hermes and I picked up our horses and packed our skimpy belongings on a third beast. As we trotted away Hermes bounced on his saddle in a way that was painful to watch. Naturally, I laughed heartily at this. I rode passably well. When I was very small I rode gentle mares on our rural estates; and when I assumed my manhood toga, my father sent me to the circus to be trained by the riders who gallop alongside the chariots, urging on the four-horse teams. This practice served me well in Spain, for much of the guerilla chasing we engaged in among the hills was done by cavalry. Still, horses were never a passion with me, and I always preferred to see professionals doing the riding and driving from the ease of the stands. Still, it beat walking or sailing. Anything beat sailing.

Like all our roads, the Appia was beautifully kept. It was the oldest of our major highways, the stretch between Capua and Rome having been begun by Appius Claudius Caecus nearly three hundred years before, and the rest of it almost as elderly, so that the poplars and cedars planted along its length were stately and mature. The tombs built by the side of the road were for the most part of a pleasingly simple design reflecting the taste of a bygone era. Every thousand paces stood a milestone, inscribed with the distances to the nearest towns and, as always, the precise distance to the Golden Milestone in the Forum Romanum. That way, anywhere in our empire, a Roman citizen knows exactly how far it is to the center of Roman communal life. We find this comforting for some obscure reason. Perhaps it is because, when wandering among barbarians, we find it difficult to believe that Rome exists at all.

There is no finer or more enduring testament to the power and genius of Rome than our roads. People gawk at the Pyramids, which have no purpose except to contain the corpses of long-dead pharaohs. People the world over can *use* Roman roads. Barbarians seldom bother to pave their roads. Those who do are satisfied with a thin layer of cut stone, perhaps laid over a thin layer of gravel. A Roman road is more like a buried wall, sometimes going down fifteen feet in alternating layers of rubble, cut stone, and gravel to rest solidly upon bedrock.

The center of every Roman road is raised slightly to allow water to drain off. They span the world as straight as so many tight-stretched strings, crossing valleys and rivers upon bridges of prodigious ingenuity, tunneling through mountain spurs too large to be conveniently moved. What other people ever conceived of such roads? They are the pure expression of the uniqueness that is Rome.

All right, we learned road building from the Etruscans, but we build them better than they ever did. We certainly build them in places the Etruscans never dreamed of.

I was occupied with such pleasant thoughts as we rode toward Venusia. I had been too long among foreigners and I yearned to be in the great City again, even if Clodius was there.

Three days of riding brought us to Capua. The beautiful city, finest in Campania, was situated amid the richest farmlands in all of Italy. As we drew near we could hear the clatter of Capua's famed bronze works. There were foundries and smith's shops all over the city, and the din of hammering was incessant. Everything crafted from bronze, from lamps to parade armor, was made in Capua.

There was also a clatter of arms. This was not the result of war, but of training. Outside the walls of the city were a score or so of gladiator schools, for Campania was always the heartland of the sport. Romans were fond of gladiators, but in Campania they were something of a cult. As we rode past one of these, I think it was the school of Ampliatus, an idea came to me.

"Remind me when we get to Rome to enroll you in the Statilian school."

"You aren't going to sell me?" Hermes asked, alarmed.

"Of course not, idiot, although the idea has its attractions. But if you're going to be of any use to me, you'd better learn to defend yourself. You're old enough to train now." Hermes was about eighteen at the time, a handsome youth and accomplished in all sorts of criminal rascality. It was perfectly legal to train slaves to fight and as yet there were no laws forbidding a slave to bear arms, as long as he was outside the City and accompanying his master.

"The gladiator school, eh?" I could see that he liked the thought. He had no idea how rough the training would be. Like most young boys, he thought the gladiator's life was exciting and glamorous, unaware that a few splendid moments in the arena, dressed in plumes and gilded armor, was the result of years of bone-crunching work beneath the beady eyes of brutal overseers who enforced discipline with whips and hot irons. Of course I had no intention of having him trained for the arena, but he had to learn enough to stay alive in the sort of street fighting and midnight ambush that had become norms of Roman political life.

The Latina proved to be the wiser choice for the final stretch from Capua to Rome. Along the way we stayed at inns or at the villas of friends and relatives. Nine days of travel, with frequent changes of mounts, brought us, sore and bedraggled, within sight of the walls of Rome.

2

MY FATHER LOOKED UP FROM the scrolls on the table before him. "What took you so long?" he demanded. It was his usual greeting.

"The weather, the sea, the time of year, a few balky horses, the usual. I rejoice to see you well, Father." In fact he was carrying his age well. The scar that nearly bisected his face and nose looked deeper than ever, and he had more lines and less hair, but he seemed as vigorous and energetic as always. With the censorship he had achieved the pinnacle of Roman life, but that had not lulled him into retirement. He campaigned on behalf of other family members as aggressively as ever.

"Nonsense. Like all sons, you're panting after your inheritance. Sit down."

I sat. We were in the courtyard of Father's town house. The walls kept out the wind, and the late morning sun made it almost warm. "Why am I needed here? I'm far too late for Celer's funeral."

He brushed off the question. "Creticus wrote to me about that foolish business in Alexandria. You might have gotten yourself killed over matters of no importance to Rome."

"It turned out to be of utmost importance to Rome!" I protested.

"But that isn't why you got involved!" he said, slapping a palm down upon the table, making pens and ink pot jump. "It was your obnoxious love for snooping and, I don't doubt, your weakness for the company of loose women."

"Not women," I murmured, "muses."

"Eh? Stop vaporing. There is important business afoot, and for once you'll be able to snoop to your heart's content with the family's blessing."

This sounded promising. "What about Clodius?"

He shifted uneasily, not a common thing for him to do. "We've patched things up somewhat with Caesar, so as long as he's in the city the little swine will probably leave you alone. But Caesar leaves Rome at the end of the year and so will you. Have you had word of Caesar's proconsular command?"

"In Egypt we had word that he and Bibulus were getting the upkeep of the Italian goat paths and dung heaps, but in Rhodes word came that Vatinius had secured Cisalpine Gaul and Illyricum for Caesar."

"That is true. Now the Senate has given him Transalpine Gaul as well, with his proconsulship to run for five years."

My jaw dropped. "No one has ever had such a territory or such a period of office!" I said. "Everyone knows Gaul is about to erupt like a volcano. And they gave it all to *Caesar?*"

"My thoughts exactly. Most of the Senate hopes he'll disgrace himself or get killed. At any rate, he'll be out of Rome for five years."

"That is foolish," I said. "Caesar has more brains than the rest of the Senate combined. In five years he'll build up a *clientela* bigger than Marius had and he'll be powerful enough to march against Rome."

"Do you think you are the only one to have thought of that?" He waved a hand dismissively. "It's not your concern. Now that you're back I will call a meeting of the family leaders. Be back here just before sundown this evening." He returned his attention to his scrolls. That was all. I had been dismissed.

I was mystified, but I felt a profound relief. I had performed my primary duty in calling on my father. Now I could do what I wanted. So, naturally, I went to the Forum. A Roman separated from the Forum for too long suffers an illness of the spirit. He languishes and pines. He knows that, however important his work, however abandoned the pleasures of the locale, he is far from the center of the world. It felt wonderful to be approaching the spot all those hundreds of milestones had led me to.

Emerging from the warren of narrow streets and alleys into the Forum was like coming out of a narrow mountain pass onto a great plain. The vista opened up and I could see more than a narrow strip of sky overhead. The great basilicas, the monuments, the *rostra*, the Curia where the Senate met and which had not been burned down recently, and, most beloved of all, the temples. From the beautiful little round Temple of Vesta, they ascended to culminate in the glorious crown of the Capitol, seat of Jupiter Optimus Maximus.

But even more than the architecture, the population made the Forum. As usual it was thronged, even on a rather chilly December day. Citizens, freedmen and slaves, women, foreigners, and children of indistinguishable status, they bustled or lounged or played as the mood suited them. And the mood was one of excitement. To one closely attuned to the heartbeat of Rome, and I am one of these, the mood of the city may be sensed as a mother senses the mood of her child: frightened, sad, hilarious, indignant, angry, all are apparent to one who knows how to read the signs.

I knew it could not be simply the anticipation of Saturnalia, which was to commence in a few days. As much as Romans love the revelry of Saturnalia, there is something glum about the holiday, for it is the time when we have to pay our debts. No, this was something else, another intriguing little mystery to plumb.

I plunged into the crowd and began greeting old friends and making dinner appointments. For all its awesome power and glory, Rome is just an overgrown farm town and I could not look in any direction without seeing someone I knew. With Hermes dogging my heels, I slowly made my way through the Forum and up the Capitol, where I made a sacrifice in thanks for my safe return.

With the commencement of afternoon, I sent Hermes to my house for my bath things and relaxed amid steam and hot water while friends and acquaintances gossiped about charioteers, gladiators, scandalous women, and so forth. Nobody seemed to want to talk much about politics, and I found that strange. It was not as if they were fearful, as might be the case when a lunatic tyrant or a ruthless dictator held power, as it was during the last year of Marius or the proscriptions of Sulla. Rather, it was as if they were confused. The last thing a Roman wants to admit is that he doesn't know what is going on.

So I made my next call the Egyptian embassy. Lisas, the

ambassador, had been in Rome forever and collected all the gossip in the world, since he spent almost all his time entertaining and bribing the Roman government and all the other embassies. The fat old pervert received me hospitably as always. I noted with some dismay that beneath his heavy cosmetics, his face was spotted with a number of tiny lesions. Perhaps we would soon need a new Egyptian ambassador. That would sadden me, for the man, to use the term loosely, was an invaluable resource.

"Welcome, Senator, welcome," the old man enthused. He clapped his hands and slaves came running to wash my hands and feet, even though I had just come from the bath. One took my toga, another thrust a beaker into my hand. Others fanned us vigorously. It wasn't hot and there were no flies, but maybe the slaves just needed the exercise. We went into a small, circular dining room that was one of the many eccentric features of the Egyptian embassy, which followed no architectural convention I was ever able to discern.

"His Majesty informs me that you performed some signal favors for him last year. He is most grateful." Even as he spoke, as if by magic, viands appeared on the table between us. It always amazed me that, no matter what hour I called upon Lisas, it was always dinnertime. Romans are punctilious about mealtimes, but not Lisas. Even for an impromptu courtesy call, he had not just the usual fruit and cheese and olives ready, but fresh-baked bread still hot from the oven and whole roast fowl with its skin still crisp.

While we ate we spoke of inconsequential things. I inquired about the health of Ptolemy's latest son, who had been just a bump in his mother's belly when I left Alexandria, and Lisas asked about my stay in Rhodes, hoping that I had been

13

on some sort of secret mission. Alas, it was just one of my many unofficial exiles.

"I'm a little puzzled about Rome's political state," I admitted, as a slave poured a sweet dessert wine. "I've been out of touch for a long time and my friends are unenlightening."

"Hardly surprising," Lisas said. "The events of recent months have been unprecedented. Caesar's has been a most productive consulship."

"Most consuls just sit out their term and hope for a rich province to govern afterward," I said.

"Exactly. Not Caesar, though. Almost immediately he rammed through the settlement for Pompey's veterans. Then he remitted a third of the contracts to Crassus's friends, the tax farmers for Asia."

I shrugged. "Campaign debts. The three of them are as tight as my maiden aunts. Caesar would never have been made consul without the help of the other two."

"Quite possibly. Of course, it helps that he is acting as if he were sole consul."

"How did that come about?" I asked. "Granted, Bibulus has the spine of a squid, but couldn't he even try to overrule his colleague?"

"Indeed, he did try." Lisas spread his hands in an Egyptian gesture of futility. "But he was driven from the Forum by open threat of violence and took refuge in his house. There he announced that he was watching for omens."

At this one I laughed aloud. "That one's been tried before!" By ancient law all public business had to be suspended while an augur watched for auspicious omens. It was a common way for connivers to delay legislation, but it was rarely good for more than a day or two, certainly not for the duration of a consulship.

"Caesar ignored him and proceeded to act unilaterally. You have noticed that by now everyone has dropped the Caius and Julius and refer to him merely as Caesar? It disturbs some people."

"As it should," I said. "Only kings and slaves are called by a single name. Somehow I don't see Caesar fancying himself a slave."

"Just so. Most graciously, Caesar has also persuaded the Senate to ratify His Majesty's position as king of Egypt and as friend and ally of the Roman people." Lisas oozed contentment.

I forebore to ask what sort of bribe Ptolemy must have offered, knowing it had to be immense. But it was worth whatever he paid. From now on no foreigner could invade Egypt without going to war with Rome, and no usurper could do away with Ptolemy without giving Rome an excuse to annex Egypt. I went back to an earlier point.

"You say Bibulus was driven from the Forum by violence. Was Clodius by any chance involved?"

"Who else? His mob supports Caesar and the popular party."

"What about Milo?"

"They brawl, but for the moment Clodius is in the ascendant. Milo is allied with Cicero, and Cicero is probably packing his belongings right now. When Clodius takes office as tribune, he will make it his first order of business to drive Cicero into exile, using the executions of the Catilinarian conspirators as an excuse."

"It was necessary," I said uncomfortably. I hadn't liked the idea of the executions myself, but for once Cato and I were in agreement: It was folly to accord constitutional protection to men who were in the very act of the violent overthrow of the Constitution.

"You needn't convince me," Lisas said. "It is only an excuse. Cicero fought Clodius's transfer to the plebs with all the legal and political skill at his disposal, and that was considerable. Clodius does not forget." He took a sip of his wine and set the cup aside. "But Caesar's term of office draws to a close. Events in Gaul beckon."

"I was there on an embassy with Creticus just before we went on our mission to Alexandria. The people there are very unhappy with us."

"They are unenlightened barbarians. The allies of Rome are falling away and joining those who would resist Roman expansion into free Gallic territory."

"Can't really blame them for that. The free ones, I mean. We are sometimes a little nonchalant about helping ourselves to other people's territory. That's no reason for our allies to desert us though."

"There is a new factor, however," Lisas said, spinning it out for the sheer delight of keeping me after him for details.

"New factor? Not an invasion from that island up north, Britannia or whatever it's called?"

"Oh, no. The eastern Gauls have been fighting among themselves for several years now."

"I knew about that. One faction is led by the Aedui and the other by the Averni, I believe. The situation changes so fast there that it's hard to keep track."

"That is still the lineup. Anyway, word has it that the Averni were losing and so they decided, foolishly, that they needed, well . . . allies."

I all but let my cup clatter to the floor. "Jove preserve us! You mean the Germans are across the Rhine again?"

"So it would seem. Only mercenaries so far, but they have a new and apparently ambitious king, one Ariovistus. Last I heard, the king was still east of the Rhine; but my sources say that there may be more than a hundred thousand German warriors on the western bank already, and the Germans have coveted the rich lands of Gaul for a long, long time."

I groaned. As a rule, foreigners come in three sorts. There are the comical ones, like Egyptians and Syrians. Then there are the ones who are both comical and scary, like the Gauls. And then there are the Germans, who are just plain terrifying.

"Surely the Senate isn't sending Caesar into Gaul with a mandate to drive the Germans out?"

"By no means. I suspect that Caesar will first ensure that the Helvetii do not migrate into Roman territory. That is what has been feared for years. He cannot very well march to the Rhine and leave them at his back. I think he intends to crush the Helvetii, then wheel northeast and take on the Germans and their Gallic allies." He gave me a self-deprecating smile. "Of course, that is just my theory. I am not a military man."

Lisas dealt with the world from his embassy, but he knew how to interpret a map and he had a sound grasp of politics as it is played on a world scale. I did not doubt that he was very close to the truth of the situation. Roman territory did not extend to the Rhine, but for generations we had considered it our unofficial border. If the Germans crossed, it was a sign of hostility.

"Nobody ever gained great wealth fighting Germans," I said. "Gauls are a wealthy people by comparison."

"But one may win glory and a triumph," Lisas pointed out. "And who was the last Roman to defeat the Germans?"

"Marius, of course," I said. "At Aquae Sextiae and Vercellae."

"And what is Caesar's dearest wish except to be the new Marius? He has courted the *populares* for his whole career, always stressing that Marius was his uncle by marriage."

"It makes sense," I admitted. "But it amazes me that even a man like Caesar can believe that he has what it takes to beat the Germans! A few victories in Spain don't amount to all that much. By the time Marius fought those battles, he'd all but built his legions from scratch and led them to victory for twenty years. You can't just take charge of established legions as a new proconsul and expect that sort of performance and loyalty." I knew as I said it that I was probably wrong. Everyone, myself included, had underestimated Caesar for years.

"Caesar has a genius for persuading the common people. Men don't come any more common that legionaries. They are the most powerful force in the world, more powerful than politicians and consuls, more powerful than the Senate. Marius knew that and so did Sulla. Pompey never understood it, and so his sun is setting."

As I took my leave of him, Lisas led me out by the arm. "Decius, my friend, as always I rejoice to see you, but I did not expect to see you until after the tribuneship of Clodius should expire at the end of next year." He had given me some inside information, now he expected the favor to be returned.

"I must confess that I am surprised as well. I was recalled from Rhodes unexpectedly. It has something to do with Celer's death."

His eyes lit up with conspiratorial delight. "A most distinguished man. We were stricken with grief at his untimely passing. Your family expects you to exercise your . . . unique talents in the matter."

"I can't imagine why else they want me here. I'm not a family favorite."

"But you have a brilliant future before you," he effused. "I am sure that, in a decade or two, you shall be the most prominent of all the Metelli. You must come see me often while you are in Rome. I may be able to help you. I hear things." And, of course, he wanted me to pass on anything I might learn. It might be a fair trade.

I had little confidence in his predictions about my bright future. At that time the only way to achieve prominence in Roman life was through military glory or extreme longevity (Cicero, as always, was the exception). I detested military life and my prospects of reaching my fortieth year were exceedingly slim. Oddly, I actually have reached the distinction Lisas predicted so many years ago, although in a way neither of us could have dreamed. I am the only Caecilian of my generation still alive.

But he was wrong about Caesar. Caesar wasn't interested in being the new Marius; he wanted to be the one and only Julius Caesar.

3

THE MEETING WAS HELD IN MY father's house. The *janitor* opened the door when Hermes knocked and we went inside. The old mansion was eerily quiet.

"The Master and the others are in the triclinium," the aged gatekeeper informed me. "Your boy will have to stay in the back of the house with the other slaves." That explained the quiet.

Hermes made a face. "I'll just wait out front, in the street."

"You mean in that tavern on the corner," I said. "Get on in back." He stalked off with ill grace. I could sympathize. The real reason he didn't want to be exiled to the rear was that my father had no young, pretty slave girls in his town house.

Besides my father, there were three Caecilians gathered

in the triclinium, all of them named Quintus, my family not being imaginative in the way of names: Creticus, with whom I had served in foreign lands several times, and now the most prominent of the clan, a former consul and a pontifex; Nepos, who had been praetor the previous year, and an adoptive Caecilian who went by the ringing name of Quintus Caecilius Metellus Pius Scipio Nasica, was a pontifex and was serving as Tribune of the People that year. The rest of the distinguished men of the clan were away from Italy that year.

We exchanged curt greetings. The usual wine and refreshments were absent. There was not so much as a pitcher of water in the room. These men were here for serious business.

"I'm surprised to see you still in Rome, Nepos," I said. "I thought you were given Sardinia."

"I passed on it," he said. "Vettius took it instead." Nepos was a tall, soldierly man, who alone among our clan leaders supported Pompey. This was tolerated because that way, should Pompey become dictator, at least one of us wouldn't be executed or exiled, and the family would keep most of its lands.

"I can sympathize," I told him. "I wouldn't accept Sardinia if I won it at dice."

Creticus made a face. "You've not changed, Decius. You're an utter political moron. Nepos stays in Rome because he's going to stand for consul next year."

"That explains a lot," I said. "A proconsular province beats Sardinia any day. What's up for grabs?"

"Barring a foreign emergency, he'll be assigned Nearer Spain," Father said. Nobody suggested that Nepos might be defeated or that, barring emergency, he would fail to secure the desired province. When the Caecilia Metella settled on one of their own for consul, he got it. And Spain had been

Metellan territory for almost two hundred years. We had been governing there for so long that it was a major power base, second only to our Italian lands.

"Next year will be a bad one," Creticus pointed out. "It will be Clodius against Cicero, and a tribune can do real damage. We'll need to have as much influence as possible the year after to undo whatever's been done. Scipio will stand for curule aedile as well."

Scipio nodded. He was a pale, distinguished man of about thirty-five. "As aedile I will be celebrating my father's funeral games. I intend to give a gladiatorial display of special magnificence." His adoptive father, the elder Metellus Pius, had died four years earlier. It had become customary to delay funeral games until an heir held the aedileship, in charge of the public spectacles. That way he could discharge his civil and filial duties at the same time and win popularity for higher election. When Caesar was aedile he set incredibly high standards of spectacle outlay.

"Clodius will have the commons stirred up, and nothing buys back their loyalty like a good set of games," I observed. "But it will be expensive."

"You will be expected to contribute," Father said. I should have kept my mouth shut.

"All of which is strictly secondary to the evening's business," Creticus said. "Decius, you know that Celer was poisoned, don't you?"

"I knew that he was dead and that he didn't die by violence, disease, or accident that anyone witnessed. People always suspect poison when a prominent man dies without visible cause, but there are a hundred illnesses that can kill without warning signs."

"He was poisoned," Creticus said flatly.

I released a sigh. I had been afraid of this. "And I can just guess who you suspect did it."

"No need to guess," Creticus said. "It was his wife, that slut Clodia. We want you to gather evidence so that we can bring charges against the bitch and have her executed or exiled."

"You don't quite understand how this works," I said. "If I am to investigate, I will gather evidence *then* decide who the murderer is, if indeed he was murdered."

"Whatever it takes," Creticus said.

"It may not be Clodia," I said.

"Who else could it be?" Father demanded.

"I have no idea, but no man ever became consul and commanded armies in the provinces without making plenty of enemies. He fought the Catilinarians and executed plenty of them. Their families will not have forgotten. He might have been dallying with the wrong man's wife. Married to Clodia, I can well imagine that he sought female companionship elsewhere."

Nepos snorted. "What man ever commits murder over a little trifling adultery? Celer's enemies were not the sort to resort to poison."

"Right," said Scipio. "If he'd been decently attacked and cut down in the street, we could be certain that it was a political enemy behind it. Poison is a woman's tool."

"Why would she have killed him?" I asked. At this they all looked surprised.

"The woman is a murderess many times over," Creticus said. "Why not?"

It was typical of these men. Murder was all too common in Rome, but they knew that a man would have a sound political or personal reason for resorting to the act. A scandalous woman, on the other hand, would kill because it was her nature to. And any woman whose name was bandied about in public was scandalous. Highborn Roman ladies were supposed to live anonymously.

"Very well. What is to be my authority?"

"We want this handled with discretion," Creticus said. "After all, this is within the family. But if you encounter difficulty, you may say that you are acting for Scipio. As tribune, he will bring charges against the *venefica*." He used the old word for witch poisoner.

"You understand that poisoning is perhaps the most difficult of all murders to prove?" I said.

"I've prosecuted and judged such cases," Father said. "So has Creticus. Just bring us evidence for a credible charge and we'll get rid of her."

"Why did Celer marry her in the first place?" I asked.

"We needed an alliance with the Claudians at the time," Creticus said. "What else?"

What indeed?

At the door of Father's house, Hermes took a torch from the stand and began to light it from the doorside lamp.

"Don't bother," I told him. "There's decent moonlight tonight."

I preferred to avoid torches in Rome except on the inkiest nights. Their light is flickering and they destroy your night vision. An attacker need only throw a cloak over it or douse it with water and you are utterly blind until your eyes readjust. Besides, a torch draws attention.

We went outside and stood by the gate for a few minutes while our eyes grew accustomed to the dim light. After that, the streets were fairly negotiable. The moon was three-quarters full and almost straight overhead, casting her beams upon even the narrowest alleys.

"What did you learn?" I asked Hermes as we set out.

"Not much. Your father isn't exactly chummy with his slaves."

"But they hear things," I said. "What do I keep you around for if not to pick up slave gossip?"

"Near as I can tell, the old man's just like always. Doesn't use the whip as much as he used to. Maybe he's mellowing." He paused. "There've been several of these late meetings where the staff were sent to the back of the house in the last few months."

"That doesn't mean much," I said. "Not for political connivers like my family. Has there been talk about Metellus Celer? Or his wife, Clodia?"

"They say she poisoned him, but that's just city gossip, not inside family information. Is that what this is all about?"

"Exactly. The family wants to punish Clodia and they are sending me out to dig up evidence." I talked about these things openly to Hermes. Despite his criminal inclinations, he could be an invaluable help in my investigations and had a real feel for the work. This caused me some disquiet. Did Hermes have the instincts of an investigator, or did I have the instincts of a slave?

"This is your chance!" he said. "That woman's been a sword hanging over your head for years. Now you can be rid of her for good."

"I know. I ought to be rejoicing, but I'm not."

"Why? Oh, well, she is the sister of Publius Clodius. It'll give him one more reason to hate you."

I shrugged. "That isn't it. He can only kill me once, and he intends to do that as soon as possible. No, something else

26

feels wrong about this business." I brooded for a while, and we walked across the ghostly, moonlit Forum. Dead politicians glared down at us from their pedestals as if we were Gauls come back to loot the Capitol again. I paused.

"What is it?" Hermes asked.

"Something just became clear to me. Everyone seemed awfully cheerful in the streets and the Forum today."

"I noticed. Is it because of Saturnalia?"

"No. It's because the year is almost over and next year will be one of utter political chaos. I just realized that Romans *like* political chaos!"

"Maybe citizens do," Hermes said.

"Don't be mealy mouthed. Slaves love civil unrest more than anybody else. They can get away with a lot more then. When men can brawl in the streets, they don't vent their anger by beating their slaves."

"That's what you know about it," he said, but I had lost interest.

What I was wondering about was why they had recalled me from Rhodes. Certainly I had a reputation as an investigator, but any halfway competent *iudex* could come up with enough material of the sort that passed for evidence in a Roman court, where eloquence of denunciation was more important than proof of guilt. Maybe they just didn't want to run afoul of a woman with Clodia's reputation. Poisoning is not only difficult to prove, but it is also difficult to avoid.

4

CATO WOKE ME FAR TOO EARLY and Cassandra brought in my breakfast tray. My two aged house slaves were intrusive and officious as usual, but they were always good for a few days of cheerful service immediately after one of my returns from foreign parts. After that they would revert to their customary cranky selves.

"Are my clients outside?" I asked.

"No, they've not yet got word you're back in town, Master," Cato said. "You should send your boy to summon them."

"Absolutely not!" I said. "I don't want them calling on me in the mornings. The longer they're in the dark, the better." I took the napkin off the tray, revealing hot bread, sliced fruit, boiled eggs, and a pot of honey. Breakfast was one of those degenerate, un-Roman practices to which I was addicted.

Fed and dressed, Hermes in tow, I went to a corner barber to be shaved and have my hair trimmed. It had grown a little shaggy around the ears during my voyage and long ride. Besides being necessary, there was no better place to hear the gossip of the streets.

"Welcome back to Rome, Senator," said the barber, one Bassus, who was shaving the head of a burly butcher. The other men waiting their turn welcomed me back effusively. I was popular in my neighborhood, and in those days even patrician senators were expected to mix with the citizenry, especially in the mornings.

"It's good to breathe Roman air again," I said, taking an ostentatious breath through my nostrils. It smelled foul, as it usually did in Rome. "Is the district still Milo's?"

"Solidly," said the butcher, running a hand over his newly smooth scalp. It gleamed with oil. "Next year will be rough, but the year after's ours." The others agreed heartily.

"How is that?" I asked.

"Because Milo's standing for the tribuneship next year," said Bassus.

"Milo a tribune!" I said.

"He swears if Clodius can hold the office, so can he," chuckled a fat banker. The gold ring of an *equites* winked from his hand. "And why not? If that little ex-patrician rat can be elected tribune, why not an honest, upstanding rogue like Milo?"

Milo and Clodius ran the two most powerful gangs in Rome at the time. But Clodius was from an ancient, noble family that, like mine, regarded the higher offices as theirs by birthright. Milo was a nobody from nowhere. He had been elected quaestor and was now a senator, which was difficult enough to picture. But tribune? I would have to call on him.

Actually, I had a number of calls to make. If I was going to conduct an investigation, I would have to learn how much support and help I had available to me in the City. Men of importance spent much of their time away from Rome. I also needed to learn how my enemies were disposed.

"How is Clodius behaving these days?" I asked, taking my seat on the barber's stool.

"Almost respectably, for him," said the banker. "He's so happy with the prospect of taking up his office in a few weeks that he just preens and struts around, and his men don't fight with Milo's unless they happen to bump into one another in an alley. Both of next year's consuls are his sympathizers, too. I hear Cicero's already packing."

"Who are the consuls?" I asked. "Someone told me in a letter, but I've forgotten."

"Easy ones to forget," Bassus said. "Calpurnius Piso and Aulus Gabinius. Clodius promised them fat provinces after their year in office. They'll do as he wants." Next year was sounding more and more like a good one to be away from Rome.

"Clodius isn't going to have a tribuneship," I said. "It sounds something more like a reign."

"We got Ninnius Quadratus in as tribune," the butcher said. "He hates Clodius. Terentius Culleo won as well, and he's supposed to be a friend of Cicero. But they won't be able to do much. Clodius's gang rules the streets in most districts and they have the Via Sacra, and that means the Forum." Everyone agreed that this gave Clodius an unfair and nearly unbeatable advantage.

If this all seems confusing, it is because Rome had two sorts of politics in those days. The great men like Caesar and Pompey and Crassus wanted to rule the whole world, and this meant they had to spend much of their time away from Rome. But Rome was where the elections were held that determined

31

everyone's status and future. Many communities had Roman citizenship; but if they wanted to take part in the elections, they had to journey all the way to Rome in order to vote. Thus, voting power remained a virtual monopoly of the City populace.

Hence, men like Clodius and Milo. These contended for control of the City alone. Each of the great men needed representatives to influence the elections, by force if need be, and watch out for their interests while they were away. The politics of the gangs and the City districts each controlled were as complicated as those of the Senate and the Empire. The gangs of Clodius and Milo were by no means the only ones, merely the most powerful and numerous. There were dozens of others, and these operated within a complex web of shifting alliances.

All of this was greatly aided by the fact that Rome was not so much a single city, like Athens, as it was a cluster of villages within a single continuous wall. In very remote times, it really had been seven separate villages atop seven distinct hills. As the villages gained population, they grew down the sides of the hills until they merged. The Forum back then was their common pasture and marketplace. This is why the ancient and revered hut of Romulus is not near the Forum, nor even on the Capitol, as one would think. Rather it stands amid several other sacred sites at the foot of the Palatine near the cattle market. That is probably all there was to Rome when he founded it.

The result is that Romans identify themselves as much with their districts, or ancestral villages, as they do with the City. Only outside of Rome do they really think of themselves as Romans. My neighbors were Suburans, who took pride in their famously noisy, raucous district where, they contended, all the toughest Romans were bred. They looked down upon the Via Sacrans, who thought they were holier than anyone else because they dwelled along the old triumphal route. The two districts had a famous traditional street fight at the ritual of the October Horse. And they were only two districts among many.

These things, plus the fact that Rome had no police, made gang control of the streets possible, and I would have had it no other way. It is all gone now. The First Citizen gives us peace, security, and stability; and most people these days seem happy to have them at long last. But in accepting them, we gave up most of what made us Romans.

It didn't occur to me at the time. I was concerned mainly with getting through the next few weeks alive and trying to decide where to wait out the next year. I loved Alexandria, but people there wanted to kill me. Gaul was to be avoided at all costs. It was full of Gauls, and now there would be Germans and Caesar fighting them. There was fighting in Macedonia as well. I had spent too much time in Spain and was bored with the place. There were always the family's rural estates, but I detested farming as much as I did the military life. Perhaps I could get posted with Cicero's brother in Syria. It sounded like an interesting place, if the Parthians would just keep quiet. It would bear thinking about.

I rubbed my smooth-shaven jaw, detecting the usual stubble along the jagged scar left by an Iberian spear years before. It has defeated the efforts of barbers ever since.

"Hermes," I said, "I have an errand for you."

He looked around uneasily. "You don't intend to go wandering around alone, do you? Here in the Subura's fine, but nowhere else. Get Milo to lend you some of his gladiators as a guard."

"I'm touched by your concern, but if my neighbors are right I should be safe enough in daylight. Clodius is being a jovial man of the people again. I want you to run to the house of Lucius Caesar and find out if the Lady Julia Minor is home. Her last letter was from Cyprus months ago. If she's here, I want to call on her."

Hermes set off at the slow amble that was his usual pace except when heading for a dice game, a gladiator fight, the races, or a meeting with some unlucky family's pretty young housemaid.

Julia was Julius Caesar's niece and my betrothed. Since all marriages among the great families were political, they were waiting for the political atmosphere to be correct before setting a date for the wedding. It was pure accident and a matter of no concern to my family or hers that she was the one lady I truly wanted to marry. The Metelli wanted a link with the Julii and we were to provide it. I am not sure whether these arranged marriages did any good or not. Creticus had married his daughter off to the younger Marcus Crassus, and they were deliriously happy. Caesar's daughter married Pompey, and they seem to have gotten on well enough until she died in childbirth. Celer married Clodia for the sake of a temporary alliance with the Claudians, and I was there to find out whether she had decided to divorce him with drastic finality.

I was in the dark about one matter, and I decided to rectify it before proceeding further. I turned my steps west toward the river and began the long walk to the Transtiber district.

I found Asklepiodes in his spacious surgery in the *ludus* of Statilius Taurus. His intelligent face broke into a smile when he saw me come in. His hair and beard were a little grayer than when I had last seen him in Alexandria, but otherwise he was unchanged. He was directing a slave, who was rubbing liniment into the shoulder of a massive Numidian.

"Rejoice!" he said, taking my hand. "I hadn't heard of any recent, interesting murders in Rome. What brings you home so suddenly?"

"The usual," I said. "Just not recent."

"You must tell me all about it." He dismissed the slave and the injured gladiator. "Wrenched shoulder," he commented. "I keep telling Statilius that training with double-weight shields causes more injuries than can be justified by any good that they may do, but it is traditional and he will not listen."

I took a seat by his window. The clatter of arms drifted musically up from the exercise yard below.

"It is upon the mysteries of your profession that I wish to consult you," I told him.

"But of course. How may I help?"

"What do you know of poisons?"

"Enough to know that I am forbidden by oath to prescribe them."

"Sophistry," I said. "You use them all the time in your medicines."

"True, the line is a fine one. Many beneficial medicines, in excessive quantities, can kill. A drug that slows the heart can stop the heart. But I presume that your interest is in those poisons favored for homicide?"

"Exactly. My family wants me to look into the death of Metellus Celer."

"I suspected as much. Like everyone else, I have heard the rumors. An important man, married to a notorious woman, a sudden, unexpected death, ergo, poisoning."

35

"I must snoop," I said. "I must ask questions. But what am I looking for?"

Asklepiodes sat and pondered. "First, you must discern the symptoms. Were there convulsions? Did the victim foam at the mouth? Did he complain of stomach pains or chills? Did he vomit ejecta of unusual form or color? Was there a bloody flux of the bowels?"

"That sounds simple enough," I said.

"It is perhaps the only simple part. You must realize that, when the subject is poisoning, there is far more superstition than learning involved."

"I know," I admitted. "Here in Italy the whole subject is associated with witches more than with physicians or apothecaries."

"As you say. Few poisons act with terrible swiftness, few are lethal in minute quantities, few can be administered undetected. In fact, some are given in very small quantities over a very long time. Their effect is cumulative. Thus the victim may appear to have died of a lengthy illness."

"You are saying that poisoning is a job for experts."

He nodded. "Or for a murderer with access to expert advice. There are always a few professionals in the field, and they are never without practice. Remember, many approach poisoners for purposes of suicide. Among those not under the oath of my profession, this is a quasilegitimate practice. Neither gods nor civil authorities forbid suicide."

"How do real poisoners get their victims to take the stuff?" I asked him.

"The most common fashion, one you are familiar with since it has been tried upon you without success, is orally. This is almost always accomplished through food or drink as

36

the transmitting agent, although it is not unheard of for poison to be disguised as genuine medicine. The difficulty with oral transmission is that most poisons have powerful, unpleasant flavors."

"That's where disguising it as medicine would help," I commented. "Most medicines taste awful."

"Very true. Most poisons take the form of liquids or powders. They may be mixed with drink or sprinkled over food. A few occur in the form of gums or pastes and a very few can be burned to give off a poisonous smoke."

"Say you so? That's a new one on me. I knew the smoke of hemp and opium are intoxicating; I didn't know there were lethal smokes."

"Poisoning by inhalation is perhaps the rarest sort and it is usually accidental, not deliberate. Artisans who work with mercury, especially where it is used for extracting gold from ore, sometimes inhale poisonous fumes. There are places where poisonous fumes occur naturally, as in the vicinity of volcanoes, and certain swamps are notorious for the phenomenon."

"Not likely to be used for murder then?"

"It would be difficult. Poisons may also be administered rectally. It presents difficulties, but the amatory preferences of some persons could render intimate companions access to that area. The poisons may be the same as those taken orally, although of necessity their administration must be somewhat more forceful."

"I would think so." Well, nothing was beyond Clodia.

"Poisons may also enter the body through an open wound. Poisoned daggers and other weapons are not uncommon. In fact, in the Greek language the very word for poison, *toxon*, comes from a word meaning 'of the bow,' owing to the once common practice of poisoning arrows. It must be admitted, though, that often soldiers think they have been wounded with poisoned arrows when in fact the wounds have merely become infected."

"Soldiers are a credulous lot," I said.

"Poison may also be absorbed through the skin. Added to one's bathing or massage, oil would be a subtle means of administration. And some authorities believe that those unfortunate workers in mercury are subject to absorbing poisons through the skin, as well as inhaling deadly vapors."

"A hazardous trade," I observed.

"As is yours." He stroked his neatly trimmed beard. "In speaking of poisons, one must not neglect the possibility of animal vectors."

"I suppose one shouldn't," I admitted. "What do you mean?"

"The occasional poisonous serpent found in a victim's bed may not always have wandered there by chance. And some persons are especially sensitive to bee and wasp stings. A hornet's nest tossed into the window of such a person is an effective means of disposal. And at least one pharaoh is said to have died when a rival filled the royal chamber pot with scorpions."

I winced at that one. "There are more ways of poisoning someone than I thought."

"There are few subjects upon which so much ingenuity has been lavished as murder. This should present you with a unique challenge."

"I must confess, old friend, that for the first time I approach an investigation in a spirit nearing despair. If the woman has acted with even the minimum of competence, murder will be all but impossible to prove. And I know that Clodia is more than competent when it comes to murder."

"A veritable Medea. Suspected of incest with her brother, too, I hear. And a great beauty to cap it all. A fit subject for poets and tragedians." He had a Greek's appreciation of such things.

"Catullus used to think so. I heard he finally got over his infatuation and found some other vicious slut to follow around like a puppy."

"He has become much more of a sophisticate," Asklepiodes said. "You remember him as a wide-eyed boy, just come to Rome and smitten by Clodia's wiles. You were not immune to them yourself, if I recall correctly."

The memory pained me. "And now I'm supposed to find evidence against her that probably doesn't exist. She will laugh at me."

"Many men have endured worse from her. You may come to me for treatment."

"You have a medicine for humiliation? You should be rich as Crassus."

"I have some excellent Cyprian wine. It produces the mildest of hangovers."

I stood. "I may take you up on it." I scanned the walls of the surgery. Asklepiodes had samples of nearly every weapon in the world. Each had attached a scroll describing the wounds it produced. "I wish everyone would use honest weapons like these," I lamented.

"What a simple place the world would be," Asklepiodes sighed. "We should then live in a golden age. As it is, the choice of weapons is broad. Even the subtlest poisons are crude compared to the weapon of choice favored in Rome today."

"Which is?"

"The spoken word. I try to stay aloof from Roman politics, but you are a noisy lot."

"We learned it from you Greeks," I pointed out. "Pericles and Demosthenes and all that wordy pack."

"You should have chosen the Spartans to emulate rather than the Athenians. They were stupid louts, but they had a soldierly appreciation of brevity in oratory. Anyway, I do not refer to your distinguished rhetoricians like Cicero and Hortensius Hortalus. Rather, I speak of the rabble-rousers."

"Caesar and Clodius?"

"There are many others. I will not presume to address your own realm of expertise, but you would do well to inform yourself of their activities. I fear civil war is in the offing."

"That's a bit extreme. We haven't had one in more than twenty years. A little rioting now and then does no great harm. It clears the air and drains off excess resentments."

"A most Roman attitude. But this time it will not be aggrieved allies and *municipia*. It will be class against class."

"Nothing new about that either. It's been going on since the Gracchi. Probably earlier. It's in our nature."

"I wish you joy of it, then. Please feel free to consult me at any time."

I thanked him and left. Actually, I was not as sanguine as I pretended with Asklepiodes, but I was reluctant to bare my fears about the Roman social ills with a foreigner, even if he was a friend. And if war between the classes was coming, the rabble-rousers among the commons were by no means solely to blame. My own family shared a good deal of the responsibility.

I was born an aristocrat, but I had few illusions about my peers. We had brought endless ills upon ourselves and upon Rome and its empire through our own stupid intransigence. The extreme end of the aristocratic party resisted any improvement in the lot of the common Roman with the thoughtless, reflexive hostility of a dog guarding its dinner.

I pondered upon these things as I made my way back into the City proper. Rome had long since expanded beyond the walls marked out by Romulus with his plow. The Port of Rome, an extramural riverside district, had leapt the river to form the new suburb of the Transtiber. Huge building projects were in progress out on the Field of Mars, where once the citizens had formed up every year to enroll in their legions and vote upon important matters. They still went there to vote, although few bothered to serve with the legions anymore.

Before long, I thought, there would be more of Rome outside the walls than within. And where was all this excess population coming from? Certainly not from an increasing birth rate. In fact, many old families were dying out from lack of interest. The fertility of the Caecilii Metelli was a distinct exception.

No, Rome was filling up with peasants from the countryside and freed slaves. The peasants, once the backbone of the community, had been forced to sell their lands, bankrupted by huge, inefficient plantations worked by cheap slave labor, another ill my class had visited upon the Republic. And the slaves were themselves the loot of our endless foreign wars. The unfortunates who ended up on the plantations or in the mines were worked to death, but many were used for less arduous service in Rome, and few of them remained slaves for life. Instead, they were manumitted; and within a generation, two at the most, their descendants had full rights of citizenship.

In a street near the cattle market I saw a pompous, self-important senator parading with his troop of clients behind him. Actually, some of them were in front, clearing the way for the great man. There must have been a hundred of them, and that was one reason for the proliferation of slave manumissions. One way to show off your importance was to be seen with a large *clientela,* and freed slaves automatically became your clients, bound by ties of duty and attendance. Really rich men had thousands. To top it all, I happened to know that that senator (he shall remain nameless; his sensitive descendants are very powerful these days) was himself the grandson of a freed slave.

I wander. I do that a great deal. In my youth I detested all the old bores who were forever lamenting the degeneracy of the times and the low estate to which the Republic had fallen. Now that I am old, I rather enjoy it.

In the cattle market itself I walked among the pens and cages and was very careful where I stepped. The air was redolent of the massed livestock and raucous with their bleats, bellows, cackles, and other noises. Despite its name, the Forum Boarium sold very few cattle except those intended for sacrifice. There was plenty of other animal life, though, from asses to sacrificial doves. You could buy them alive or a piece at a time, already butchered.

Besides the butchers, farmers, and livestock vendors, there were many other sorts of vendors' stalls. But I was not looking for something to buy. In the Forum, I had noticed that the fortune-tellers' stalls were gone, undoubtedly driven out by the censors or the aediles. This happened every few years, but they always drifted back. They had to be set up someplace and the cattle market was a good place to look, but I saw none.

Then I saw a man haranguing a goat vendor. The speaker wore a senator's tunic like mine, but his toga was plain. He held out his hand and the vendor sullenly handed over a number of coins. Collecting fines in the market meant this must be one of the plebeian aediles. The curule aediles wore a toga with a purple stripe.

"Pardon me, Aedile," I said, walking up behind him.

He turned, his eyes automatically going to the purple stripe on my tunic. "Yes, Senator? How may I . . ." Then, at the same instant, we recognized one another. "Decius Caecilius! When did you get back?" He stuck out his hand and I took it, managing not to grit my teeth. It was Lucius Calpurnius Bestia, a man I detested.

"Just yesterday. Your rank suits you, Lucius. You've lost weight."

He made a face. "Wretched office. I never have time to eat, and I spend my days crawling all over buildings looking for violations of the construction codes. It keeps me in shape. Ruinously expensive, too, since the sums contributed by the state were laid down about three hundred years ago and prices have gone up since. We have to make up the difference out of our own purses. I can't tell you how grateful I am that the year's almost over." Then he laughed jovially. He really did not understand how much I disliked him. "When will you stand for aedile, Decius?"

"In about five years, if I live that long. That's when I meet the age qualification."

"Start borrowing for it now," he advised. "What brings you to the cattle market? I'd never come here if the job didn't call for it."

"I was wondering where the fortune-tellers had got to. They're not in the Forum, and I don't see them here either." I felt a tug at the hem of my toga and looked down. A kid was nibbling on it. I jerked it away from the little beast and determined that no serious damage had been done. The kid looked disappointed and went to join its nanny.

"We ran them out of the City back at the first of the year," Bestia said. "You know what a passion for order Caesar has. As consul and *pontifex maximus* he made it our first order of business to drive them outside the gates. They can't even come into the city to shop without a permit from one of the aediles."

"Where are they now?" I asked.

"They've pitched their tents out on the Campus Martius by the Circus Flaminius. I thought you were one of those people who don't believe in omens. What do you want with a fortune-teller?"

"It always pays to be careful," I told him. Bestia was one man with whom I definitely did not wish to discuss an investigation.

"Well, that's where you'll find them. Come on, admit it: You've got some well-born lady pregnant and you need to arrange for an abortion."

"You've guessed it. Caesar's wife."

He hooted. "And she's supposed to be above suspicion!" After four years Romans still found Caesar's incredibly pompous and hypocritical pronouncement hilarious. We were laughing less and less at Caesar though.

I thanked him and left. Bestia had been neck deep in Catilina's crackpot conspiracy and had almost certainly been involved in murder. He'd gotten away clean, though, because he'd been acting as Pompey's spy within the movement. There was little use in striking a pose of moral superiority. It was all but impossible to accomplish anything in Roman public life without having to deal with odious men like Bestia. He wasn't even among the worst of them.

It was a long walk out to the Circus Flaminius, but who

minds walking after days at sea and on horseback? I left the City proper through the Porta Carmentalis near the southern base of the Capitol. This is the spot where the Servian Wall has two gates within a few paces of each other, but only one of them could be used because the other was opened only for triumphal processions.

I wasn't looking for any fortune-teller in particular, but I needed to test the atmosphere of a world that was almost entirely unknown to me: the strange underworld of the witches.

Italian witches came in three sorts that I knew about. There was the *saga*, or wise woman, who was usually a fortune-teller and learned in herb lore and occult matters. They were seldom perceived as malevolent and the authorities periodically drove them from the City only because they sometimes predicted political events and the deaths of important men. These predictions could easily come true, considering how superstitious the citizenry were, and how heavily Rome relied on rumors for information.

Next there was the *striga*, a true witch or sorceress. These women were known to cast spells, lay curses, and use the bodies of the dead for unclean rites. They were much feared and their activities were strictly forbidden by law.

Last of all was the *venefica* previously mentioned: the poisoner. I did not plan to go looking for one of those just yet. And, for obvious reasons, they did not publicly cry their wares like ordinary vendors.

The Campus Martius had once been the assembly and drill field for the City's legions, but its open spaces were getting fewer as buildings encroached. Once the only really large structure there had been the Circus Flaminius, but everything was now dominated by the huge Theater of Pompey and its extensive complex, which included a meeting hall for the Senate. Since its completion, most Senate meetings had been held there. At least the place had enough room. Sulla had almost doubled the number of senators without building a correspondingly large Senate chamber. Now, twenty years later, despite deaths and purgings by the censors, there were still far too many to fit comfortably in the old Curia.

I saw the tents and booths immediately upon coming in sight of the Circus Flaminius. They were brightly colored and painted in fanciful designs with stars, serpents, and lunar crescents being favored motifs. They also seemed to be doing a brisk business, another sign of unsettled times. As in so many other matters, Rome had two distinct traditions in fortune-telling: the official and the popular.

On an official level, the state had augurs who were elected and who interpreted omens according to a strict table of significance, mostly concerned with birds, lightning, thunder, and other things of the air. They did not foretell the future, but rather, they received the will of the gods concerning a given subject at a particular time. This was a bit rarified for the common people, so from time to time the state resorted to the Etruscan *haruspices*, who interpreted the will of the gods by the robust technique of examining the entrails of sacrificial animals. Rarest of all were consultations of the Sibylline Books, which occurred only at times of calamity or extraordinary omens and were in the keeping of a college of fifteen distinguished men.

These were lofty personages, whose pronouncements were of general concern to the state and community. There were private augurs and *haruspices* who offered personal consultations and charged a fee for their services, but they were rather despised by officialdom. Hence the wise women, whom the common people consulted incessantly upon matters both important and trivial. Unlike the official omen readers, who made no pretence to special powers, the seeresses often claimed the ability to foresee the future. Like their betters, the commons never lacked for credulity, and the frequency of failed predictions never shook their faith in the efficacy of these prophetesses.

The first booth I came to was small and shabby, not that the rest would have been mistaken for *praetoria*. I passed inside and immediately began choking on the thick incense smoke. With smarting eyes I could just make out an aged crone seated pretentiously upon a short-legged bronze tripod, as if she were a genuine sibyl.

"What would you have of Bella?" she hissed. "Bella finds that which is hidden. Bella sees what is to come." Her near-toothless mouth made the words come out a bit mushy, robbing them of their intended awe-inspiring effect.

"Actually, I was looking for someone skilled with herbs and medicines," I told her.

"Six booths down on the left," she said. "Beneath the circus arches. Ask for Furia."

I thanked her and backed out. Before proceeding I stood taking deep breaths while facing the wind. When my eyes stopped tearing, I went in search of the one called Furia.

The crone's talents obviously did not include a facility with numbers, because there were at least twelve booths between hers and the circus. I hoped for the sake of her clients that her gift of prophecy was greater than her arithmetic. From the tents I passed I heard rattling and fluting and the sounds of wailing chants. Some of these women claimed to be able to put customers in contact with dead relatives. I have never understood why these shades never seem to speak in a normal tone of voice but always resort to shrieking and moaning. Neither could I see the point of consulting them. My living relatives gave me enough trouble as it was.

The deep arcade at the base of any circus makes a near-ideal impromptu market, and those beneath the Flaminius had been curtained off, with further curtains providing interior partitions. Quite illegal, of course, but even a small bribe will work wonders. With a bit of asking and poking about, I soon located the booth of Furia.

Luckily, she did not favor incense. The hanging that covered the arch was embroidered with vines and leaves, mushrooms, and winged phalli. The interior was dim but I could see baskets of herbs and dried roots, some of them pungent. In the rear a peasant woman sat cross-legged on a reed mat, dressed in a voluminous black gown and wearing an odd hat of what appeared to be black horsehair woven into a thin, stiff fabric. Its brim spread as wide as her shoulders and its crown was shaped into a tall, pointed cone.

"Welcome, Senator," she said, apparently unawed by my rank. "How may I serve you?"

"Are you Furia?"

"I am." Her accent was that of Tuscia, the land just across the Tiber. These latter-day Etruscans enjoy a great reputation as magicians.

"I am Decius Caecilius Metellus the Younger and I . . ."

"If you're one of the aedile's assistants, I've paid my fees." By this she meant her bribe.

"For a fortune-teller your powers of anticipation are not great. I have nothing to do with the aediles."

"Oh, good. I've had quite enough of them for this year. Bad enough having to look forward to the next lot." She was a handsome, big-boned woman with straight features and the very slightly tilted eyes common to those of Etruscan descent. Her dark brown hair was pinned up beneath her headgear. "So what may I do for you? When folk of your class want to consult with me, they usually send their slaves."

"Do they? Well, there are some things I prefer to do for myself. Things concerning certain, shall we say, very private matters."

"Very wise. I don't suppose you need medicinal herbs. I'll wager you consult with a Greek physician to treat your ills." She looked down her high-bridged nose as she said it, to show her contempt for such newfangled foreign practices.

"I enjoy excellent health at the moment."

"An aphrodisiac, then? I have some excellent medicines to restore virility."

"I'm afraid not; and before you suggest it, I do not require an abortifacient."

She shrugged. "Then you've about exhausted my store." Her attitude was strange. Vendors usually press their wares upon you whether you want them or not. This one seemed almost disdainful.

"Suppose I found myself plunged into deepest despair?"

"Try a skilled whore and a jug of wine. That should fix you up nicely. Improve your outlook no end."

I was almost beginning to like her. "But this is a melancholy beyond bearing. I must end it."

"Try the river."

"That would be ungentlemanly. You get all bloated and fish nibble at you."

"You look like you've spent some time with the legions. Fall on your sword. You can't get nobler than that." She was amused, but she also seemed angry.

"I want an easy and painless way out of my troubles. Is that so difficult to procure?"

"Senator, your talk may be good for making the flowers grow, but that's all. What is it you're after?"

"I want to know why you are so reluctant to sell me a perfectly legal means of suicide."

She stood, unwinding gracefully from her cross-legged seat without using her hands. She was taller than I had expected. Standing in her bare feet she was able to look me straight in the eyes. Her own were green and startlingly direct. She stepped very close, within a few inches of me. As a trained rhetorician, I knew that she was making use of her great physical presence to intimidate me. It worked.

"Senator, go away. Words like 'legal' may have some sort of meaning in the Senate, but not among us." Her breath smelled sweetly of cloves.

"What do you mean?"

"I mean I'll not end up like Harmodia, and neither will anyone else in this market. Try as you will, nobody will sell you what you want."

"Who is Harmodia? And why this sudden coyness concerning poison?" But I was already talking to her back. She stepped delicately to her mat and pirouetted as gracefully as a dancer, then settled on it as gently as a cloud. I couldn't do that without my knees popping like sticks in a fire.

"The subject is closed, Senator. Now leave. Unless you want your fortune told?" Now she showed a hint of a smile. I wondered if she were badgering me.

"Why not?"

"Then come sit here." She gestured to the mat before her as graciously as a queen offering a seat to the Roman ambassador. I sank onto the reeds, trying not to make too awkward a job of it. We were almost knee to knee. She reached behind her and brought out a wide oval tray of very ancient design, made of hammered bronze with hundreds of curious little figures chased on its surface. I knew the work to be Etruscan. She balanced it across our knees and picked up a bronze bowl with a lid and handed it to me. Then she took off the lid.

"Shake this thirteen times, circling to the left, then pour it onto the tray."

The bowl contained a multitude of tiny objects and I did as I was bidden, rotating the bowl violently in leftward circles thirteen times. Then I upended it and the things inside tumbled out. There were stones and feathers and a great many tiny bones; the reedlike bones of birds and the knucklebones of sheep. I recognized the skulls of a hawk and a serpent, and the yellow fang of a lion old enough to have been killed by Hercules. She studied these, muttering under her breath in a language I did not recognize. The light coming in over the door curtain seemed to dim, and a cold breeze touched me.

"You are rooted to Rome, but you spend much time away," she said. "Your woman is high-placed."

"What other sort of woman would I have?" I said, disappointed. "And what senator doesn't spend half his time away from Rome?"

Furia smiled slyly. "She is higher than you. And there is something about her that you fear." This took me aback. Julia was patrician. But fear her? Then I remembered what there was about Julia that I feared; I feared her uncle, Julius Caesar.

"Go on."

"Oh, you want a special fortune told?" Now her smile was openly malicious. She gathered up her things and replaced them in the pot and covered them. Then she put away the tray. "Very well. But remember that you requested this."

Now she settled herself and her face went blank, hieratic, like the face of an Asian priestess.

"Give me something to hold that is yours. Have you something that has belonged to you for a long time?"

All I had with me were my clothes, a small purse, my sandals, and the dagger I usually hid in my tunic when I went out during uncertain times. I took out the dagger.

"Will this do?"

Her eyes glowed eerily. "Perfectly. I won't have to use a knife of my own." That sounded ominous. She took the dagger and held it for a moment.

"You've killed with this."

"Only to preserve my own life," I said.

"You needn't justify yourself to me. I don't care if you murdered your wife with it. Give me your right hand."

I held it out. She took it and gazed into my palm for a long time and then, before I could pull it back, she slashed the tip of the blade across the fleshy pad at the base of the thumb. The blade was so sharp that I felt no pain, just a thrum like a plucked lyre string that went all through my body. I made to jerk my hand away.

"Be still!" she hissed, and it was as if I was rooted to the spot. I had lost all power of motion. Swiftly, she drew the blade across her own palm, then she gripped our two hands together, with the hilt of my dagger between them. The bone grip grew slick with blood.

I was almost beyond astonishment, but she further amazed me. She raised her free hand to the neck of her gown and jerked it down, baring her left breast. It was larger than I would have expected, even on so Junoesque a woman, full and slightly pendulous. In the dimness the white of her flesh was almost luminous against the black fabric. She drew my hand toward her, and held both hands and dagger against the warm softness of her breast.

For a moment I thought, half-crazily, *This beats gutting a sacrificial pig any day!* Then she began to speak, in a rapid monotone, running her words together so that they were difficult to follow as her brilliant green eyes lost focus.

"You are a man who draws death like a lodestone draws iron. You are Pluto's favorite, his hunting dog to chase down the guilty, a male harpy to rend the flesh of the damned and blight their days, as yours will be blighted." She released my hand, almost throwing it back at me. As I fumbled the dagger back into its sheath, she contemplated the spiderweb of our mingled blood that nearly covered her breast, as if she read some significance in the pattern. A heavy drop gathered on the bulbous nub of her nipple, mine or hers, who could tell?

"All your life will be the death of what you love," she said.

Unnerved as I seldom had been in my life, I scrambled to my feet. This was no mere fortune-telling *saga*. This was a genuine *striga*.

"Woman, have you cast a spell on me?" I demanded, unashamed at my shaking voice.

"I have what I need. Good day to you, Senator."

I fumbled beneath my toga, trying to extract some coins from my purse. Finally, I cast the whole thing before her. She did not pick it up, but looked at me with her mocking smile.

"Come back any time, Senator."

I stumbled toward the curtain, but even as I grasped it she spoke.

"One more thing, Senator Metellus."

I turned. "What is it, witch?"

53

"You will live for a long, long time. And you will wish that you had died young."

I staggered out of the booth into a day that was no longer wholesome. All the long way home, passersby avoided me as one who carried some deadly contagion.

5

By MIDAFTERNON I WAS OVER the worst of my fright and wondering what had happened. If, indeed, anything had happened at all. I was a little ashamed of myself, panicking like some bumpkin at the words of a peasant fortune-teller. And what had she said anyway? Just the sort of gibberish such frauds always used to dupe the credulous. Live a long, long time, would I? That was a safe enough prediction, since I certainly wouldn't be able to confront her with it should it prove false.

Then I remembered the dense, choking fumes in the first tent. Surely the woman Bella had been burning hemp and thorn apple and poppy gum to soften up her victims. I had been under the influence of these vision-inducing drugs when I sought out Furia. Thus did I comfort myself and salve my wounded pride.

Hermes came in as I was bandaging my hand.

"What happened?"

"I cut myself shaving. What took you so long? Lucius Caesar's house isn't that far away."

"I got lost." A patent lie, but I chose to ignore it. "Anyway, Julia's at home and she sends you this." He held out a folded papyrus, which I took.

"Fetch me something to eat, then get my bath things together." He went off to the kitchen. He came back a few minutes later with a tray of bread and cheese. I munched on this dry fare, washed down with heavily watered wine, while I read Julia's hastily scrawled letter.

Decius, it began, without any of the usual greetings and preliminaries, *I rejoice to learn that you are in Rome, although this is not a good time for you to be in the city. I can only guess that your being here means trouble.* Ah, my Julia, always the romantic. *My father is with Octavius in Macedonia, but my grandmother is here, keeping close watch on me. I will find some pretext to meet with you soon. Stay out of trouble.*

Thus ended Julia's letter. Well, it had been written rather hurriedly. I remembered that there was a marriage tie between the Caesars and Caius Octavius. As I finished my frugal luncheon, I tried to unravel the connection. His wife was Atia, and now I remembered that Atia was the daughter of Julia the sister of Caius and Lucius Caesar by a nonentity named Atius. This Octavius was the birth father of our present First Citizen, a fact of which we were blissfully unaware at the time, and that is the extent of the First Citizen's connection with the Julians, although he likes to pretend that the blood of the whole clan fills his veins.

From my house Hermes and I walked to a street near the Forum where one of my favorite bathhouses was situated. It was a fairly lavish establishment, although the baths of those days were nowhere near the size of the ones built recently by Agrippa and Maecenas, with their multiple *thermae* and exercise rooms, libraries, lecture halls, plantings, statuary, and mosaics. This one had a few decent sculptures looted from Corinth, skilled masseurs from Cyprus, and hot baths small enough for a dozen or so men to converse easily. Good conversation with one's peers is half the pleasure of the baths, and it is difficult to be heard in the vast, echoing *thermae* of today, which will accommodate a hundred or more bathers at a time.

The bathhouse I used was patronized mainly by senators and members of the equestrian order and was therefore a good place to pick up on the latest doings of the government. Leaving my clothes in the atrium under Hermes's less than watchful eye, I went as quickly as possible through the cold plunge, then into the *caldarium* to soak luxuriously in the hot water. As I entered the dark, steamy room I was disappointed to see that there were only two others in the bath; men I did not know.

I greeted them courteously and stepped into the deliciously hot water, then settled chin deep to soak. I had my back to the door and had been in place no more than a few minutes when my new companions looked up toward the entrance with alarm on their faces. I did not bother to look around as men filed in behind me and climbed into the bath, big, hard-faced men, covered with scars. They were arena bait of the worst sort. My two erstwhile companions hastily vacated their places. Soon six hulking brutes shared the water with me, and they left a space to my right. Another man lowered himself into that space, youngish, good-looking in a dissipated fashion, and decorated with only a few minor scars, some of which I had given him.

"Welcome back to Rome, Decius," he said.

"Thank you, Clodius." He had me cold. There was absolutely no way I could fight or escape, and it would be undignified to try. So much for my predicted long, long life.

"Be at ease, Decius. I'm a tribune designate and I have a great many important things on my mind just now. You are the least of my concerns for the moment. Don't cross me and you have nothing to worry about."

"I rejoice to hear it," I said, meaning every word.

"I won't even hold your friendship for that mad dog Milo against you as long as you don't ally yourself with him against me."

"I'm not looking for trouble, Clodius," I said.

"Excellent. We understand one another then." He seemed marginally more sane than usual, not that this was saying much. "As a matter of fact"—he was oddly hesitant—"there is a way we might patch things up between us, start off clean, so to speak."

This was truly mystifying.

"What do you mean?"

"By now you know that my brother-in-law, your kinsman Metellus Celer, was poisoned?"

"I know he is dead," I said cautiously. "I have only heard rumors that he was poisoned."

"Oh, yes, I'd forgotten. You're one of those philosophers of logic."

I let the insult pass. "I prefer solid evidence to hearsay," I told him.

"Well, rumor then has it that Celer was poisoned by his wife, my sister, Clodia. My enemies and the common herd are whispering behind my back that she is guilty, just because she flouts convention and champions my cause."

"The world is full of injustice," I averred.

"You're supposed to be good at finding things out, Metellus. I want you to find out who killed Celer and clear Clodia's name."

I was so stunned that I almost slid beneath the water. He took my hesitation for reluctance.

"Do this and you can have anything of me you ask, and as tribune I can do a great deal for you: honors, appointments, whatever you want. I can push them through the Popular Assemblies almost without effort."

"I don't require a bribe to find out the truth," I said pompously. The temptation was powerful though, which may be why I was so haughty.

He waved it aside. "Of course, of course. But I'm sure you wouldn't object to a generous Saturnalia present, would you?" This was a common way to proffer a bribe.

I shrugged. "Who could take offense at that?" I would like to believe that I only said this because I knew that I would never leave the room alive without agreeing to his proposal. Men have drowned in the baths before.

"It is agreed then," he stated with great finality. "Good. Begin at once. You will need to call upon Clodia. She is having a dinner tonight. You are invited."

"This is all rather sudden," I said.

"I am busy and have little time. You won't be in Rome long, will you, Decius?" The way he said it brooked little disagreement.

"Only long enough to settle the matter of Celer's death."

"Excellent, excellent. I don't mean that we must resume our feud when this disagreeable matter is over, but to be frank the fewer friends Milo and Cicero have in the city during my tribuneship, the happier I'll be." He clapped me on my wet shoulder. "We're men of the world, eh? We all know how politics work. Just because men disagree on certain matters doesn't mean they can't cooperate harmoniously on other matters of mutual interest." Like all professional politicians, Clodius could turn on the charm when necessary.

"It goes without saying," I murmured.

"Precisely." He splashed water over his face and hair. "For instance, Cato and I loathe one another. But I have an extremely important post for him next year, one that I would entrust to none of my friends."

"Permit me to guess that it's a position that will keep him away from Rome," I said.

He grinned. "No reason why I can't accomplish two beneficial acts with one piece of legislation, is there?"

"What's the post?" I asked, genuinely interested. Everything Clodius did as tribune was likely to affect myself and my family in one way or another.

"Our annexation of Cyprus is coming up. I'm going to give Cato an extraordinary position as *quaestor pro praetore* to oversee the transfer and render a full accounting to the Senate, his authority to last as long as he thinks fit to get the job done."

"He's a good choice," I admitted grudgingly. "The island is strategically important and rich. In the hands of most men that would be a license to loot the place and sow bad will among the natives for a generation to come. Cato is utterly incorruptible; not that it makes him any more likable. He'll render an honest accounting."

"My thoughts exactly."

"I take it you don't intend any reconciliation with Cicero?"

His smile dropped away and the real Clodius flashed through. "Some things are beyond even the demands of political expediency. I'm going to drive him into exile and I've made no secret of the fact."

"You realize that you'll be robbing Rome of one of her best political and legal minds, don't you? Cicero is one of the most capable men of our age."

Clodius snorted. Maybe he had water up his nose. "Decius, like most of the aristocrats, you're living in the past. Between the dictatorship of Sulla and the present we've had this little revival of the old Republic, but it won't last. The important figures of our age are the men of action, men like Caesar and Pompey, not lawyers like Cicero."

"Let's not forget Crassus," I said, annoyed at his all-too-accurate assessment of the times. "Men of wealth are of paramount importance, too."

Clodius shrugged. "When has that not been the case? Even kings are primarily rich men, forget about the blood lineage. But wealthy men who are not also powerful soon lose their wealth to men with many followers and sharp swords. During Sulla's proscriptions, wealthy men were routinely condemned so their property could be seized."

"You seem to have all the answers," I said.

He nodded. "I have." He stood and his flunkies rushed to bring him towels. "I really must be going, Decius. I have a great deal to accomplish. The transition to the new government is already in process. I will see you this evening at Clodia's."

"Is she still living in Celer's house?" I asked.

"Yes, for the moment. She will be moving back into the Claudian mansion after Saturnalia. It's more secure."

I interpreted this to mean that Celer's will had been read and he had left nothing to Clodia. This meant that the house would probably go to Nepos, who was half-brother to Celer. He was Pompey's man, and Clodia was aligned with her brother, who was Caesar's. This was a not particularly complicated matter of property, family, marriage, and politics, and typical of the times.

When Clodius and his men were gone, Hermes came tiptoeing in.

"Master, I never saw them coming. I'd have warned you, but I looked up and there were those gladiators and Publius Clodius and I . . ."

"Quite all right, Hermes," I said, studying the ceiling, rejoicing in the fact that I was breathing. "I rather expected that they had killed you. Clodius does so love his little surprises."

"I thought I'd find you floating facedown," he admitted. "I'm glad to see he let you live."

"Then let us rejoice in our mutual survival." I almost felt that I could get out of the bath without my knees wobbling too disgracefully. I had never been reluctant to fight Clodius one-to-one, or each of us with his own followers behind him, armed or unarmed. We'd had it out in the streets more than once, and I did not fear him on anything like an even footing. But there is something unmanning about being caught by your deadliest enemy when you are alone, hugely outnumbered, cornered without means of escape, and stark naked to boot. From a proud and pugnacious Roman, I had become something resembling a jellyfish.

"What's happened?" Hermes asked.

"Well, how shall I explain?" I studied the ceiling some more. "The good part is, we are safe in the streets for a while. Clodius has called off his dogs. The bad part is, he, too, wants me to investigate Celer's death, but only because he wants me to clear Clodia of guilt. I fear a certain conflict here."

Hermes didn't take long to figure out the problem. A

slave always knows exactly where the danger is coming from.

"Prove her innocent and you alienate your family," he said. "Prove her guilty and Clodius will kill you."

"That is how I read it," I affirmed. "Of course, Clodius plans to kill me anyway, no matter what I do. It's not as if a threat from him was anything new. And my family at least won't have me killed. I can, however, look forward to spending the rest of my life draining the swamps on the worst of the family estates."

"You could throw your support to Pompey," said Hermes. He was learning fast.

"No, I can't. I won't back Pompey or Caesar or Crassus. I am a Republican."

"Don't they all claim that?" His grasp of reality was improving.

"Of course they do. But they are lying and I am not. Sulla claimed that he was restoring the Republic, and he proved it by murdering half the Senate and then making his supporters senators whether they'd served in office or not. Pompey was made consul without having ever served in elective office, against all constitutional law and precedent! And Caesar is the worst of the lot because nobody knows what he is up to, except that he intends to be dictator!"

"You know," Hermes said, "your voice sounds really good in here, the way it echoes off the walls, I mean."

"Bring my towel," I told him. Wearily, I climbed from the hot bath and made my way to the massage tables.

An hour later, dressed, massaged, rubbed down with fresh oil, and over my second fright of the day, I felt ready to resume my activities. Life in Rome was nothing if not stimulating. I was already wondering what Clodia would have for dinner.

I STILL HAD A FEW HOURS BE-
fore going to Celer's house. Clodia, I recalled, liked to start
dinner late. This was regarded as scandalous, which was probably why she did it. That gave me time to make another es-
sential call.

Milo's house, or rather fort, was located in a tenement
warren that made it difficult to attack directly. He had planned
it that way. He had once told me that a house fronting on a
public square is imposing, but it gives your enemies plenty of
space to run and build up momentum with a battering ram. It
was because of such foresight that Milo had risen to the prestige and dignity of Rome's most prominent gangster. Always
with the possible exception of Clodius.

At that time Milo was allied with Cicero. As Cicero's star
was descending, Milo's preeminence was likewise fading. It
was one of the many ironies of the political and social scene
that the aristocrats were championed by Cicero, a *novus homo*
from Arpinum, whose favored gang leader was Milo, a nobody
from nowhere, while the representatives of the common people
were Caesar and Clodius, both of them patricians from incredibly ancient and prestigious families.

The guard at the gate was, as usual, Berbix. He was an
ex-gladiator of Gallic origin, who was well known in Roman
courts. He had uncommonly good eyesight, making him especially apt for spotting Clodius supporters at a distance and
concealed weapons closer up.

"Welcome back, Senator," he said, favoring me with a
gap-toothed grin. I was beginning to wish people could find
something more original to say.

"Is Milo in?" I asked.

"He always is, except when he's in the Forum," Berbix answered. "His door's always open to any who want to see him. Go on in." He ignored the dagger beneath my tunic. I was one of the few men who were allowed into Milo's presence armed. Not that anyone, with or without weapons, presented much threat to Titus Annius Milo Papianus.

This accessibility of his was part calculated political wisdom and partly the fact that he wanted people to think of him as a tribune. By ancient custom, the doors of the Tribunes of the People were to be open at all times. Milo felt that political power grew from close contact with the citizens, not hobnobbing with senators. He was always ready to do people favors. Then, of course, they were expected to do favors for him.

I found him sitting at a small table with another man, a hard-faced character in a senator's tunic who looked somewhat familiar. The two of them were going over scrolls that seemed to contain lists of names. Milo looked up at my approach and a huge grin spread over his face.

"Decius!" He sprang to his feet and enveloped my comparatively diminutive hand in his huge paw, the palm of which felt as if it were covered with articulated metal plates. He had been a galley rower in his youth, and he had never lost the horny hands of that profession.

"I hear you're prospering, Titus," I said.

"So I am," he said, self-satisfaction enveloping him like a toga. In another man it might have been a repellant attitude, but Milo accepted the largesse of *Fortuna* the way a god accepts worship. He looked like a god, too, which never hurt him with the voters. He turned and gestured toward his companion. "I believe you know Publius Sestius?"

Now I remembered. "Of course. We were both quaestors

when Cicero and Antonius Hibrida were consuls." It was coming back to me and I held out my hand, which Sestius took. "We never saw much of each other. I remember that you were returned first at the polls and got attached to the consuls' personal staff. I was in the treasury."

"It was a memorable year," Sestius said, which was a diplomatic way to put it. He had the look of an aristocrat who was also a street brawler. The same, I suppose, might have been said of me.

Milo clapped his hands and a thug brought in a tray with a pitcher of wine and cups, along with the usual nuts, dried figs, dates, parched peas, and so forth. Despite his wealth, Milo had no comely serving girls, cultured valets, or entertainers among his staff. Every member of the household was eminently capable of defending the house and their master.

"Publius and I are working out our strategy for next year's tribunician elections," Milo said. "We'll probably spend most of our time in office undoing all the harm Clodius will do next year. Clodius will get Cicero exiled, so we'll get him recalled. That's going to take some hard work."

"I've just had an odd encounter with Clodius," I said, glancing significantly at Sestius.

"And you're still alive? Speak freely, Publius is no friend of Clodius."

Briefly, I sketched out my odd interview with Clodius. Milo listened with his customary intense attention. No nuance of anything he heard ever escaped Milo. At the end of it, he tossed a handful of salted peas into his mouth.

"I fear you are not going to make Clodius a happy man. That harpy poisoned Celer as sure as the sun comes up every morning."

"Why?" I asked. "She's malevolent and she despised her

husband; but she had to be married to somebody, and Celer wasn't as objectionable as most she would have been attached to. He had a fine house, and he left her free to do pretty much as she pleased." This constituted a happy marriage, among my class.

"Celer got a bit too hostile toward her little brother toward the end," Milo said.

"That's right," Sestius concurred. "Decius, you've been away from Rome too much of late. Last year Metellus Celer, as consul, opposed Clodius's bid to transfer to the plebs. He was certainly not alone in that, but he got downright violent about it. He was losing his sense of moderation in his last months in office."

"It was a busy year," I observed. "I heard that Caesar and Pompey and Crassus made up their political differences."

"Temporarily," Milo said. "It won't last. But for now the usual feuds are dormant. Caesar got Clodius transferred to the plebs to clear his path to the tribuneship, got him adopted by a man named Fonteius to do it, and guess who presided as augur at the adoption?"

I ran the list of augurs through my memory, trying to recall which of them were still alive and in Italy. "Not Pompey!"

"Pompeius Magnus himself," Milo confirmed.

"The world is getting to be a very odd place," Sestius said. "If you can't count on people like that to slit one another's throats, what can you count on?"

"Things will be back to normal soon," Milo said. "Clodius is going to make such a mess of things next year that people will demand a return of order."

I had my doubts. "Clodius is ridiculously popular," I

said. "Is it true that he plans to make the free distribution of grain a guaranteed right of the citizens?"

"A radical concept, isn't it?" Sestius said.

"It won him his tribuneship as nothing else could," Milo commented, picking up a few nuts. "I wish I'd thought of it first."

"You're joking!" Sestius said. "If the grain dole becomes institutionalized; instead of an emergency measure, not only will we lose one of our most powerful political tools, but every freed slave, ruined peasant, and footloose barbarian in Italy will head straight for Rome to sign up!"

"They already do that anyway," I pointed out.

"It's no cause for rejoicing," Sestius grumbled.

"We'll sort things out," Milo said confidently.

It may seem odd that men like Clodius and Milo and Sestius could speak with such sanguine assurance, as if they were about to reign as kings rather than serve as elected officials, but the tribuneship had made a great comeback in the last few years. Sulla had all but stripped the Tribunes of the People of all their powers, but one after the other, each year's tribunes had passed laws in the Popular Assemblies restoring them. Now they were more important than ever, and they had the immeasurable power to introduce new legislation and carry it through the assemblies. This was the power that gave or withheld proconsular appointments, apportioned the state's treasure, and got people exiled. The consuls themselves were relatively powerless by comparison, and the Senate had become a debating club. Real power lay with the commons and their elected representatives, the tribunes.

I promised to keep Milo apprised of the situation and

left his house, wondering whether I should go to Clodia's house armed. I also regretted that I had not thought to ask Asklepiodes whether there existed a reliable means to *avoid* being poisoned.

6

THE HOUSE OF THE LATE METEL-
lus Celer was located low on the slope of the Esquiline, in a
district that had somehow escaped the worst of the fires that
periodically swept the city. It was a relatively modest structure. It had been in the family for several generations and so
was on the scale common to the days before the Punic Wars,
when even the greatest families were little more than wealthy
farmers.

Hermes accompanied me in a mixed state of alarm and
anticipation. Clodia frightened him as she frightened everybody. But she also belonged to that new generation of Romans
who affected to love things of beauty for their own sake, rather
than for their value as loot. To this end she surrounded herself
with beautiful things, including slaves. Clodia was a familiar
sight in the slave markets, always shopping for new beauties
as she discarded those past their peak of comeliness.

This was another of her many scandalous traits. Most well-bred people, including my own family, pretended that they never bought slaves but used only those born within the household. When they wanted slaves from the market, they discreetly sent stewards to do the buying. Not Clodia. She liked to look over the livestock herself, examining teeth with her own eyes, punching for wind and squeezing for muscle tone with her own hands.

"Try not to get caught doing anything improper with the girls," I cautioned Hermes.

"Of course not, Master," he said with patent insincerity. "But you do want me to pump them for information, don't you?"

"Quit drooling. Yes, I want to know if they have any knowledge of Celer's death or if Clodia had any strange visitors. Well, I know she has all sorts of strange visitors, but what we're looking for are witch women, mountebanks, the sort of people who are likely to be peddling poisons."

This was a pretty far-fetched hope. Clodia had traveled widely for a woman, and she might have picked up exotic poisons almost anywhere. It was the sort of thing she would shop for. But there was a chance that she had acquired her poison openly, right here in Rome. Aristocratic felons like Clodia often took few precautions to conceal evidence of their crimes. They considered themselves above suspicion, or at least above prosecution.

I knew I was in for an interesting evening the moment the door opened. In the past, Clodia had been allowed to exercise her taste only within her own quarters. The rest of the house was a typically drab, stuffy Metellan establishment. That rule had gone up with the smoke of Celer's funeral pyre.

The *janitor* who opened the door to us looked like one of

those Greek statues of ephebic athletes, all flowing muscles and perfect skin, and dense, curly locks. Except for his scalp he had been fully depilated, a common affectation of highborn women but rarely encountered in men except for Egyptian slaves, and this boy was clearly not Egyptian. The only concession to modesty Clodia had allowed him was a gauzy pouch that bagged his genitals, supported by a thin string about his hips. His only other covering was a gilded and jeweled neck ring by which he was chained to the doorpost.

"Welcome, Senator," the boy said, smiling to show perfect, white teeth. "My Lady and her guests are in the triclinium."

We passed through the atrium with its flanking rooms and its niche for ancestral death masks and on into the peristyle. It was usually open to the sky, but an elaborate awning, decorated with golden stars, had been drawn across it to keep out the cold breeze. Beneath the awning the pool now featured a graceful sculpture of a dancing faun, and fat, ornamental carp disported themselves in the water below. Between the pillars bronze chains supported beautifully wrought Campanian lamps.

Everywhere I looked I saw splendid works of art and craftsmanship. I also noticed that Clodia hadn't bothered to inlay the floors with mosaic in the new fashion. Not much point in it, since she wouldn't be staying. All of her treasures were portable and would go with her.

"Decius!" Clodia came for me, her gown floating around her body like colored air. She was still one of the most beautiful women in Rome and about thirty-three years old that year, her body unmarked by childbearing, hence the near-transparent Coan gowns she favored. The sheer stuff was woven on the island of Cos and the censors always tried to ban it from the City, or at least keep respectable women from wearing it. Clodia's respect for public morals laws was minimal. Her face was youthful, marred only by a certain hardness about the mouth and eyes. She used cosmetics sparingly, unlike so many women.

"How good to see you," she cried, taking my hands in both of hers. "It's been far too long since I've seen you. Fausta told me all about that exciting business in Alexandria. The court there sounds wonderful." Clodia and Fausta were best friends, even though Fausta was soon to marry Milo, the deadliest enemy of Clodius. Politics.

"I am sure Princess Berenice will receive you like a queen should you choose to visit," I assured her. Berenice was even loonier than most Egyptian royalty.

"Come along and meet my other guests. You know some of them."

"Lead on," I said. "But sometime this evening I must speak with you privately."

"I know," she whispered conspiratorially. Conspiracy was something she enjoyed. "But you mustn't bring up the subject at dinner. Oh, Decius, I am *so* glad that you and my brother have made up your silly quarrel!" She was laying it on a little thick, even for Clodia. But then she practiced moderation in nothing, not even insincerity. "Now come with me." She looped an arm through mine and we went into the triclinium, which opened off the roofed portion of the peristyle.

Here some changes had been made. Clodia did not favor the cozy intimacy of the common dining room, so she had knocked down a couple of interior walls and made one room out of three. As I recalled the layout of the house, she had sacrificed Celer's bedroom and study to expand her triclinium.

The couches and cushions were as lavish as any I had seen in Rome, even in the house of Lucullus.

"Well, Clodia," I said, "it isn't quite as princely as Ptolemy's palace, but it's close."

She smiled, accepting it as a true compliment. "Isn't it splendid? There's hardly a furnishing in the room that hasn't been forbidden by the censors at one time or another."

"Sumptuary laws never work," I said. "The people who pass the laws are the only ones who can afford to break them." This wasn't strictly true, because rich freedmen, barred from higher office, were becoming more and more a fixture in the City.

Some of the guests were admiring the wall paintings. These, at least, were not forbiddingly expensive and had been applied to smooth out the effect of knocking three different rooms into one. They were of a style just coming into fashion: a black background with ornamental pillars painted on at intervals. The pillars were strangely spindly and elongated, as if they had been stretched. Here and there along their length were little platforms holding potted plants and bowls of fruit, similarly elongated. Atop the pillars were fanciful terminals consisting of stacked globes or drooping cones. I suppose they were intended to be whimsical, but I found the style dreamlike and faintly disorienting, as if you were seeing something you half-remembered and couldn't quite place.

"Decius, have you met the tribune Publius Vatinius?" She took me to a tall, soldierly man. He looked like the sort who loves to carry out his superior's most atrocious orders.

"I am always happy to meet another Caecilius Metellus," he said. The ubiquity of my family was a byword in Rome.

"Tribune Vatinius was responsible for securing Caesar's extraordinary commission in Gaul," Clodia gushed. If there was anything she loved more than luxury it was power politics.

"A most unusual expedient to deal with the Gallic situation," I said.

"It's a reform long overdue," Vatinius asserted.

"Reform? Do you mean this is something we can look forward to seeing again?"

"Of course. We have to stop pretending we live in the days of our ancestors. We have a vast empire all over the world, and we try to govern it as if Rome were still a little Italian city-state. The way we change offices every year is absurd! A man no sooner learns his task or the territory he is to govern when he is out of office."

"Who would want to hold an office like the quaestorship or the aedileship for more than a year?" I objected.

He chuckled. "Very true. No, I spoke of the offices that hold *imperium:* praetor and consul. Most specifically, propraetor and proconsul. A one-year stint governing a province was one thing when our holdings were just a few days' march from Rome, but it's utterly obsolete now. You can take weeks if not months just getting to your province. Just about the time you've learned your way around, it's time to go home."

"You can usually get a command prorogued for another year or two," I said.

"But you never *know!*" he said with some heat. "And if you want to stand for office again, you have to drop everything and hurry back to Rome, even if you're in the middle of a war. This new way is better. Caesar goes to Gaul knowing he has five years to sort out that situation and bring it to a satisfactory conclusion. Plus, he has *imperium* over both Gauls plus Illyricum; so if he has the barbarians on the run, they can't just duck across the border where he'll have to coordinate with another proconsul." It was one of the rules that a promagistrate wielded *imperium* only within the borders of his assigned province. If he tried to use it outside them he risked being charged with treason.

"It is a well thoughtout policy," I admitted.

"Believe me, it is the only policy from here on," he insisted. "And we need further legislation to allow a serving promagistrate to stand for office in absentia. If a legate can run a province or an army in the magistrate's absence, why not one to conduct an election campaign back home?"

There was considerable justice in his reasoning. The truth was that our ancient system of republican government was dreadfully awkward and unwieldy. It was aimed at thwarting the dangerous practice of concentrating too much power in the hands of one man. Sensible as his solution was (and I had no doubt that it was Caesar's solution, not his), I still hated the idea of giving anyone that much power for that long a time. After five years, especially if he was victorious in battle, all the legions in Gaul would belong solely to Caesar and to no other. Not that this was anything new. Pompey's legions were Pompey's, not Rome's.

"Oh, and you must know the aedile Calpurnius Bestia," Clodia said.

"We spoke just this morning," Bestia said. "Did you find your fortune-teller, Decius?" His beefy, intelligent face creased into a smile as he took my hand.

"Fortune-teller?" said Clodia, lifting an eyebrow in my direction. "Decius, you've changed. What happened to your renowned scepticism?"

"Egypt does that to you," I said. "It puts you in touch with otherworldly things."

"Come along, Decius," she said, tugging at my arm. "If you're going to lie to me, you might as well get drunk and do it convincingly." She took me to a table that was covered with goblets and picked one up and handed it to me. "Now, who haven't you met?" As she scanned the room I set the goblet down and picked up another. She gestured and a tiny, stunningly voluptuous young woman came to us.

"Decius, have you met Fulvia? She and my brother are to marry."

"Yes, I met her here about two years ago. You are more beautiful than ever, if that is possible, Fulvia. But I expected you to be married by now." She truly was stunning, with white-blonde hair piled atop her head in the latest style, held in place by tortoise shell combs and silver skewers.

"Clodius intends to celebrate our nuptials after he takes office." I remembered that furry, palpitation-inducing voice. "He plans to throw a vast celebration for the whole populace, with games and a free distribution of food and oil and everyone's attendance at the baths paid for for the whole month."

"Sounds like a wonderful party," I said, trying to figure out what such a thing would cost.

"He's hired more than a hundred gladiators from Capua to come up to Rome to fight another troupe from the Statilian school," Fulvia said with unmaidenly relish.

"*Munera* at a wedding?" I said, aghast.

"Oh, technically the *munera* will be in honor of our late father, to keep everything legal," Clodia explained, "and they'll be on a day set aside solely for that purpose, but everyone will know that it's part of the wedding celebration."

"And it will win Clodius no end of popularity, I'm sure," I said. *Oh, well,* I thought, *so what if the old boy died almost twenty years ago. It's never too late for funeral games.*

"He's already the most popular man in Rome," Clodia

purred. "This, plus his enactions in office, will make him the next thing to king of Rome."

This was just the sort of thing I liked to hear. Yes, next year would definitely be a good one to stay as far from Rome as possible. If, of course, I survived this year. I was about to make some ill-considered remark about the annually sacrificed King of Fools when I was saved by the arrival of another guest, none other than Marcus Licinius Crassus Dives, third of the Big Three after Caesar and Pompey and richer than the other two and the rest of the world put together. I exaggerate, but he was awfully rich. Clodia dragged him over.

"When did you get back, Marcus?" Clodia crowed. Another returnee. "When I sent my invitation to your house I really didn't expect you'd be there. How lucky for me you were!" She didn't bother with introductions. Everyone knew who Crassus was, and if he didn't know you, you probably weren't worth knowing.

"My dear, you know I'd have run all the way from Campania to attend one of your gatherings," he said, grinning and showing some new, deep lines in his face. In fact, he looked tired all over. "I got back to the City last night, and I've given my slaves orders to tie me up if I ever talk about leaving again."

"Is that where you've been, Marcus Licinius?" I asked.

"Got away from Rhodes, eh, Decius Caecilius? Lucky you. Yes, I've been most of the year organizing the new Capuan colony and a duller, more onerous job I've never had. The Senate formed a judicial board to oversee the settlement of Pompey's veterans and Caesar's paupers on the new lands under the new agrarian law, and they named me to head the board. When Caius Cosconius died last summer the Senate asked Cicero to replace him, but he had the brains to refuse."

"Oh, but such important work, Marcus," Clodia said. "It's the biggest and most important task to face the government since the wars with Carthage. No wonder the Senate wanted you and no other to be in charge." I had never rated such flattery from Clodia.

Crassus shrugged. "A clerk's job, but it had to be done." His words were blunt and commonsense, but I could see the self-satisfaction oozing all over him with her words. Clodia dashed off to deal with a new guest, Fulvia in tow, leaving me temporarily with Crassus.

"It may have been a strenuous task," I told him, "but I'm relieved to hear that it's settled. The business dragged on far too long."

"Largely because of our hostess's late husband," Crassus grumbled, taking a goblet from the table, "though I shouldn't say so under his own roof."

"He was an obstinate man," I admitted. "But he wasn't obstructing Pompey single-handed."

"He nearly was, last year."

"Was it that bad?" I asked.

"Didn't you hear? But I suppose most of the information you got was from your family. They probably spared you the embarrassing details. First, he got in trouble with the moneylenders by continuing to uphold Lucullus's remission of the Asian tax debt. He fought tooth and nail against Clodius's transfer to the plebs. The infighting got extremely nasty and personal, especially since they were in-laws. Then, to cap it off, he attacked the tribune Flavius over yet another agrarian law to provide land for Pompey's troops. It got so openly violent that Flavius charged him with violation of tribunician immunity and had him haled to prison!"

"Prison! A serving consul!" This was bizarre even for our sort of politics.

"Well, it was only for an hour or two. There was a lot of argument whether the sacrosanctity of the the tribuneship overrode the constitutional immunity of the consulship. Caesar was called in to rule on it as *pontifex maximus*."

"Incredible," I mumbled into my wine. "They must've been lining up to poison him."

"Eh? What's that you say, Decius?"

But we were interrupted by Clodia hauling in her latest prize. He was a splendid-looking young man who seemed vaguely familiar to me. He was somewhat flushed with wine, and he had a smile as dazzling as Milo's.

"Sometimes," Clodia announced, "I invite someone just for being wellborn and handsome. This is Marcus Antonius, the son of Antonius Creticus and nephew of Hibrida."

"My greetings to you all," the boy said, gesturing like a trained actor and amazingly assured for one so young. Now I thought I remembered him.

"Didn't we meet at the time of Lucullus's triumph?" I asked.

"Did we? Then I am doubly honored to meet you again, Senator."

"Decius Metellus," Clodia told him.

"Ah, the famous Decius Metellus!" I could see that he had no idea who I was, but he was one of those rare people who could make you like them even when they were being rude.

"Got a military tribuneship for next year didn't you, Antonius?" Crassus said.

"Yes, and I'll be joining the staff of Balbus in Asia. I wish I could have gotten attached to Caesar in Gaul, but all the other candidates were senior to me and they were all clamoring for Gaul."

"You'll have your chance," Crassus assured him. "That's going to be a long war in Gaul."

Dinner was announced and we took our places on the couches. Hermes took my toga and sandals and hurried upstairs, where all the slaves not attending in the triclinium or the kitchen were banished for the duration. There were the usual nine at dinner, although Clodia never felt bound to honor the old custom. It was probably just coincidence. I have named six others besides myself, and I no longer remember who the other two were. Parasites, I suppose, probably poets. Clodia had a fondness for poets.

I was on the right-hand couch, with Clodia to my left and Vatinius to my right. As highest in rank, Crassus had the honorary "consul's place" on the right of the central couch, with Bestia and one of the poets. The other couch held Antonius, Fulvia, and the other poet. Clodia and Fulvia flopped right down on the couches alongside the men, flouting yet another convention. This time, I approved. I would always rather share a couch with a beautiful woman than an ugly man. Or a handsome one, for that matter.

The food was wonderful. Clodia had better taste than most, and while her spread was lavish and included rare viands and spices, she never indulged in the vulgar extravagance flouted by the newly rich. Her wines were the best and nobody seemed to be keeling over from the effects of poison.

The serving slaves were another matter. Like the *janitor* they were exceptional beauties, and like him, they were minimally clad, only ornamented here and there with jewelery and sporting Clodia's specialty: the jeweled neck ring. As a further exotic refinement, they were all of differing races. The wine server was an Arab boy with enormous brown eyes. Towels were passed by a tawny-skinned Asian girl. The carver was a muscular Gaul, who wielded a pair of curved knives with incredible dexterity. The main courses were borne in on platters by southerners who came in gradations of ever darker skin: the eggs were brought in by a pale-brown Mauritanian, the fish by a slightly darker Numidian, the meats by a deep-brown Nubian, and the sweets by a soot-black Ethiopian.

The music, on the other hand, was provided by a small ensemble of albinos, their extraordinary skin like polished, blue-veined marble and their cascading hair like sea foam. Unlike the others these wore gauzy blindfolds that allowed them some vision. I presumed the reason for this oddity was that Clodia disliked their reddish eyes.

In such a company the talk, naturally, was of politics and war and foreign affairs. This was not one of Clodia's artistic gatherings, so the two parasites kept quiet, grateful for a free meal and the radiance of their distinguished betters. The conversation stayed light while we stuffed ourselves, but with the after-dinner wine we got back to the one thing everyone really cared about. The legislations of the year that was ending were discussed, especially the amazing number of new laws rammed through by Caesar (most of them excellent and long-needed, although it pains me to admit it).

Crassus, to whom all deferred, reeled them off, counting ostentatiously on his fingers like a a fishwife totting up the price of a basket of mullets. Crassus had an excellent memory and a politician's grasp of the relative importance of everything.

"First and most important, he passed his Agrarian Law, using public money to buy up the state lands in Campania and distribute them among twenty thousand of Pompey's vet-

erans and a few thousand of the urban poor, to ease the over-
crowding of the city. The Senate balked at that one. Decius,
you should have heard Cato bray!"

"I'm not surprised," I said. "We've called it 'public land,'
but the senatorial families have been leasing them at almost
no cost for generations."

"Including yours, Decius," Clodia said.

"Including mine," I acknowledged.

"Well," Crassus continued, "there was Cato, railing and
foaming at the mouth for almost an entire day, until Caesar
threatened him with arrest."

"Cato is a tiresome man," Antonius said. Fulvia had
moved closer to him than would have been deemed decent in
any other household.

"That he is," Crassus agreed. "Anyway, by next day the
crowd was so big the assembly had to be held in front of the
Temple of Castor, with Caesar reading off his new law from
the steps. Pompey and I were there backing him, naturally,
neither of us serving in any capacity but adding a little much-
needed weight to Caesar's side of the balance.

"Then Bibulus threw in his tame tribunes: Ancharius,
Fannius, and Domitius Calvinus, to interpose their veto. The
crowd grabbed the fasces away from Bibulus's lictors, broke
the rods, and used them to beat the tribunes. How can tribunes
claim to represent the people when the people themselves
rebel against them? Anyway, that was when Bibulus stormed
off to his house and said he was watching for omens. He even
said he was going to sanctify the whole rest of the year, so no
official business could be transacted!" This raised a general
laugh.

"What archaic nonsense!" Vatinius commented.

"Besides," Bestia put in, "Caesar's *pontifex maximus* and

has the last word on any matter touching religion. I suppose Bibulus had to try though. It was the only weapon he had."

"The result was," Crassus continued, "Caesar not only got his law passed by the Popular Assembly, meeting in extraordianry session, he made the entire Senate confirm it and swear an oath to uphold it."

The sheer gall of it was breathtaking. This was far more radical than the peevish reports I had received overseas.

"Except for Celer, I take it?" I said.

"Celer, Favonius, and the ever-reliable Cato held out the longest," Vatinius said. "But in the end they swore to it along with the rest of us."

"Who's Favonius?" I asked.

"We call him 'Cato's Ape,' " Bestia said. "That's because he's as loyal as a dog but not as dignified." Another general laugh. I suddenly realized that Antonius and Fulvia had arranged their clothing, cushions, and coverlets so that their hands could not be seen. The boy's face was redder than ever, and his mind did not seem to be on politics.

"That was the last significant resistance to Caesar," Crassus said. The fingers began to go down in quick succession. "He remitted a part of the Asian taxes to help out the tax farmers, and he confirmed Pompey's arrangements for the government of Asia. That took care of the three biggest issues."

More fingers went down. "There was a reaffirmation of the absolute inviolability of a magistrate while in office—that one will cause Cicero trouble—a law for the punishment of adultery . . ."

"A marvelous piece of legal impartiality, coming from Caesar," Clodia said. More laughs.

". . . a law to protect the individual citizen from public or private violence; a law forbidding anyone who lays hands on a citizen illegally from holding office; a law to deal with judges who accept bribes; several laws to deal with tax dodgers; laws against debasing the coin; laws against sacrilege; laws against corrupt state contracts; laws against election bribery; and, finally, a law to regulate the accounting each promagistrate renders to the Senate concerning his period of governance abroad, one account to be filed in Rome, the other in the province, and any discrepancy to be made up from the governor's own estate."

"Don't forget the *Acta Diurna*," Clodia said. "He decreed that a daily record be kept of all the Senate's debates and activities and published the next morning."

"And," Crassus said with satisfaction, "he rammed every bit of that legislation through over the heads of the Senate, addressing the Popular Assemblies in a group, directly."

It was a staggering circumvention of custom. "From what you say," I put in, "it sounds as if Caesar is not acting as consul at all; he's behaving like a sort of supertribune!"

"That is very much the case," Vatinius said. "And it was necessary. Most of those laws have been bandied around in the Senate for years, and they never got anywhere because the Senate has become an intransigent body of self-seeking little men who will always ignore the best interests of the state in favor of their own."

I found it profoundly depressing. An arrogant, ambitious demagogue like Julius Caesar passed a huge, just, and enlightened body of laws, while my own class behaved like pigheaded Oriental lordlings.

"How did Cicero stand in all this?" I asked.

"With the aristocrats, as usual," Crassus said. "He's getting into deeper and deeper trouble, but he won't face it. We've given him every opportunity to work with us, then he'd have nothing to fear, but he won't believe he's in any danger. He thinks the people love him! Pompey and I can put up with him and Caesar actually admires Cicero, but he's become totally self-deluded and thinks he doesn't need us."

"What a waste of fine talent," Clodia said. "Years ago I thought Cicero was the coming man in Roman politics. The most brilliant mind I'd ever encountered; and coming from outside as he did, without all the baggage of a family history in Rome and a lot of useless political ties . . ." She paused and sighed. "He could have had the world, and in the end all he wants is to be accepted as some sort of pseudoaristocrat."

The talk got looser and more frivolous as the wine flowed and I took little part in it. During it all I brooded on one inescapable fact: Quintus Caecilius Metellus Celer had been a man with enemies.

After a while we rose, groaning and full-bellied, from our couches. Some went out to the peristyle to walk off their dinner, for the house had no formal garden. Antonius and Fulvia slipped away somewhere. The two parasites made fulsome thanks and left. Such men, if they are skillful at both cadging and timing, can work in two free dinners a night.

I now realized that Rome, along with myself, was now suspended in a brief breathing space between the upheavals of Caesar's consulship and the one to come. This frequently happened at the end of a year, when the outgoing consuls were getting ready to proceed to their provinces and the newcomers were arranging their staffs and, often as not, collecting bribes prior to taking office. It was at this time that the whole populace was celebrating Saturnalia, giving gifts, settling debts, and sloughing off the old year for the new. After that, it would be shield up and sword out, and the fighting would start all over.

And the year to come would surely be worse than the last.

Clodia came to me when most of the guests were gone. I hadn't seen Antonius take his leave.

"Now I think we can talk, Decius. I have a sitting room just off my bedroom. It's very comfortable. Come along." I followed her into a small, neat room furnished with two lounge chairs with a small table between them. Much of one wall had been turned into a large window overlooking a small, delightfully picturesque gully carpeted with myrtle, from which rose the sounds of night insects. Thirty yards away, on the other side of the little gorge, was a circular temple of Venus in one of her many aspects.

"I had no idea this house commanded such a prospect," I said, leaning out the window and hearing the sound of a spring running over the gravel below.

"Isn't it lovely? Celer never would have noticed, since this is the rear of the house. This was a storeroom until I took it over and had the window made. My maids make me up here in the mornings. It catches the early light." She clapped her hands and a pair of slave girls brought in a pitcher of wine and goblets. They were typical of Clodia's purchases. They were twins, barely nubile, and quite beautiful, except for the barbaric designs tattooed over their faces and bodies.

"Scythians," said, noticing my interest. "Only the children of the nobility are tattooed like this." She stroked the tawny hair of one. "The pirates wanted a fortune for them. They claimed they'd lost a number of men kidnapping them, but I doubt it. Even nobles can fall on hard times. They probably sold these two rather than have to feed them."

"Lovely creatures," I said, wondering how I would fare as a slave among foreigners. "However, it's getting late and we must talk of serious matters. Speaking of which, you should keep a tighter rein on Fulvia. She and Antonius were behaving shamelessly tonight."

"Decius, you are such a prude." She smiled as she poured wine for us.

"I don't care if they dance naked on the *rostra,* but Clodius is apt to take offense."

"Why should he? They aren't married yet."

"Why, indeed?" They were a strange family. "Anyway, Clodia, I must inquire into the death of your husband." I took a seat on one of the lounge chairs and she took the other. The lamps cast a bronzy glow over us and the room. The air was sweet from the nearby countryside. Luckily, the breeze blew from the northeast. If it had come from the southeast, it would have passed over the notorious lime pits where the bodies of slaves and the unclaimed indigent were disposed of. We were far from the fetid heart of the city.

"And why are you doing this?"

That took me aback. "Why? Just this afternoon, Clodius all but ambushed me at the baths and . . ."

"Yes, yes, he told me." She waved it aside with elegantly painted nails. "He thinks you can put an end to the suspicion that I killed Celer. But I am equally certain that Celer's relatives want you to prove just the opposite. Is that why you are back in Rome?" Her eyes were direct, clear, and steady, even though she had done more than justice by the evening's liquid refreshments and was even then putting away more.

"You know what my family wants and what Clodius wants. Why don't you ask me what I want?"

"All right. What do you want, Decius?"

"I want the truth."

She laughed. "Oh, you're such an honest drudge, Decius.

I don't know how you manage to lead such an interesting life. You have Cato's rectitude, although you aren't as boring." She laughed again and then stopped and glared at me with dagger-point eyes. "You think I did it, don't you?"

"I am witholding judgment until I have evidence," I said. "Why do you think I judge you guilty?"

"Because you haven't touched your wine, and I know you have a thirst like Sisyphus. And you don't get to drink wine of this quality every day, either."

I knew my face was flaming as bright as Antonius's had earlier that evening. Ostentatiously, I took a large gulp from my cup. It was a wonderful Massic, as smooth as Clodia's complexion. She leaned forward and studied my face solemnly.

"I do wish we had better light," she said. "I'm trying out a new one, and I'd like to observe the effects."

"You bitch!" I said, pouring myself another cupful. As she had said, it might be a long time before I had a chance to taste such a fine vintage again. "Now tell me how it happened."

She sat back, smiling. "That's better. You aren't too objectionable when you're not pretending to be Romulus. Where shall I begin?"

I thought about what Asklepiodes had said. "Was Celer's death sudden, or did it come after a lengthy illness?"

"It was unexpected. He was always a powerful, vigorous man, and anger didn't weary him as it does most men. He was like my brother in that."

"Anger?" I asked.

"Weren't you listening at dinner?" she said impatiently. "His whole term as consul was one battle after another, and it didn't stop when he stepped down. He was being prosecuted continually for his actions in office so that he had to keep putting off leaving for his proconsular province."

"Which province was he to have?"

"Transalpine Gaul. Afranius, his colleague, was to have Cisalpine. But that tribune, Flavius, was after Celer like a Mollossian hound. Finally, he got Celer's appointment revoked."

I made a mental note to visit this firebrand. "Men have been known to drop dead from such provocation. Might his anger have brought on a seizure?"

She shook her head. "No, he never got carried away. His anger was of the cold, deliberate sort. He was a Metellus, after all."

Meaning that my family was famed for moderation, unlike the Claudians to whom she belonged, who had a streak of criminal insanity.

"He was going to take Flavius to court again," Clodia went on. "The year had gotten so far advanced that it would have been useless to go to Gaul even if he could have gotten his appointment back, but he planned to sue for another appointment for the next year." This was not unheard of. Pompey had once had a delay of three or four years between sitting as consul and being assigned a proconsular province.

"But he died before he could take Flavius to court?"

"He rose that morning to go to the Forum. He was the old-fashioned sort, like most of you Metelli. He just threw on his tunic and toga and went out to receive his clients."

"Did he take breakfast?"

"Never. While he went through his greeting round, he always had a cup of hot *pulsum.* That was all." She made a face and I sympathized. The old soldier's drink of vinegar and water had never agreed with me either. "Since he was going to court, they were all supposed to follow him there. As he was going out the door, he collapsed, clutching his chest and breathing heavily. The slaves carried him back to his bedroom, and someone went running for a physician."

"Did you see any of this?"

"No. We maintained separate bedrooms on opposite sides of the house, and I rarely rise before noon. The steward came and summoned me when he collapsed."

"And you went to see him immediately?"

"Of course not!" she said testily. "Do you think I am going to go out among important people with my hair tangled and my face in disarray?"

"There is precedent," I said. "It is even customary, along with breast-beating and lamentation."

"He wasn't dead yet. For all I knew he wasn't even in serious danger."

"Who was the physician?"

"Ariston of something or other. He wasn't much use."

"Ariston of Lycia. I know of him. My family retains his services." Under a common arrangement, the Metelli gave this physician a fat present each Saturnalia and he attended us at need. By law, physicians in Rome, like lawyers, could not charge fees for their services.

"He'd arrived by the time I got to Celer. My husband was having great difficulty breathing and his face was turning blue, as if he were choking, but that was not the case. He felt Celer's belly and said something about paralysis of the diaphragm and tried to sound very wise, but I could see that he had no idea what to do."

Ariston. Another man to see. Before this was over I was going to have to talk to everyone who had been in Rome that day. I might have to make a tour of the provinces, to find those who had left. This was getting more complicated, and it had started out complicated enough.

"When did Celer die?" I asked her.

"Just before nightfall. His breath grew more and more labored, until he stopped breathing entirely just after the sun set."

So much for spectacular symptoms. "If he had been a bit older," I said, "or in less than perfect health, there would be little suspicion of poisoning."

"Of course there would be!" she said, revealing for the first time the strain under which she lay. "Because I am his wife! When a prominent man dies and it is not because of age, violence, or a recognizable disease, poisoning and witchcraft are always suspected. As it happens, his wife was a scandalous woman. Everybody knows how he and Clodius hated each other, and that I have always supported my brother. Hence, I must be the poisoner."

"I won't be hypocritical and pretend I think you incapable of such a crime," I said. "Nor that I think you wouldn't do it without a qualm if you thought you had sufficient reason. It's just that there are so many candidates that you are not even at the top of the list. Clodius, Flavius, and Pompey had plenty of motive, and they are just the three most prominent."

"Yes, but they are *men!*" Clodia said. "Everyone thinks they would have murdered him in an open and respectable manner, with swords or daggers or clubs. Poison is supposed to be the weapon of women or contemptible foreigners." She was beginning to get wrought up. "And I am a scandalous woman! I speak my mind in public, no matter who is listening. I keep company with poets and charioteers and actors. I indulge in religious practices not countenanced by the state. I pick my slaves personally, right in the public market, and I wear gowns forbidden by the censors. Of course I must have poisoned my husband!"

"You forgot to mention incest with your brother," I pointed out.

"That is just one of the rumors. I was speaking of the things I actually do. The truth is, it doesn't take much to be a scandalous woman in Rome; and if you are guilty of one impropriety, then you must be capable of anything."

I shook my head. "Clodia, what you say is true enough of Sempronia and the elder Fulvia and a few others. They are just unconventional and have a taste for low company and are public about it. I happen to know from personal experience that you are capable of murder."

She held my gaze for a few seconds, then lowered her eyes. "I had no reason to poison Celer. He wasn't a bad husband, as such things go. He didn't pretend that our marriage was anything more than a political arrangement, and he allowed me to do as I pleased. After the third year, when he was satisfied that I was not going to bear him any children, he no longer objected to any men I cared to see."

"He was a model of toleration."

"We would have reached an amicable divorce soon anyway. He was looking for a suitable woman. I wouldn't have killed him for his property. He left me nothing, nor did I expect him to. I had no reason to kill him, Decius."

"At least now you're not pretending that you don't care whether I believe you."

"It isn't that I prize your good opinion. Do you know the punishment for *venificium?*"

"No, but I'm sure it's something awful."

"*Deportatio in insula,*" she said, her face bleak. "The poisoner is taken to an island and left there, with no means

94

of escape. The island chosen is always exceedingly small, without population or cultivated plants, and with little or no freshwater. I made inquiries. Most last only days. There is a report of one wretch who lasted several years by licking the dew from the rocks in the morning and prying shellfish up with her bare fingers and eating them raw. She was sighted by passing ships for a long time, howling and raving at them from the waterline. She was quite a horrid sight toward the end, when her snaky white hair almost completely covered her." She was quiet for a few moments, sipping at her Massic.

"Of course," she added, "that was just some peasant herb woman. I would not wait to be carried off. I am a patrician, after all."

I stood. "I will see what I can do, Clodia. If someone poisoned Celer, I will find out who it was. If I find that it was you, that is how I will report it to the praetor."

She managed a very small, tight smile. "Ah, I can see that I've snared you with my feminine wiles again."

I shrugged. "I'm not an utter fool, Clodia. When I was a child, like most children, I burned myself on a hot stove. That taught me to be wary of hot stoves. But while I was young I still burned myself through incaution. Now I am careful of approaching even a cold stove."

She got up laughing. Then she took my arm and led me from the room. "Decius, you are not as adept at striking down your enemies as a hero should be. But you may just outlive them all."

Hermes met me at the door and an aged *janitor* let us out. Apparently the beautiful youth was just for show. This one wore a plain bronze neck ring and wasn't even chained to the doorpost. As usual I refused a torch, and we stood outside for a few minutes, allowing our eyes to adjust. In a sense, Clodia's words have proven to be prophetic. I have outlived all of my enemies but one. The problem is, I outlived all my friends but one as well.

"Did you learn anything?" I asked Hermes as we made our way back toward the Subura.

"There's hardly a slave in the place who was there when Celer died. Clodia didn't like his slaves because they weren't pretty enough, and she sent them off to his country estates. Most of them she bought since he died. Some of her personal slaves were there at the time, but it was like the two of them lived in different houses and their staffs didn't mix much."

"Well, you can't expect slaves to speak readily about a murder in the house."

"Can you blame them?" Hermes asked. "I think they're happy that Clodia is the suspect, because if she weren't, it might be one of them. Then every slave in the house might be crucified."

Rome has some truly barbarous laws, and that is one of them.

The moonlight was tolerable and the route was familiar. We would simply work our way downhill to the Suburan Street and thence continue downhill into the valley between the Esquiline and the Viminal, where my house lay. I was steady enough, having moderated my intake of wine for a change. In such a place and in such company I knew better than to incapacitate myself. I wasn't truly worried about being poisoned, not much.

It was not terribly late. Here and there people wended their way home from late parties, their torches winking like lost spirits among the narrow alleys and tall apartment buildings. A fat man passed by us, weaving, supported on each side by a slave boy. An ivy wreath sat askew on his bald head, and he sang an old Sabine drinking song. I envied someone who could carouse so carelessly these days.

An odd religious procession passed by, with much wailing and clashing of cymbals and tootling of flutes. It might have been a wedding or a funeral or a premature celebration of the coming solstice. Rome is full of foreign religions and strange little cults.

Everywhere people were working late into the night decorating their houses and public squares for Saturnalia, hanging wreaths, painting over the malediction graffiti on the walls, and replacing them with good-wish slogans, heaping small offerings before neighborhood shrines, even washing down the streets.

"That's a marvel worth traveling all the way from Rhodes to see," I commented.

"The decorations?" Hermes asked.

"No. Clean streets in Rome. I . . ." That was when I noticed we had followers.

"Well, it's only for one day." Back then, Saturnalia was celebrated for only a single day, not for three, as recently decreed by the First Citizen. "I'm looking forward to . . . what's wrong?"

"Eyes front, keep on walking as you were," I ordered him. "We've acquired some admirers." My hand went inside my tunic and gripped my dagger. I chided myself for not carrying my *caestus* as well. A metal-reinforced punch is a great help in a street fight, and it is always unexpected.

The question was: What did these men want? I knew there were at least two. Did they want to rob me? Kill me? Or were they just out for some fun? All three were reasonable expectations. Any well-dressed man was a target for thieves, especially after dark. I was engaged in a rather murky investigation involving a number of people who seldom hesitated to kill anyone they found inconvenient. And there were always those amusement seekers who found the sight of blood and teeth on the street infinitely pleasing. Ordinarily, thieves and bullies were easily discouraged by the prospect of armed resistance. Hired killers might take more persuading.

"I see two," I remarked. "Do you see any more?"

Furtively, Hermes glanced around. "Not much light. It's the two behind us, isn't it? The ones pretending to be drunk?"

"That's right." Somehow, sober men can seldom imitate drunks convincingly, unless they are trained mimes.

"No, I don't see any others."

"Good." We were nearing my home. "When we get to the shrine of Ops on the corner, I want you to dash ahead and get the gate open. Be ready to shut and bar it behind me when I come through."

"Right," he said, relieved that I wasn't asking him to stand and fight.

As we neared my house the two "drunks" behind us began to walk more quickly, losing their wobbly gait in the process. The moment we passed the corner shrine, Hermes broke into a sprint and I hurried after him, considerably hampered by my toga. I would have cast it aside, but a good toga is ruinously expensive. Besides, the cumbersome garment is not without its uses in a brawl. I almost made it to my gate before they caught up to me. When I sensed they were within arm's reach, I whirled, unwilling to risk a knife in my back as I went through the gate.

My move was unexpected and they checked their pursuit, almost skidding on the cobbles. Even so, the one on the right barely escaped impaling himself on the dagger I held out at full extension. Both men had knives in their hands, short *sicas* curved like the tusk of a boar. While the two stood disconcerted, I whipped off my toga and whirled it, wrapping my left forearm with a thick pad and leaving a couple of feet of it dangling below.

"What will it be, citizens?" I asked. "Shall we play or would you rather walk away in one piece?" As usual, frustration and puzzlement had put me in just the right mood for a brawl. Sometimes I am amazed that I survived those days.

They hadn't been expecting this, which meant they didn't know my reputation. Both men wore short tunics, the *exomis* that leaves one shoulder and half the chest bare. Both had identical scrubby beards and pointed, brimmed felt caps. In a word: peasants.

"Leave off this snooping, Metellus," said the one on the right, waving his blade at me.

"Get out of Rome and leave be," said the other. They had an accent I had heard before but could not quite place. But then, every village in Latium, even those within a few miles of Rome, spoke its own distinctly accented brand of Latin.

"Who sent you?" I asked. The one on the left tried to slide in, but I snapped a corner of my toga at his eyes and took advantage of the distraction to cut the other one, nicking him lightly on the hand. The left-hand peasant got over his surprise and took a cut at me. He was creditably skillful but not quite fast enough. I blocked with my impromptu shield and punched him in the nose with my wool-wrapped fist. The other slashed toward my flank, but I jumped back and evaded the stroke. They weren't as unskilled as their appearance suggested. If they got their attack coordinated, I knew, they would get to me soon.

"Back off, you louts!" The cry came from behind me and

a second later Hermes was beside me, my army *gladius* in his right hand, the moonlight gleaming along its lethal edges. "You two may be terrors in your home village, but you're in the big city now!" He grinned and twirled the sword in his hand, an excellent act, considering he had no slightest knowledge of swordplay. But he loved to hang around Milo's thugs, and he knew their moves.

Now thoroughly disconcerted, the two backed away. "Stop poking into things as don't concern you, Metellus," said one of the rustic gemini. "If you don't, there'll be more of us back soon. Leave Rome now, if you want to live." With that, the two backed to the end of the block, then turned and darted around the corner and were gone.

"That was well done, Hermes," I said, as we walked the few steps to my gate. "I really must get you enrolled in the *ludus*. I think you'll do well."

"When I saw it was just a couple of bumpkins that had ridden into town on a turnip wagon, I ran to get your sword," Hermes said. "What was that all about?"

"That's what I'd like to know," I told him. "Clodius would have sent trained killers. Clodia would have poisoned me. All my enemies have competent murderers for their dirty work. Who sends hayseed bullies from the hills?"

We went inside and barred the gate. Cato and Cassandra stood there, blinking, wakened by the commotion from a sound sleep. "What is it, Master?" Cato asked shakily.

"A couple of cutthroats," I told him, holding my toga out to Cassandra. "There may be some cuts in need of reweaving."

She took it, yawning. "I hope there aren't any bloodstains this time. That's always the hard part, getting the blood out."

"None of mine," I assured her. "But I punched one of them in the nose and he may have bled on it."

"Who cares whose blood it is?" she grumbled. "Blood's blood."

Yes, my tearful welcome home was definitely a thing of the past.

7

MY CLIENTS SHOWED UP THE
next morning. Word had gotten out. Burrus, my old soldier,
was there. So were several others I knew well, along with quite
a few that I didn't. Celer had died childless, and it seemed
that his clients had been divided among the rest of the family.
There were so many of us that none was burdened with too
many of them, but it seemed to me that, as the most penurious
of the lot, I should have inherited no more than two or three.
Instead, I had eight of them, almost doubling my crowd. I
suppose I should have been flattered. It meant that my family
believed I had a political future, if they thought I would need
so many.

After a lot of greeting and learning of names, I had a
sudden thought and took Burrus aside.

"Burrus, it occurs to me that you've been over much of
Italy on maneuvers and military operations. Have you ever

heard this accent?" Here I spoke a few words in the fashion of my attackers. I had been particularly struck by the odd way they used *p* for *c* and placed strong emphasis on dipthongs. Burrus frowned at my amateurish recital, but he also showed recognition.

"If anyone talks that way, it's the Marsi, up around Lake Fucinus. We did a lot of fighting in that area in the Social War. I was with Pompeius Strabo's army in that one. It was my first war and bloodier than any I ever saw afterward. Strabo was a hard one. Why, in one day we executed so many prisoners that . . ."

"Yes, yes," I interrupted, knowing he could go on all morning. "Strabo was a savage of the old school. But have you heard anyone talking like that lately?"

He shrugged. "Just about every day. The Sabellian lands aren't far from here, and they bring their livestock and produce to the markets in Rome all the time. Why do you ask?"

"Oh, I had a few words with some men who spoke that way recently and I was curious." The market was probably where I had heard the dialect, among a score of others. Like most Romans I separated accents into "City" and "country" and seldom drew further distinction. The Sabellians were among the many ancient races of Italy, their most prominent people being the Marsi, with whom we had fought a terrible war thirty years before over the demands of the Marsi and other peoples to have their rights as Rome's allies acknowledged. They were ruthlessly put down, and then, in an almost whimsical fashion, almost all of their demands were granted. Now they were full citizens and an invaluable well of manpower for our legions.

I needed to be able to move about freely that day so I dismissed my clients, reminding them that I would require them all to attend me for the upcoming rites at the Temple of Saturn. Then, with Hermes at my heels, I went out for my morning shave and a walk to the Forum.

The whole month of December is sacred to Saturn, so very little official business is transacted in that month. There are no Senate meetings unless there is an emergency; there are few trials or other judicial proceedings. The outgoing officials are wrapping up their affairs and preparing to be sued for their actions in office, and the incoming ones are preparing for a year of unrelenting toil. December is Rome's breathing space. In the old days, it was a time of recovery from the sheer physical exhaustion of the harvest and the vintage. Now slaves do most of that work. At least they get a holiday on Saturnalia, although not for the whole month of December.

The Forum was filled with citizenry, many of them putting up decorations, the rest gawking at those doing the work. Everywhere there were sheaves of grain and quaint figures made of plaited corn stalks. Wreaths and garlands of vine leaves were draped from all of the Forum's many points of attachment. Marquees, stalls, and booths were being set up, bright with dyed awnings and new paint. For the holiday, most restrictions on vending in the Forum were relaxed. Most of the booths would be hawking food, but many would sell masks, wreaths, and chaplets. Others sold the wax candles and the little earthenware figurines that were the traditional Saturnalia gifts.

"Hermes," I said as we surveyed the preparations, "I plan to be in the archive for a while. I want you to wander among these vendors and keep your ears open. You remember how those two louts last night sounded?"

"I'm not likely to forget"

"Find out if there are many speakers of that Marsian

dialect in town selling their wares. If you see those two, come running to get me."

"The light wasn't very good last night," he said doubtfully. "I'm not sure I'd recognize them if I saw them. Peasants mostly look alike."

"Do your best." I went to the *tabularium,* trudging up the lower slope of the Capitoline, where the temples clustered thick on our most sacred ground. The state archive was housed in a huge, sprawling building graced with rows of imposing arches and columns and statues on the side overlooking the Forum. The rest of it was as undecorated, inside and out, as a warehouse.

And warehouse it was, after a fashion. In it reposed all the records of state that were not kept by ancient tradition in one of the temples. There were various religious explanations given why the treasury records were in the Temple of Saturn and the archive of the aediles was in the Temple of Ceres and so forth, but I think it was just so that we wouldn't lose all our records in a single fire. The walls of the *tabularium* were lined with shelves and honeycombed with cubbyholes containing documents in every conceivable form: Scrolls predominated, but there were wooden tablets, parchments, even foreign treaties written on palm leaves. Those of a more grandiose frame of mind left tablets inscribed on sheets of lead, impressed on slabs of baked clay and carved in stone. Those wishing special magnificence for their documents had them carved on polished marble.

Much of this was an exercise in futility. Personally, I think the clay slabs will last the longest. Lead melts at a low temperature, and many people are unaware of how easily marble is damaged by fire. Not that much of the stuff cluttering the *tabularium* would be missed anyway, however it might perish.

On the second floor, on the airy side facing the Forum, was the Hall of Court Documents. Like the rest of the establishment, this division was presided over by state freedman and slaves. They were all experts in the sole task of storing and caring for the documents and memorizing where everything was. At the time the freedman in charge was one Ulpius, a man of dry and musty manner, no doubt absorbed from his surroundings.

"How may I help you, Senator?" he asked. His Latin had the faintest Spanish tinge, although he must have come to Rome as a child.

"My friend, I need information about one Harmodia." I smiled at him benevolently. It is customary to be chummy with slaves and freedmen around Saturnalia.

He blinked, not buying it. "Harmodia? Is this a woman?"

"The form of the name makes this the logical conclusion," I said. "I am looking for any court records concerning a woman named Harmodia."

"I see. And you have no information concerning this woman save her name?"

"That is correct," I told him happily.

"Hm. It might help to know if she is slave, freedwoman, or freeborn."

"I'm afraid I wouldn't know."

"Living or dead, perhaps?"

"Wouldn't have the foggiest."

"Have you considered consulting the Cumaean sibyl?" Still dusty dry, but with a definite edge of sarcasm.

"Listen," I told him, "I am engaged upon an important investigation . . ."

"For which consul, praetor, tribune, *iudex*, investigative committee, or other authorized person or body? Or have you, perhaps, a special commission from the Senate?"

Trust a fussy bureaucrat like Ulpius to ask questions like that. I was so accustomed to talking my way around such embarrassing inquiries that I had to think for a moment before I remembered that I actually *had* official backing, of a sort.

"I am acting for the tribune Quintus Caecilius Metellus Pius Scipio Nasica"—ah, that great, thumping name—". . . and the tribune-elect Publius Clodius Pulcher."

"I see," Ulpius said, sighing, disappointed that he wouldn't be able to turn me away with a few withering words. "But I have very little hope of assisting you if you have nothing but a name."

"As I was about to say, one of my informants in this investigation mentioned a Harmodia who may have met with a lamentable fate. I think it must have been within recent weeks."

"Anything else that might narrow the field, as it were?"

"She was probably from the countryside or the nearby villages, and I think she may have been an herb seller."

"I suppose that helps," he said, gloomily. "It would help further if we knew what district the woman is, or was, from. That would at least tell us whether a case involving her was brought before the *praetor peregrinus* or one of the others." He turned and snapped his fingers. Immediately, six men sprang forward. He reeled off instructions, as if they were needed. Of course, all of them had been listening. They went to their shelves and began sifting the documents with amazing speed and efficiency. This called for prodigious feats of memory, because there was very little system in the way the documents were filed. Each slave or freedman and his apprentice simply had to keep a mental picture of everything in his area.

While they searched, I walked over to one of the arches and looked down over the bustle of the Forum while leaning against a bust of Herodotus. The old Greek didn't seem to approve of Rome's prosperity from the way he was scowling. He probably thought Athens should be running things. Well, it's just what they deserved for being political and military idiots.

Despite Ulpius's gloomy forecast, a young slave boy was back in a few minutes with a papyrus that looked almost new.

"This is the morning report brought before the *praetor urbanus* on the ninth day of November," the boy said. "On that morning, a woman named Harmodia was found murdered on the Field of Mars, near the Circus Flaminius. Nearby stall keepers identified the woman as an herb seller from Marruvium."

I felt that little surge that I get when a piece of the puzzle fits. Philosophers probably have a Greek term for it. Marruvium is the very heart of Marsian territory.

"Is there anything else?" I asked.

"I checked the morning reports and court records. No one has been apprehended as the murderer." No surprise there. Criminal investigation in Rome was a haphazard affair at best and a peasant woman who wasn't even from the city would have rated even less attention than most victims.

"If you need to learn anything more about the woman," Ulpius said with deep satisfaction, "then you will have to consult the archives of the aediles."

"And so I shall," I told him. "I thank you all." I made certain to memorize the face of the boy who had found the report so quickly. Next time I needed to find something in the *tabularium* I would know who to ask.

I found Hermes prowling the Forum and told him to come with me.

"Any Marsi?" I asked him.

"Quite a few, although I didn't spot anyone who looked like those two from last night. They're mostly selling herbs and medicines. I asked around. Everyone says the Marsi are famous for it."

"Somehow, I'm not surprised. Hermes, we aristocrats are losing contact with our Italian roots. We've been employing Greek physicians for so long that we forgot what every other Italian knows: that the Marsi are famed herbalists."

"If you say so."

While we spoke, we walked at a fast pace toward the Circus Maximus. "And I'll wager," I went on, "that they are poisoners and abortionists of note, as well as witches and general practitioners of magic, for those things always seem to go together."

"Makes sense to me," Hermes mumbled.

The Temple of Ceres is a structure of great beauty and dignity, and its basement holds the cramped offices of the aediles. Inside I learned, without surprise, that there were no aediles present. Like everyone else who could, they were taking an early holiday. Not so the freedman who had charge of keeping an eye on the records and the slave boy who swept out the offices.

The archive of the aediles was nowhere near as voluminous as the great *tabularia* but it was extensive enough. Luckily, I now knew exactly what date I wanted, and the old man shuffled off to fetch what I demanded. A few minutes later, he shuffled back.

"Sorry, Senator. There's nothing about this dead woman."

"What?" I said, astounded. "There must be! This happened in the market area on the Campus Martius, and it involved a stall keeper who must have paid her . . . fees, I suppose, to the aediles. How could there not be a report?"

"I couldn't say. The aediles are only in charge of markets and streets and so forth; they don't handle criminal investigations."

I left very dissatisfied. Granted that it is always difficult to find anything in the state archives, something this recent should be available. We were almost to the plaza surrounding the circus when the slave boy from the temple ran up to us.

"What do you want, you little mouse?" Hermes said, with the usual contempt of a personal slave for one owned by the state.

"I have something that may be of use to the senator," the boy said.

"What is it?" I asked.

"Well, they don't give me much back there," he said insinuatingly.

"You're a slave," I informed him. "They don't have to give you anything."

"I'm owned by the state, so they have to feed me and give me a place to live. On the other hand, I don't have to tell you anything if I don't feel like it."

Hermes was about to punch the boy, but I grabbed his shoulder.

"What makes you think you have something worth paying for?"

"You want to know about that report, don't you? The one about the woman Harmodia?"

I took out a copper and tossed it to him. He tossed it back. "You'll have to do better than that." This time Hermes

111

did punch him. He merely got up off the pavement and held his hand out. I dropped a silver denarius in it.

"The woman Harmodia was found by the Circus Flaminius, murdered," he said.

"I already know that, you little twit," I said. "What else?"

"The aedile Caius Licinius Murena was in the offices that morning and he went out to the Field of Mars to look into it. He came back a couple of hours later and dictated a report to his secretary and gave it to me to file. A couple of days later, a slave from the court of the *praetor urbanus* came and said the aedile needed the report for his presentation to the praetor. I was the only one in the offices that hour and I fetched it. It never came back."

"Who came to report the killing?" I asked him.

"A watchman. I think he was one employed at the Circus Flaminius." The primitive organization of *vigiles* we had in those days did not extend beyond the old City walls. They weren't very efficient within the walls, for that matter.

"Do you know the name of the man who came to get the report?"

The boy shrugged. "He was just a court slave." Court slaves, obviously, were inferior to temple slaves.

"Anything else?"

"I told you what happened to the report, didn't I?"

"Away with you, then," Hermes said, jealous of the boy's financial success. "That wasn't worth a denarius," he said when the temple slave was gone.

"You never know," I told him. "Let's go pay a visit to the Circus Flaminius."

As we walked I thought about the aedile, Caius Licinius Murena. The name was vaguely familiar to me. Gradually, I straightened it out. During the Catilinarian fiasco he had been a legate in Transalpine Gaul and had arrested some of Catiline's envoys who had been stirring up the tribes. His brother, Lucius, had been proconsul there but had returned to Rome early for the elections, leaving Caius in charge. Lucius had been elected consul for the next year along with Junius Silanus. Afterward he had been prosecuted for using bribery to get elected, but Cicero had gotten him acquitted. And that was as much as I knew about the aedile Murena.

We retraced my steps of the day before, across the cattle market, which was more crowded than ever, what with people buying supplies for the feasting to come and animals for sacrifice. The whole city, in fact, was filling up as people poured in from the countryside to celebrate the holiday.

The Campus Martius, in sharp contrast, was nearly deserted. I saw immediately that the previous day's horde of tents, booths, stalls, and so forth had temporarily moved into the City proper, taking advantage of the relaxed market laws. I felt obscurely relieved, not having to pass by Furia's booth.

A bit of asking and poking around turned up the watchman, one of several employed by the circus to keep thieves away from the expensive decorations and prevent indigents from kindling fires beneath the arches on cold nights and perhaps burning the place down. He lived in a tenement near the circus. In common with most of Rome's *insulae*, his was a five-story building, its ground floor mostly let out for shops and its lower living quarters rented to the better-off classes. The upper floors, divided into small, waterless, and nearly airless rooms, were rented to the poor. The object of my search lived on the top floor, beneath the eaves.

Hermes and I toiled our way up four flights of stairs amid the noises of squalling infants and arguing children and adults. The smells of poverty were not pleasant, but I was so familiar with them that I didn't bother to wrinkle my nose. Most of my neighbors lived no better. When I found the door, Hermes pounded on it, hard. For a long time we heard nothing.

"Maybe he's not in," Hermes said.

"He's in. He's a watchman. He sleeps days."

After repeated knocking we heard shuffling and scraping noises from inside. In time, the door opened fractionally and I got a vague impression of a bleary-eyed, unshaven face.

"What is it?" Then he recognized my senatorial insignia and the door swung wide. "Oh. Pardon me, Senator. How may I help you?" He seemed to be equal parts bewilderment and trepidation, unable to fathom what this strange visitation could portend. Also, he was still half-asleep.

"I am Senator Decius Caecilius Metellus the Younger, and I am engaged upon an investigation. Are you Marcus Urgulus?"

"I am." He nodded vigorously. He was a middle-aged man, once robust but running to fat, with more lines in his face than teeth in his mouth.

"Did you, on the ninth day of last month, discover the body of a murdered herb woman named Harmodia?"

"Yes, yes, I did." He looked uncomfortable and embarrassed. "Ah, Senator, I hesitate to invite you into my crib. One reason I took the job of watchman was so I wouldn't have to spend my nights here."

I, too, had little eagerness to enter.

"Is there a tavern nearby? If so, I'll stand you to a cup or two while I hear your report."

"Just a moment, sir." He went back in and I could hear water splashing into a basin. A minute later he reappeared. His eyes were clearer and his hair had been smoothed to a semblance of order. "There's a little dive at the corner of the *insula* next door," he said, leading the way.

We descended and walked out of the tenement with a sense of relief. A walk to the corner and across a tiny street brought us to a low doorway, above which was carved a relief of a charioteer driving a *quadriga*, the four horses depicted in full gallop and painted in garish colors. The area around the Flaminius had for many years been the only developed part of the Campus Martius, and the building was an old one.

"This is the Charioteer," Urgulus said. "It's where most of the men who work at the Flaminius hang out."

We ducked beneath the lintel and went inside. The shutters were propped open, lightening the gloom of the smoky interior. The smoke came from a number of charcoal braziers that warmed pots of spiced wine and pans of sausage. The smell hit my nostrils, and my stomach reminded me that I was neglecting it. I handed some coins to Hermes.

"Fetch us a pitcher of wine and something to eat," I told him, making a mental note to count the change when he came back.

"There's a good table back here where we can talk," Urgulus said, walking back to the murkiest corner, where a square table was placed beneath a sign warning against loud arguing and disorderly dicing. We walked past the tavern's half-dozen or so other patrons. If they were impressed by the presence of a senator in their midst, they didn't show it. Circus people are a notably tough and aloof breed.

We took our seats and a minute later Hermes arrived with a pitcher, a platter of bread and sausage, and three cups. He was taking liberties, but I did not bother to upbraid him for his presumption. It was almost Saturnalia, after all. The wine was not bad at all, only lightly watered, with steam rising from it and flecks of spices floating on its surface. I tasted clove and fennel as I drank, and the hot drink warmed my insides agreeably.

"Now," I said, "tell me about your discovery."

"It was just getting light," Urgulus began, "and I went to the circus watchmen's office to turn in my club and my keys. I'm in charge of the passageways and the gates on the second level, south side." He rolled the cup between his hands and gazed as if into a great, far distance. "I left the circus and walked out from beneath the arches, and I hadn't gone three steps before I tripped over the woman's body." He gave me a strained, sheepish grin. "I was already half asleep, and this side of the circus," he nodded toward the hulking structure visible through the open door, "was still in deep shadow. I landed right in a big puddle of blood."

"Did you recognize her?" I asked.

"Not just then. It was still too dark. I tell you, sir, I almost went home and didn't report it. There I was with blood all over me, and I thought people might think I'd killed her. But I got over my first scare and realized the blood and the body were both plumb cold and the woman had gone stiff. She must have been lying there all night.

"So I went to the fountain and washed the worst of it off, and when I went back it was light enough to see that it was Harmodia."

"You knew her?"

"Oh, yes. She'd had her stall beneath arch number nineteen for years. Can't say I knew her well. I try to avoid those countrywomen unless I need some doctoring, like when I get the toothache or belly cramps."

"Describe her," I said. The man's cup was empty and Hermes refilled it.

116

"She wasn't really a big woman but built sort of stocky. About thirty years old, not bad-looking. She had brown hair and blue eyes and all her teeth. She talked with a Sabellian accent, you know . . . Marsian. A lot of the herb women are from there, or Tuscia."

"How was she killed?"

"Throat cut," he said, drawing his stiffened fingers across his neck in the universal gesture. "And cut good, right down to the spine. That's why all the blood."

"Any other wounds?"

"Not that I could see. Of course, her dress was soaked with blood and for all I know she was stabbed as well. When the other countrywomen came in to set up their stalls, they took charge of the body and I went to the aedile's office to report what I'd found. The aedile Murena came back with me and talked to the people who knew her for a while, then he left. That's all I know, Senator."

"Who claimed the body?" I asked him.

"Some of the market women said they'd take her back to her home. I think it was up around Lake Fucinus somewhere."

"Did no one come forward who had witnessed the murder?"

He gave a cynical laugh. "Do they ever?"

"Seldom. Have there been any rumors?"

"Not that I've heard, and I guess that says something in itself."

"What do you mean?" I asked.

"Well, there are *always* rumors, aren't there? If no one's talking, it probably means somebody important is involved."

"And the other herb women have said nothing?"

"Like I said, Senator, I don't have more to do with them than I have to." He looked as if his wiser nature was telling

117

him to shut up, but the hot wine was warring with his wiser nature and in such a contest, wine always wins.

"Why is that?"

"Well," he looked around, as if someone were trying to eavesdrop. The men at the other tables were rattling dice and knocking back wine, paying us no attention. "Well"—he went on—"they're all witches, you know. They can put the evil eye on you, cast spells, all sorts of things."

"But most are just harmless *saga,* surely?" I prodded.

"Not all of them," he said, leaning forward, speaking low and earnestly. "Some are *striga,* and there's no way of telling which are which until you get on the wrong side of them!" He sat back. "And people say they're especially powerful right about this time, too."

"Why should that be?"

He looked surprised. "Tonight's one of their most important festivals, isn't it? The eve of Saturnalia is when they dance and sacrifice and perform their rites, out on the Vatican field."

This was the first I had heard of such a thing. "Why the Vatican?"

"There's a plot of sacred ground out there," he said. "It's said to have a *mundus* and the witches can call up the dead through it or contact the gods of the underworld. Mark me, sir, at midnight tonight you won't find a *striga* in the city. They'll all be out there."

"You've been very helpful, Marcus Urgulus," I said, handing him a few denarii. "Here. Have a fine holiday."

He thanked me and hurried off, leaving me to sit and ponder. Rome contains worlds within worlds. This world of the witches was a new one to me. It was a part of the world of the peasants and the small country towns, as the politics of the Senate and the rites of the great temples were parts of my own world. Witches and spells and poisons; the thought made my cut palm throb.

"Why all this talk of witches and their rites?" Hermes asked, the hot wine working on him as well. He looked uncomfortable with the subject.

"I don't know," I admitted. "I thought this would be a straightforward murder investigation, just a simple poisoning for sound personal or political reasons. Now we're off into the realms of the occult and the supernatural."

Like most educated people I was sharply sceptical of all superstitions and persons claiming supernatural powers. On the other hand, I knew better than to take chances. And the woman Furia had unnerved me. I couldn't help but wonder: Just what did they do out there on the Vatican field?

I just knew that my curiosity was leading me into something incredibly foolish.

8

THAT EVENING WE MADE PREP-
arations for the rites at the Temple of Saturn. My clients gathered in their best clothes, everyone merry, having dipped into
the wine well in advance of the official holiday, which would
not begin until after sundown and which took full effect only
the next morning, with complete license for the slaves and the
peculiar demands of dress and behavior belonging only to the
day of Saturnalia.

I had my slaves bring out trays of refreshments to keep
the mood going and mingled with the clients, saying all those
inane expressions of goodwill that are demanded upon such
occasions. Despite the pervasive air of jollity that had seized
the city, I had both dagger and *caestus* stashed inside my
tunic. Streets jammed with noisy, celebrating crowds make
even better conditions for an ambush than those same streets,
deserted in the black of night.

Leaving my house, we made our slow way down to the Subura Street and thence toward the Forum, our progress paralytically slow because every last inhabitant of Rome who was not on his deathbed was out in the streets, greeting and dancing and making noise. The wine sellers had clearly been doing a great business, and most of the flutes were being played by persons of no musical talent.

In time we merged with the crowd coming down the Via Sacra, then past the basilicas and porticoes until we all stood before the great Temple of Saturn. The lictors and the temple slaves were there in force, ushering people into their proper places. Here I left my clients and took my place with the rest of the Senate on the steps of the temple, where, as a very junior member of the body, I stood in the back row. Still, this gave me a vantage point, and I could see all the most important members of the state who were in Rome at the time.

In the places of highest honor, near the altar that stood before the entrance, were the vestals, including my Aunt Caecilia, the *flamines* (we had no *Flamen Dialis* that year), the *pontifices,* and all the serving magistrates. Among the aediles I saw Calpurnius Bestia, and I tried to figure out which of his colleagues was Murena, but without success. I saw Metellus Scipio among the tribunes and Clodius with the tribunes-elect. The consul Bibulus had finally come out of his house for this one ritual, which required all officials holding *imperium.* He looked like a man who had eaten too many green peaches.

Looking down and to my left, I saw the patrician families standing in the first ranks at the bottom of the steps. From my vantage point it was shockingly plain how thin were those lines. Once the great power in the state, the patricians had grown so few that there was no longer any particular advantage to belonging to one, save prestige. There were about fourteen patrician families left at the time, and some of these, such as the Julii, were minuscule. Perhaps most numerous were the Cornelians, and even their numbers were much reduced.

Among them I saw Clodia, Fausta, and Fulvia standing in a group. Once I had spotted the Julii, it was easy to find Julia. She caught my eye and smiled broadly. I smiled back. But, then, everyone was smiling. We all get a little silly at Saturnalia.

Behind the patricians stood the order of the *equites,* far more numerous and collectively the most important of the classes, since it was property qualification, not birth, that gave an *eques* his status.

This rigid partitioning by rank was symbolic, for at the end of the ceremony all classes would mingle freely in memory of the Golden Age of Saturnus commemorated in this yearly rite. Unlike all other sacrificial ceremonies, no one, man or woman, slave or free, wore a head covering, for all such solemnity was banished from the happiest ritual of the year.

When all were assembled, the augurs came forward, standing near the altar, watching the sky for omens. Among them was Pompey, dressed like the others in a striped robe, holding in his right hand the crook-topped staff. The populace scarcely breathed for the next few minutes. The evening was a fine one and there was no thunder; no birds of ill omen appeared. They announced that the gods were favorable to continuing the ceremony.

Now Caesar made his grand entrance, striding from inside the temple through its great doorway. There was no ceremonial reason for a consul to arrive on the scene thus, but then, that was Caesar. Here he was doubly important; as consul and as *pontifex maximus,* the supreme arbiter of all matters touching the state religion. He halted by the altar and made a half-turn, gesturing grandly like the great actor he was.

Through the doorway we could just see the huge, ancient, age-blackened image of the god, his pruning knife in his hand. Ceremoniously, the priest and his attendants removed the bands of woolen cloth that wound around the god's legs and lower body. In the dim past we had captured Saturn from a neighboring town, so his feet were bound to keep him from leaving Roman territory. Only on his festival was he loosed. A collective sigh came from the people as the last of the wrappings fell away.

Caesar watched the horizon and the setting of the sun, as if he were personally responsible for it. Since the portico of the temple faced northeast, this was no easy task. When the last gleam disappeared from the gilded pediment of the Curia Hostilia, ancient meetinghouse of the Senate, he gestured again, and the sacrifice was brought forward.

Since Saturn is primarily a god of the netherworld, his rites take place in the evening. For the same reason, his sacrifice was a black bull instead of a white one. The beast led up the steps by the attendants was a magnificent animal, dark as the nighttime sky, his horns gilded, draped all over with garlands. The crowd watched anxiously, for if the animal balked or made loud noises, it would be a bad omen.

But the bull made it to the altar with perfect equanimity and stood patiently, waiting for the rest of the ceremony. The priest and his attendants came forth to stand by the bull with their various emblems of office, and the heart of the ritual commenced. One attendant held up the tablet bearing the written prayer, and the priest began to chant it in a loud voice. Like all such ancient prayers it is in language so archaic that nobody knows what it really means, but it must be recited precisely, hence the tablet. Behind him a flute player blasted away for all he was worth, so the priest would not be distracted by an unseemly sound like a sneeze or cough. Getting the entire population of Rome to stand still for the duration of a lengthy prayer without sneezing or coughing is a marvel in itself.

We all stood with our arms slightly extended, our hands at waist level, palms facing downward, as is proper when addressing a deity of the underworld. The prayer ended, the attendant swung his great hammer, and the bull collapsed to its knees without a sound, already dead when the priest cut its throat. Other attendants caught the gushing blood in golden bowls and carried it to the channel before the altar and poured it in, to drain away through a hole that led to the earth beneath the temple. For a sky god, the blood is poured over the altar.

Now the *haruspices* came forward in their Etruscan robes, chanting their Etruscan chants. They slit open the bull's belly and the entrails tumbled out. They examined the intestines and lungs, then conferred for a while over the liver, turning it this way and that, inspecting its crevices, looking for lumps, malformations, discolorations, or other oddities to interpret, for each part of a liver has a specific significance concerning the will of the gods in particular matters. They said something to the priest, and he spoke to the chief of the Herald's Guild, who stood beside him.

Solemnly and with great dignity, the head herald strode to the front of the portico and stood at the top step. He took a deep, deep breath. This man had, perhaps, the loudest voice in the world.

"*IO* SATURNALIA!" he bellowed, and was probably heard in Cisalpine Gaul.

With that the crowd erupted and the celebration was on. Cries of "*Io* Saturnalia!" went up from all directions. Every citizen, from consul to freedman, took off his toga, the garment that distinguishes the citizen from the slave and the foreigner. For the duration of the holiday, we were all equal. We pretended so, anyway.

Folding my toga and tucking it beneath my arm, I descended the steps to where the patricians were rapidly merging into the general populace. Amid the sea of bobbing heads it was difficult to find one small woman. But I was taller than most and not so difficult to locate.

"*Io* Saturnalia, Decius!" Julia cried, slamming into me like one galley ramming another, throwing her arms around me and giving me a resounding kiss. The license of the season allowed such an indelicacy, unthinkable at other times. Besides, we weren't married yet.

"*Io* Saturnalia, Julia!" I said, when I could draw breath again. "Let's find someplace less deafening where we can talk."

As we pushed through the mob, I caught sight of Hermes. Without thinking, I held my toga out to him.

"Take this to my house!" I called out.

"Take it yourself, Decius," he said, turning away. "*Io* Saturnalia!"

Julia laughed until tears ran down her face while, our arms around each others' waists, we lurched around until we found a wine booth in front of the Basilica Sempronia, bought two rough clay cups full of even rougher wine, and sat on the base of a statue of Fabius Cunctator at the corner of the basilica steps. The old boy got his odd title, "the delayer," from being so cautious about engaging Hannibal in combat. It was a rare case of a Roman leader being honored with a title for showing some plain good sense.

Twilight does not last long at that time of year. As the

sky darkened, torches were kindled, braziers flamed with pine knots, and from them people lit the traditional wax tapers. There is an old story that, in ancient times, the god demanded heads for his sacrifice. Then somebody realized that the old word for "heads," with a slightly different accent, meant "lights," and we've been giving each other candles ever since.

"This has always been one of my favorite sights since I was a child," Julia said, as the flickering or blazing lights spread over the Forum and the rest of the city. "It's how I pictured Olympus or the cities in old Greek myths. How sad that it's only for a day and two nights."

"But the whole point of holidays is that they're unlike other days of the year," I pointed out.

"I suppose so," she said, taking a long swallow. I had the distinct feeling that, like everybody else, she had started much earlier in the day. "All right, Decius, why are you here? I've already heard gossip that you and Clodius have called a truce, and that's like hearing somebody discovered a lost book of the *Iliad* where Patroclus catches Hector and Achilles in bed together. Tell me what you're here for and let me help you."

So I told her. I knew it was useless trying to keep secrets from her, although I didn't see how she could help out in this case. Something kept me from giving a full account of the episode in the *striga*'s booth. The experience still upset me. I had to go back for refills before I got the whole account out.

"You've done a lot, considering you've been in the city less than three full days."

"I pride myself on my diligence," I said.

"Clodia! I wish you could stay clear of that woman. She's perfectly capable of poisoning, and I was sure she has. Do you really think she might be innocent?"

"Only because so many others seem to have had equal if not greater reasons to do away with him. I am sure now that he was poisoned, else why kill the herb woman? It must have been to cover whoever bought the poison from her. But why are these Marsi threatening me? I would think they should want the killer brought to justice."

Julia's brow wrinkled in deep thought. There were times when she could see the patterns in things better than I could, probably because she didn't have to deal with all the violence that kept me continually on my toes. She always claimed that it was because she drank so much less.

"There is one common factor that keeps cropping up in all this, if you can ignore the witches long enough."

"They're pretty hard to ignore," I said. "What factor?"

"Gaul. Murena and his brother were in command there not so long ago. Celer was to have Transalpine Gaul for his proconsular province, but Flavius took it from him and Celer died before he could get the courts and the Senate to give it back. He spent his whole consulship fighting Pompey, and Pompey wanted that Gallic command."

"Instead," I said, turning over the possibilities in my mind, "your uncle Caius Julius got the whole of Gaul for five years."

"My uncle had nothing to do with killing Celer!" she insisted. She still had a blind spot for Caesar, although by then his ambitions were plain to everybody.

"Gaul. I don't know, Julia. We've been occupying and colonizing and fighting in that place for so long that hardly anyone of public consequence *hasn't* had some connection with it. I've been there myself more than once on military or diplomatic duties."

"But so many of them connected with the murders, and

so recently! Right now, Gaul is the biggest plum to be picked. I'm surprised they haven't tried to poison my uncle. You know Pompey wants Gaul."

"Caesar is too smart for that," I said, with the clarity of vision that wine sometimes bestows upon me. "He finally got Pompey's veterans their settlement. With his disgruntled soldiers behind him, Pompey was a force to be reckoned with. Even with a good war in view, they may be difficult to pry off their fat Campanian farms now." It had been a neat bit of maneuvering now that I thought of it, the way Caesar had protected himself from treachery by Pompey.

"Besides," I went on, "Lisas told me that it may turn into a fight with the Germans, not just the Gauls. There's precious little loot to be had fighting the Germans."

"Germans?" she said sharply. "What's this?"

So I had to explain my talk with Lisas in some detail. She followed my recital closely, with a Caesar's quick grasp of political and military nuance.

"Do you think you can trust that scheming Egyptian?"

"I don't see what advantage there would be for him in making it up," I told her. "It could be catastrophic for your uncle. It won't be the war he was counting on."

"Don't be ridiculous. He is equal to anything, including big armies of bigger barbarians. When he comes back from Gaul, he'll celebrate the biggest triumph ever seen in Rome."

I didn't think he stood a chance, which shows how much I knew about it.

"Decius, for the holiday I have full freedom to move around the city without my grandmother's supervision." Julia's grandmother was the frightening Aurelia, mother of Caius and Lucius Julius Caesar. She was not above demanding my public flogging and execution for impropriety with her granddaughter, and had done so more than once in the past.

"Even so, I don't see what you can . . . ?"

"What is there to do in this case except pick up rumors, gossip, and malicious innuendo? I can do that as well as you!"

"Well, yes, but . . ."

"Then it's settled." And so it was.

By this time we needed another refill, and as I handed Julia her cup, she noticed the bandage on my hand.

"What happened to your hand?" She set down her cup and took my wounded paw in her delicate, patrician fingers, as if she could heal it by contact.

"On the voyage here we were attacked by pirates," I told her. "I received this wound when I drove them back to their ship and slew their captain."

She dropped my hand. "You probably cut yourself shaving."

For the remainder of the evening we wandered among the stalls, admired the many mountebanks performing their various arts, and generally got into the mood of the season. We saw performing animals, boys dancing on tight-stretched ropes, troupes of beautiful youths, and maidens performing the ancient dances of the Greek islands, Nubian fire-breathers, Egyptian magicians, and others too numerous to recall.

A Persian magus made a bouquet of white flowers appear from within Julia's gown, and as she cried out in delight and tried to take them in her hands, the flowers became a white pigeon and flew away. We had our fortunes told by a benevolent-looking old peasant woman who gazed into our palms with rheumy eyes and predicted that we would enjoy long years of happy marriage with many children, prosperity, and distinction. She was predicting the same for everyone who came to her. Long lines stood outside the booths of the many more professional seers as people waited to hear their fortunes for the coming year. I looked for Furia's booth but did not see it.

Everywhere, people were rolling dice at folding tables, monument bases, or just on the pavement. On Saturnalia, public gambling was allowed. The rest of the year, one could bet openly only at the circus. As the evening wound down, the torches began to burn low, smoke, and flicker. Then only the diehard gamblers remained at the tables, rolling their dice and knucklebones beneath the light of Saturnalian candles.

As midnight neared, people began to trail off toward their homes, to rest up for the even greater revelry of the following day. I took Julia to the door of Caesar's great house on the Forum, the mansion of the *pontifex maximus* adjoining the Palace of the Vestals. There we were met at the door by the formidable Aurelia, who for once was constrained by custom from upbraiding me. We promised to meet the next day, but we did not dare to exchange so much as a kiss with her grandmother looking on. She was quite capable of setting her slaves on me with whips and staves.

As I walked home, I felt not the least fatigued despite all the wine I had drunk and the food I had stuffed down my gullet. As I crossed the fast-emptying Forum, thick with the smoke of burned-out braziers, I was struck by its eerie aspect at such a time. The few gamblers crouched over their candles were like underworld spirits tormenting some unfortunate mortal singled out by the gods for special punishment. The outlines of the majestic buildings were soft and muted, more like something willed into being by Jupiter than the work of human hands. This was the Forum as we see it in dreams.

Far up the slope of the Capitol, just below the Temple of Jupiter Optimus Maximus, I could make out the dark, forbidding crag of the Tarpeian Rock, where traitors and murderers are hurled to their deaths. From the frantic gaiety of the earlier evening, all was transformed to a sinister gloom.

It was with thoughts of this sort that I made my way through the narrow, winding streets to my home, acknowledging the greetings and good wishes of weaving drunks, stepping over the recumbent bodies of those who had partaken too lustily and hadn't made it to their own doors, thoughts of gloom and demons wended their way, inevitably, to the witches. What were they doing that night, out on the Vatican field?

At my house I had to let myself in, since my slaves weren't about to answer my knock at the door. I went to my sleeping room and finally unburdened myself of my toga, which had been making my arm sweat all evening. I began to undress for bed, then stopped, sat on the edge of the bed, and thought. I was wide awake. If I lay down, it would only be to stare at the ceiling until the sun came up.

There was no help for it. I had been in Rome for three days, being cautious, trying to cover myself, trying to restrict my investigation to talking to people. It just wasn't natural. I couldn't get my mind off those *strigae* and their fascinating rites outside the walls. Enough of safety and caution. It was time to do something stupid, dangerous, and self-destructive.

I got up, removed my sandals, and put on a pair of hunting boots that laced up tightly above the ankle. I changed my senator's tunic for one of deep blue and threw on a dark cloak that had a hood and covered me to the knee. I wasn't the helmet of invisibility, but it might do. I replaced my dagger and *caestus* and thought about belting on a sword. No, that would be overdoing it. My days of guerilla fighting in Spain had taught me that, for a spy on renonnaissance, a fast pair of feet are a surer defence than any weapon.

Minutes later I was back in the streets and hurrying, as fast as the uncertain light allowed, toward the river. From my home, the quickest way across was by skirting the northern end of the cattle market and crossing the river by the Aemilian Bridge. This access to the city was rarely closed off at night because throughout the night farmers from the countryside drove their carts in for the morning markets. The bridge gate was closed only in emergencies. According to legend it takes only one Roman hero to defend a bridge.

Once across the river, I was on the Via Aurelia and in country that was a part of ancient Tuscia. The noise of the creaking farm carts disturbed me, so I took a side lane to the north to get away from them. Soon all I could hear was the occasional hoot of an owl, for the weather was too cool for many insect sounds.

The Vatican field is very large, and I began to feel rather foolish in having followed my impulse. How was I going to find a few celebrating witches in this expanse of farmland? Still, it was peaceful and rather pleasant to be walking along so civilized a Roman road, paved even though it was just a farm lane, beneath the soft light of the moon. The air smelled pleasantly of new-turned earth, for it was time for the winter sowing. At intervals I saw herms set up, most of them of the old design: a square pillar topped with the bust of a benevolent, bearded man and, halfway down, an erect phallus to bestow fertility and ward off evil spirits. Fine family tombs were situated by the road, for the dead could not be interred within the old City walls.

This was the face of nature we Romans love, nature tamed and turned to the human purposes of production or religion. We have always preferred tilled fields to wasteland; flat, arable ground to hills and mountains; gardens to forests.

Wild nature has no appeal for us. Pastoral poets sing the praises of nature, but their dreamy idylls are really about the tame sort, with nymphs and shepherds frolicking among wooly lambs and myrtle groves and stately poplars. Only Gauls and Germans love the real thing.

I decided to give up on my mission and simply enjoy the beautiful, fragrant night, so near the city, yet so far from its crowding and bustle. Then my spine turned to ice when I heard the unearthly cry of a screech owl and I remembered that the words for witch and screech owl were one and the same: *striga.*

Let Etruscans busy themselves with the guts of animals. We Romans know that the most powerful omens come from lightning, thunder, and birds. I am not superstitious, but my scepticism wanes at night and returns with daylight.

The sound had come from my left, and I walked until I found a path leading in that direction. It was not paved, but was a well-trodden dirt lane so old that much of it was sunken two or three feet beneath the surface of the surrounding fields. It takes many, many generations for the tread of bare or sandaled feet to wear a path so deep, for the lane was too narrow for farm carts. It must have been there long before Romulus, perhaps before even the Etruscans, when only the Aborigines inhabited Italy.

The lane led me through the plowed fields away from the road, away from tombs and herms. The ground grew rougher, with heaps of stones piled up where the plows had turned them up, only some of them seemed to have been piled with greater regularity than others, and here and there I saw single, daggerlike, standing stones such as you see in some of the islands and in the more remote parts of the Empire, where ancient peoples worshipped gods whose names we do not know. I had not thought that any such were to be found so near the City. But then, I thought, perhaps I was letting the moonlight and my imagination deceive me. Maybe they were just big stones, too large for the plowmen to haul away, and instead stood on end to take up less ground.

I came to a low hill topped by a dense copse of trees. At the uttermost limit of hearing, I thought I detected odd, rhythmic sounds, thumpings as of small drums, and perhaps a chanting of human voices. I thought that now would be an excellent time to return to the City. Instead, having determined upon a course of foolishness and danger, I took a deep breath and stepped away from the sunken lane. I began to walk toward the wooded hill.

The new-plowed earth was soft beneath my boots and soon I detected something else: Besides the regular furrows there were many other indentations there. I crouched to see what they might be and the moonlight revealed that lines of footprints other than my own led from the lane to converge upon the little hill. I straightened, checked that my dagger was loose in its sheath, and my *caestus* was handy, then I went on.

At the base of the hill the sounds were far more plain. The thumping of the drums was now mixed with the skirling of flutes and the rhythmic chants were punctuated by loud, seemingly spontaneous cries. If these formed words they were in a language I did not know. The beat of the music was something primitive and stirring, touching me on a level below my overlay of Roman culture, as the sight of the standing stones had touched me.

At the edge of the trees I could see a faint, ruddy glow from within the copse. These were not cultivated orchard trees; no apples or olives for this sacred spot. For the most part they were ancient, gnarled oaks, rough-barked, their trunks home to owls and their roots the abode of serpents. Beneath my boots the dry, crenellated leaves of the trees crunched faintly, like parchment or the flaking remnants of Egyptian mummies.

From the limbs of the trees I could see dangling strange objects made of feathers and ribbons and other materials I could only guess at. Wind harps made soft music that could scarcely be heard over the noise from the center of the grove.

Placing my feet with great care, barely daring to breathe, I walked through the trees, my eyes straining through the gloom for hidden sentries. The Spaniards had always been too lazy to set sentries, but Italian witches might be more careful. I thought of what Urgulus had said: that there was a *mundus* on the sacred ground of the witches. These passages to the underworld are rare and are greatly revered, for it is through them that we communicate with the dead and the gods below. There was one in Rome and others up and down the Italian peninsula. I had never heard of this one.

I began to see shadows, as of human forms passing between me and the source of the light. Now I moved even more cautiously, stepping from tree to tree, trying to work my way closer while remaining invisible myself. I could see that I was approaching a clearing, and that it was filled with people whirling, dancing, clapping, chanting to the rhythm of pipe and drum. The trees were beginning to thin, but I saw a dense clump of bay at the very edge of the clearing between two oaks and I made my way toward it.

My nerves were on edge as I sidled from tree to tree, even though the frenzied revelers seemed to be paying no slightest attention to anything outside the clearing. I could get no clear look at them beyond an occasional glimpse of shining flesh, but the voices I could hear seemed for the most part to be those of women.

At the clump of bay I lowered myself to a crouch. I was within a few feet of the clearing, but the branches and foliage of the bush were so thickset that I couldn't see much. I lay down flat on my belly and began to creep forward. My weapons dug painfully into my belly, but that was the least of my worries. These people held their rites in remote secrecy specifically because they did not want to be observed by profane eyes. They would be inclined to punish anyone who spied on them. I was reminded of the stories of the Maenads, those wild female followers of Dionysus who were wont to tear apart and devour any man unfortunate enough to stumble upon their woodland rites. And these celebrants, whoever they were, seemed to be in a state of Maenadic frenzy.

When only a final low-hanging branch remained before my eyes, I very carefully moved it aside with my hand and had my first clear view of the revels within the glade.

In its center burned a massive bonfire that cast flame and sparks high into the black night overhead. Besides the blazing logs and faggots in its heart, I could see the shapes of what I hoped were sacrificial animals, and there was a heavy smell of scorching meat in the air. But the fire and its victims did not rivet my attention. The women did.

The only men I saw were those playing instruments and these, unlike the women, wore masks that completely concealed their faces. All the others were female, perhaps a hundred of them, all dancing with demented vigor. None of them wore proper clothing, although many were scantily draped in animal skins and all wore abundant vine wreaths and chaplets. There were no children, the youngest of them being at least nubile. There were a few aged hags, but the greater part of them were women of childbearing age. The greatest shock, though, was that not all were peasant women.

When the first patrician lady flashed before me, I doubted my senses. Then I began to pick out more of them. Some may have been of the noble plebeian families, but I recognized a few of them, and these were all of ancient patrician families. The first to whirl before my eyes was Fausta Cornelia, Sulla's daughter and the betrothed of my friend Milo. Then I saw Fulvia, who seemed to be right in her element. And, as I might have guessed, Clodia was there, managing to appear cool and languid even in the midst of such festivities.

The contrast between the patrician ladies and the peasant women was far greater than I might have imagined. Far from being leveled by the removal of their clothing, the contrast was rendered even more vivid. The peasant women had unbound their hair to let it stream wildly as they danced. Even the palest of them were darker than the noble women, their arms and faces burned darker still by exposure to the sun. Hair lightly furred their arms and legs and grew in dense thatches beneath their arms and between their legs.

The elaborate coiffures of the patricians stayed in place during their wildest gyrations. Their skins, protected from the sun all their lives, were whiter than pearl and they wore costly cosmetics. They were slender in contrast to the broad-hipped stockiness of most of the peasant woman. Most striking, though, was that except for their scalps, the patrician women had been divested of every trace of hair with tweezers, wax, and pumice stone. Next to the intense animality of the rural witches, these Circes of Rome looked like polished statues of Parian marble.

If I had not already been pressed solidly to the ground, my jaw would have dropped. They were like members of unlike species, as different as horses and deer, united only in their devotion to this orgiastic celebration. What was it Clodia had said to me only the night before? *I indulge in religious practices not countenanced by the state.* She had certainly been understating the matter.

I felt that I had no cause for surprise or shock. The state religion was just that: a public cult in which the gods could be propitiated and the community strengthened and united through collective participation. There were other religions and mystery cults all over the world. From time to time, usually when faced with a crisis, we consulted the Sibylline Books, and they sometimes directed us to import a foreign god, complete with cult and ritual. But this was only after lengthy discussion by the pontifexes, and it was never a degenerate Asiatic deity. Many religions were permitted in Rome, as long as they were seemly and did not involve forbidden sacrifices or colorful mutilations, as when the male worshippers of Cybele, in their religious frenzy, castrate themselves and fling their severed genitalia into the sanctuary of the goddess.

No, what made my spine crawl was not the nature of this celebration but the fact that it was native, not some exotic import from an Aegean island or the far fringes of the world. Its sacred grove was within an hour's walk of Rome and had probably been going on there for countless centuries. Here was a religion as ancient as the worship of Jupiter, in Jupiter's own land, yet unknown to the vast bulk of the Roman people, little more than a whispered rumor among the common people.

And there was the participation of the patrician women. That, at least, was not so astonishing. Wealthy, indulged, and pampered, but shut out from public life or any sort of meaningful activity, they were usually bored and were always the first to pick up any new foreign religious practice to appear in Rome. And the three I recognized were just the sort to seek out any strange cult, just so it was sufficiently exciting and degenerate.

A woman broke from the whirling rings of dancers and stood next to the fire, shouting something, repeating the cry until the others slowed and, finally, stilled. The noise of the instruments died away, and the woman chanted something in a language I did not understand, with a prayerlike cadence. Her face was so transformed by her ecstatic transport that I did not immediately understand that this was Furia. Her long hair was laced with leafy vines and over her shoulders was thrown the flayed skin of a recently sacrificed goat. Its blood liberally bespattered her body, as it had so recently been decorated by my own. In one hand she held a staff carved with a twining serpent, one end terminating in a pine cone, the other in a phallus.

I saw then that she stood between the fire and a ring of stones perhaps three feet across. This had to be the *mundus* through which the witches contacted their underworld gods.

Bowls were passing among the celebrants; ancient vessels decorated in a style that was vaguely familiar to me. Then I remembered the old bronze tray on which Furia had cast her miscellaneous prophetic objects. The wild-eyed, heavily sweating worshippers seemed to be unaffected by the chill of the December night. Whatever the brew was, the patrician ladies sucked it up as lustily as their rustic sisters.

The men did not partake. I noticed then that, besides their grotesque masks, the men wore cloths wrapped tightly about their lower bodies, as if to disguise the fact of their maleness, rendering them temporary eunuchs for this female rite.

Now a woman, one of the peasants and older than Furia, came forward. She wore a leopard pelt over her shoulders, and her arms had been painted or tattooed with coiling serpents. In one hand she held a leash and its other end was looped around the neck of a young man, who wore only garlands of flowers. He was a sturdy youth, handsome and well-proportioned. His skin was perfect, free from scars or birthmarks, and I was uneasily reminded of the perfect bull we had sacrificed earlier that evening. If he had an imperfection, it was in his blank gaze. He was either utterly fatalistic, half-witted, or drugged.

Two of the men came forward and seized the youth from behind by both arms. They marched him to the lip of the *mundus* and forced him to his knees beside it. Furia handed something to the woman in the spotted pelt. It was a knife, and it was as archaic as the ritual, almost as primeval as the women's own bodies. It was even more ancient than the bronze dagger I used on my desk as a paperweight. Its grip was the age-blackened antler of a beast I had never beheld, one that certainly had not roamed the Italian peninsula since the days of the Aborigines. Its blade was broad and leaf-shaped, made of flint, its edges chipped in rippling facets, beautiful and cruelly sharp.

I knew that I should do something, but I was paralyzed with a sense of futility. These were not women who would run screaming at the sight of a lone man brandishing his dagger. The men might have weapons handy. And if the dazed boy was not inclined to run, it would be the height of folly to try to bear him off. Perhaps if it had been a small child I might have added to my night's foolishness by attempting a rescue. I like to think so.

Furia held her hands out, palms downward, over the

youth's head. She began a slow, tuneless song. The others joined in, except for the men, who held their hands before their eyes and slowly backed away from the firelight into the obscurity of the trees. The song ended. The young man now was held only by the older priestess, whose left hand gripped his hair. He seemed perfectly ready to accept his fate. I wondered whether the sacrificial bull had been drugged. Furia clapped her hands three times and three times called out a name, which I will not try to reproduce. Some things must not be written.

With the tip of her wand Furia touched the side of the boy's neck. Instantly, the other priestess plunged the flint knife into the indicated spot. It went in more easily than I would have imagined, up to the antler hilt. Then she withdrew it and a deep, collective sigh went up from the worshippers as the bright, arterial blood fountained into the *mundus.* It happened in eerie silence for there was no sound of splashing from the stones within. Perhaps it truly led all the way to the underworld. Or perhaps something was drinking it as fast as it poured in.

The blood seemed to gush from the boy's neck for an impossibly long time, until his heart ceased to beat and he slumped forward, pale and already looking like a shade. Then a number of the women rushed forward, seized the corpse, and hurled it onto the blazing pyre with a strength that seemed unnatural.

I was cold and sweating at the same time, and I knew that I must look as pale as the unfortunate sacrifice. I had looked upon a great deal of death, but this was different. The commonplace slaughters of the street, the battlefield, and the arena entirely lack the unique horror of a human sacrifice. Rage and passion and cruelty, even cold-blooded calculation, are paltry things compared to murder when the gods are called upon to participate.

I was so transfixed by what was happening before me that I neglected to pay attention to what was going on behind.

I nearly fainted when something grabbed my ankles. For an insane moment I thought that one of the underworld deities, summoned by the blood offering, was going to drag me down beneath the earth. Then other hands were on me and I was twisting around, yanking out my dagger and thrusting. Bay leaves whipped my face as I was jerked upright, and I heard a deep, masculine voice cry out as my blade connected. Then both my arms were held in wrestler's locks, and my dagger was snatched away from my grasp.

Like the boy, only struggling, I was frog-marched into the clearing, and women, amazed and outraged, drew back from my defiling presence. Then, screeching, they attacked. I suffered a few nail scratches, but Furia beat them back with her wand and they quieted.

"Look what we found, Priestess!" said one of the men who held me, in the by now familiar Marsian accent.

"I think he wants to be sacrificed," said another of the men. "Shall we take him to the *mundus?*" This one was Roman, and upper class to judge by his diction. Furia lashed him across his face mask with her wand and he yelped.

"Fool! This one is ugly and scarred like a gladiator! The gods would be mortally offended if we offered them such a one!"

I thought she was being a little rough on me. No artist had ever asked me to model for Apollo, but I had not judged myself to be truly repulsive. She was right about the scars, though. I had picked up a lot of them for a basically peaceable man. I was not going to argue with her, however. She tapped the tip of her wand against my cheek.

"I told you not to look into these matters, Roman, and my two attendants warned you as well. If you had listened, we would not have to kill you now."

"You said I was going to live a long time!" I protested. "That makes you a pretty poor prophetess, if you ask me!"

She actually chuckled. "A man may always will his own destruction, even if the gods are kindly disposed. You have brought this upon yourself." Her hair was a snarled mare's nest, and her eyes were wild. She was bloody and sweaty and she stank abominably from the flayed goat's skin, but at that instant I felt a powerful lust for her, far surpassing anything I could have felt for the immaculate noblewomen. Some things are entirely beyond reason.

She noticed. Stepping close to me she said in a low voice, "We celebrate here to propitiate our gods and bring peace to our dead. If this were a fertility rite, I might have made use of you."

Clodia stood next to me. "You were always a man of peculiar tastes, Decius, but your timing is off. In the spring rites, randy he-goats like you are in some demand."

"He is on sacred ground in the presence of the gods, Patrician," Furia said. "The powers of life and death are strong in all of us at such times." She turned to the men who held me. "His blood cannot be shed on this holy ground. Take him outside the grove and kill him."

"Wait," Clodia said. "He is a well-known eccentric, but his family is one of the most powerful in Rome. His death will not be passed over lightly."

"He is one of them!" said one of the Marsian men. "We

144

should never have permitted these high-born Romans into our rites! You see how they stick together?"

"Not me," said the cultured Roman who held one of my arms. I was sure I knew the voice. He held my dagger up. "I will be more than happy to cut his throat, Priestess."

She paused for a moment, thinking. "Roman, I saw a long life for you, and I will not oppose the will of the gods in this." Then she addressed the men. "Take him from the grove and put out his eyes. He will never be able to lead anyone back here." She turned to Clodia. "Will that satisfy you, Patrician?"

Clodia shrugged. "I suppose so. He is a troublemaker and no one will credit his ravings if he shows up blinded." Then, to me, "Decius, you are like some creature out of Aesop. You are a living embodiment of human folly." I thought her eyes were trying to tell me something else, but her tone was as nonchalant as always. Somehow I didn't find her blood-speckled nudity as intriguing as that of Furia. But then I had seen Clodia naked before. Besides, I was about to get my eyes poked out with my own dagger.

"Take him away," Furia ordered. As I was dragged off, we passed close by Fausta.

"Wait until Milo hears about this!" I hissed at her. She laughed loudly. Typical Cornelian.

When we were among the trees, the Roman waggled the blade of my dagger before my face.

"You're always poking that long Metellan nose of yours where it doesn't belong," he said. "I think I'll cut it off for you, after I take out your eyes." This man was simply not in the spirit of Saturnalia. He held my right arm with his free hand while the other was held by one of the Marsians. I could not tell how many more were behind me, but I could hear at

145

least one. I wanted to say something biting and sarcastic, but I was doing my best to seem stunned and fatalistic.

"This is far enough," said the Roman, as we cleared the trees.

"I don't know," said a Marsian. "I think we should take him to the road. This is too close to the *mundus*."

"Oh, very well." The Roman was impatient for my blood. We walked out onto the plowed ground. This suited me well as the new furrows made for uncertain footing. I had to make my move before we got to the road.

The Marsian holding my left arm stumbled slightly on a ridge of plowed earth and I pretended to fall. The Roman cursed and braced himself, and in that instant I lurched against him with my shoulder and jerked my right arm loose.

"That won't save you!" he said, coming in with my dagger held low.

Most men, having taken a weapon off me, fancy that I am unarmed. That is one reason I usually keep something in reserve. My hand went into my tunic and came out gripping my *caestus*. I swung at the Roman, trying to smash his jaw, but the spiked bronze bar glanced off his cheekbone. The blow put him down, and I whirled to my left. The Marsian, foolishly, tried to grip my arm more tightly instead of letting go, springing back, and going for his own knife. The spikes of my *caestus* sank into the thin bone of his temple and he collapsed, dead as the bull beneath the hammer of the *flamen*'s assistant.

I sprang free and saw my dagger glittering in the slack hand of the supine Roman. I dived for it, caught it on the roll, and came up facing back toward the grove. I was about to cut the Roman's throat, but there were three other masked men almost upon me. I managed to slash the arm of one; then I spun and ran.

146

I could hear their feet slapping the soft earth behind me, but they weren't slapping it as hard as I was. Terror lent me the winged heels of Mercury and I had trained as a runner, as much as I disliked exercise. The men behind me were plodding peasants, unused to a fast sprint. Besides, I was wearing a good pair of boots where they were barefoot or sandaled. Still, I was sweating ice at the thought that I could easily take a fall on this uneven earth in the dim light of the low-hanging moon.

Then I was on the sunken lane and able to reach full speed. I could hear the men behind me still, but they were slowing. By the time I reached the paved road, I could not hear them at all. I went the rest of the way to the Via Aurelia at a steady lope and then I slowed to a walk. If the men were still behind me they would be awfully tired when they caught up. I wanted to get my breath back before I had to fight.

In the event, I made it into the city without further violence. This was a good thing, because I wasn't feeling up to anything really epic. My cut palm throbbed where the gripping bar of my *caestus* had transmitted the impact of the weapon's blows. I was covered with scratches and bruises and minor cuts and was horrendously fatigued.

As I walked I thought of the nightmarish scene I had just experienced. We regarded human sacrifice as uncivilized, and it was practiced by the state only in the most extraordinary circumstances. The casual use of humans, even worthless humans, as sacrificial animals we regarded as barbarous, a practice fit for Gauls and Carthaginians, but not for civilized people. but how long ago, I thought, had our Saturnalia offerings been genuine heads instead of "lights"? I thought of the thirty straw puppets we threw into the Tiber from the Sublician

Bridge on the Ides of May. When had those been thirty war captives?

As I crossed the Forum I thought of the man and woman who had been buried alive there to consecrate its founding. Their bones were still down there somewhere.

These were the last coherent thoughts to pass through my mind that night. I have no memory of getting to my home, undressing, and falling into bed. The moon was still up as I crossed the Forum, and the eastern sky was fully dark. It had been one of the longest days of my life.

9

"HEY, DECIUS, WAKE UP!" IT
was Hermes. I felt around for my dagger. It was time to murder
the boy. Then I remembered what day it was. He barged into
my bedroom, all joy and cheer.

"*Io* Saturnalia! How about some breakfast, Decius? Come
on, get up!"

Creakily, aching in every joint, I lurched up and sat on
the edge of my bed. The light hurt my eyes, and I buried my
face on my cupped palms.

"Why didn't I kill you yesterday when it was legal?" I
groaned.

"Too late," he said cheerily. "You can't even execute a
traitor on Saturnalia. Go fetch me something to eat." Then he
saw what I looked like. "What were you doing all night? You
must have been in the roughest *lupanar* in town." He inspected some of my more egregious wounds. "I'll bet it was

one of those places where the madam chains you to a post and the girls work you over with whips. You should try being a slave; then you could live like that all the time."

I found my dagger and started for him, but he pointed at it with an odd expression and I held it up. There was brownish blood all over the blade.

"I hope you didn't kill anyone inside the City," he said.

I pondered the weapon. "I'll have to wash this blood off or it's going to rust the blade."

"You can do that in the kitchen," Hermes suggested. "While you're there, find me something to eat."

Wearily, I shuffled back toward the kitchen. From Cato and Cassandra's room I heard the sound of snoring. At least I wouldn't be fetching breakfast for them. I poured water from a jug into a basin and dipped my blade into it, scrubbing away the dry, flaky blood with a rough cloth and a sponge. When all the blood was gone, I inspected it. It was too late. The fine sheen of the Spanish steel was marred with tiny pits. Blood is the worst thing in the world for weapon steel. That is an oddity, when you think about it. I made a mental note to stop at a cutler's and have it polished, when people were back at work again.

I poked around until I found some bread and cheese and a few dried figs. I was sure my slaves had stocked up for the holiday, but I had no idea where they stored the provender and was in no mood to institute a detailed search of the kitchen. I found Hermes in the courtyard seated at his ease in the chair I usually employed. I began to sit in the chair opposite him, but he waggled an admonitory finger at me.

"Ah-ah-ah. Not today, you don't."

I sat down anyway. "Don't overdo it. We're not supposed to remember how you behave on Saturnalia, but we do anyway." I grabbed some of the food and started to eat. "My clients will be here soon. Did Cato and Cassandra make up their gifts?"

"They're in the atrium," he said, munching cheese. "Speaking of which, how about some money so I can celebrate properly?" Hermes was insolent at the best of times. On Saturnalia, he was insufferable. I went into my bedroom and opened a chest. I took out a pouch, first counting to make sure he hadn't appropriated some of my money already.

"There," I said, dropping the pouch on the table in front of him. "Keep it out of sight. In the streets you like to frequent they'll cut your throat for that much money. Don't come home with any exotic diseases, and I don't want you so hung over that you'll be of no use to me tomorrow. I'm in the middle of something very bad and I expect to be busy."

"Who wants to kill you this time?" he asked, taking a swig of watered wine.

Before I could answer him my clients began to arrive. There was the usual round of greetings. They gave me presents. Since they were mostly poor men, these consisted mainly of the traditional candles. By custom, my own gifts to them had to be more valuable, although my own circumstances were modest. I gave Burrus a new sword for his son who was with the Tenth Legion, soon to be in the thick of the fighting against the Gauls and the Germans, winning glory for Caesar.

From my house we all trooped off to my father's. His mob of clients spilled out onto the street outside and had to make their way through in shifts. When I finally got in, I found Father talking with a couple of distinguished-looking men, although their rank was hard to guess since they wore plain tunics. I made my formal obeisance, and Father introduced the two as Titus Ampius Balbus and Lucius Appuleius Sa-

151

turninus, two of the praetors of the year. Balbus was to govern Asia in the next year, and Saturninus was to have Macedonia. Clearly, Father thought I should be currying favor with these two, who were up-and-comers in a position to offer me fine appointments, but I needed to confer with him privately.

"What do you want?" he asked impatiently, when we were a little separated from the others. "You know that official business is forbidden today."

"And you know that I am acting in a highly unofficial capacity. I've come upon something important and I need to know a few things. Was Celer engaged in suppressing or expelling forbidden cults within Rome and its environs?"

"What kind of idiot question is that? He was a praetor, not a censor. And when no censors hold office, that is the province of the aediles, along with public morals."

"You and Hortensius Hortalus were our most recent censors," I pressed on. "Did you take action concerning such cults?"

He frowned. But then, he always frowned. "Hortalus and I conduced the census, we completed the *lustrum*, and we purged the Senate of some very unsavory members. Beyond that, we oversaw the letting of the public contracts. I turned in my insignia of office last year, and the subject of obscene foreign cults never came up."

"Not foreign cults, Father. Domestic cults. Native Italian cults operating within and just outside of Rome. Cults numbering among their members some very highly placed Romans."

"Explain yourself," he said. So I gave him a succinct rendition of my experiences of the previous two days, leaving out nothing. Well, leaving out very little, anyway. When I got to the part about the sacrifice, he muttered, "Infamous!" and made a complex gesture to ward off the evil eye, one he must have learned in childhood from a Sabine nurse.

"A cult of witches, eh?" he said when I was finished. "Human sacrifice. A hidden *mundus*. And noble Romans involved?" Absently, he rubbed a hand across the scar that divided his face, a characteristic gesture meaning he was plotting evil against his enemies. "This is a chance to rid Rome of its three very worst women. Exiled, at the very least. After this they could never return."

"Don't forget the man who wanted to poke my eyes out," I reminded him.

"Oh, him. Yes, it's too bad you didn't get a look at his face." This was for the sake of form. If you wanted to get rid of murderous men, the best way would have been to block up the doors of the Senate house during a meeting and set fire to the place. Murder was a popular pastime among the male gentry. It was the scandalous women who outraged men like my father.

He put a hand on my shoulder. "Look, we can't stay closeted like this. People will suspect we are doing something official. I'll manage to get the aediles aside sometime today to discuss this."

"I am not sure that would be a good idea. I am not satisfied with Murena's handling of the murder of the woman Harmodia. For some reason he took the official record of the case and hid or destroyed it. He is either concealing something or protecting somebody."

"You are making too much of the matter. The slave who was sent to fetch the document probably stopped at a tavern on the way to court, got drunk, and lost it. It happens all the time. It was just another murder of another nobody.

"But if it will set your mind at ease, I'll avoid Murena

and confer only with Visellius Varro and Calpurnius Bestia and the others. I should speak with Caesar as well, although he is probably too busy preparing for his Gallic campaign to take much of an interest. Still, as *pontifex maximus* it's his duty to make a pronouncement upon the danger of a corrupting, nonstate religion. In the meantime, you should go to your gangster friend Milo and get him to assign you some protection. Since they didn't kill or blind you, they may be looking for you now."

"I can't go to Milo!" I said. "He is going to marry Fausta and he's entirely irrational about her. *He* might kill me if I threaten to have her exposed!"

Father shrugged. "Then go to Statilius Taurus and borrow some of his gladiators. Now, come along. We must make our rounds."

I accompanied him to a few more houses, but my heart simply wasn't in the spirit of the season. He was also being unrealistic. What use would hired thugs be to me when the people I was dealing with specialized in spells and poisons? I wasn't worried about any bumpkin daggermen as long as I was armed and on familiar ground. It was depressing to have to watch everything I ate or drank though. Luckily, for the duration of the holiday, food stalls were everywhere. They would have to poison the whole city to get me.

About spells I was not so sure. Like most rational, educated men I was extremely dubious of the efficacy, even the reality, of magical spells. On the other hand, recent events were causing my rationality to flake away like dandruff. Witches were supposed to be able to strike their enemies down with ailments of the heart, liver, lungs, and sundry other organs. They could cause blindness and impotence. But if they could do all that, I wondered, how did it come about that they had any enemies at all?

By late morning I managed to break away from my father and his crowd, but as I wandered through the streets the gaiety of the season transformed itself before my eyes to the menacing and the sinister. Why did so many people wear masks if not to take on the personae of demons? What was the reason for the whole hilarious occasion but a primitive midwinter fear that, if we didn't jolly the gods along a bit, they wouldn't give us springtime next year?

I knew I was just being morbid. People wore masks, for the most part, because they were taking advantage of the confusion to mess about with other people's wives and husbands. They were celebrating because, to Romans, any excuse for a party is a good one. The world-turned-upside-down aspect was just the unique fillip of Saturnalia. Even weirder things happened at our other rites. There was the *Lupercalia,* where a team of patrician boys ran through the streets naked, flogging women with thongs of bloody goatskin, and the *Floralia,* where respectable women and whores went out in public and tooted on trumpets. There were others on our year-round calendar of official holidays, each with its tutelary deities and singular rites. Saturnalia was the biggest of the year, that was all. Still, I could not shake my mood.

In the Forum the festivities were in full swing. On the judicial platforms before the basilicas, mimes were performing parodies of the trials ordinarily held there, rife with obscene gestures and indecent language. From the *rostra* men pretending to be the great statesmen of the day made speeches even more nonsensical than the real thing. On the steps of the Curia Hostilia a pair of men wearing outsized insignia of the censors solemnly forbade such activities as feeding one's children, observing the proper rituals of the state gods, serving in the legions, etc.

The music was cacophonous and deafening. People were dancing and reeling everywhere. Nobody seemed to be walking in a normal manner. I dearly wanted to consult some court and Senate records and interview a few officials and secretaries, but it was out of the question on such a day. I wandered about, scanning the crowds for faces from the ritual of the previous night. In so vast a throng it was futile. I could only be certain of the three patrician women I already knew, Furia, and perhaps one or two others.

I went to a booth next to the Curia and spoke with its proprietor long enough to establish that he was not Marsian and bought a loaf stuffed with grape leaves, olives, and tiny, salted fish, generously drenched with *garum*. To this I added just enough wine to settle my nerves and sat on the bottom step, wolfing it all down while the pseudocensors pronounced punishments for showing respect for one's parents and forbidding senators to attend meetings when sober.

I was gratified to note that my recent harrowing experiences had not affected my appetite. Come to think of it, nothing ever affected my appetite. I was finishing up the final crumbs when the last person in the world I expected to see hailed me.

"Decius Caecilius! How good to see another man in Rome whom Clodius hates almost as much as he hates me."

"Marcus Tullius!" I cried, standing up to take his hand. We knew each other well enough to use this familiar form of address. Cicero had aged since I had seen him last, but few of us grow younger. It was odd to see him entirely alone, for he was usually attended by a crowd of friends and clients. No one was paying him any attention, and it is entirely possible that no one recognized the great and dignified orator dressed as he was in a dingy old tunic and cracked sandals, his bony knees and skinny legs exposed, his face unshaven, and with his hair untrimmed. He looked as mournful as I felt. Cicero's military record was as undistinguished as my own, and in seeing him thus the reason was plain. He could never look like anything but a lawyer and a scholar.

"Surely all your friends have not forsaken you?" I asked.

"No, I just wanted to be able to wander around alone for a change, so I dismissed all my followers. This is the one day of the year when I am probably safe from attack. Not that Clodius is likely to try violence now. He wants the glory of driving me into exile as tribune. He'll have it, too. Next year is his year, and even I am not inclined to fight it."

"Go somewhere peaceful and get some studying and writing done," I advised. "You'll be recalled as soon as he's out of power. For what it's worth, I know that you had no choice in ordering those executions. Even Cato is on your side, and Jupiter knows he's a stickler for the legalities."

"I appreciate your support, Decius," he said kindly, as if I were important enough for my support to mean something.

I waved up toward the forbidding crag of the Tarpeian Rock. "There are men walking free and safe today who deserved the rock for their part in that incident."

"I know whom you mean," he said ruefully. "Calpurnius Bestia and a dozen others. Most of them escaped through Pompey's protection and the rest were cronies of Caesar and Crassus. No chance of calling them to account now. Never mind, we'll get them for something else another time."

It struck me that Cicero was a man I should consult. "Marcus Tullius, I wonder if I might beg a favor. I find myself in the midst of the strangest investigation of my career, and I am in need of your advice."

"I am at your service, Decius. I need something to take my mind off my own woes." He looked around in annoyance. "But it is too noisy here. However, there is one place in Rome that is sure to be quiet this day, and it is only a few steps away. Come along." He began to climb the broad stairway and I followed.

The interior of the Curia was a scene of ghostly quiet. Not even a slave remained to sweep up. Even the state slaves had holiday. From these tiers of seats had come the decisions that had declared and directed our wars, settled treaties with foreign powers, determined the rights and obligations of the citizens, and proclaimed our laws to the world. Here had also been concocted most of our worst follies, as well as corruption and knavery beyond measure. But even our basest transactions had at least taken place in a setting of great dignity. The old Curia had the austere simplicity that had once characterized most of our public edifices. We descended the central stair and took our seats on the marble chairs reserved for the praetors, next to the long-vacant chair of the *Flamen Dialis*.

"Now, my young friend, how may I help you?"

I could see from the sharpness of his expression that he was indeed hoping for a brain-cracking puzzle to distract him from his formidable array of sorrows, and I wondered how I could broach the matter at hand without sounding demented.

"Marcus Tullius, you are one of the most learned men of our age. Am I correct in believing that your knowledge of the gods is as deep as your scholarship in the law, in history, and in philosophy?"

"First, let me say that no man can truly know the gods.

I have studied extensively in what has been written and spoken of the gods."

"That is what I need. If I may dare so personal a question, may I ask what your own beliefs in the matter may be?"

He paused for a moment. "Twenty years ago, I took an extended trip to Greece. I did this to study, to regain my failing health, and, incidentally, to escape Sulla's notice. He was still dictator and had cause to dislike me. I studied with Antiochus, a most distinguished and learned man. At that time I also became an initiate in the Eleusinian mysteries. I had been a profound sceptic, but the mysteries provided a most illuminating and moving experience. It is of course forbidden to discuss them with one who is not an initiate, but suffice it to say that I have remained since convinced, not only of the possibility of a good life, but of the immortality, or at least the continuity, of the soul."

I had not been expecting anything quite so deep. "I see. And yet, most people, in most parts of the world, have their own gods, which they believe to regulate the cosmos. Have these any validity?"

"What people have, for the most part, is fear," Cicero said. "They fear the world in which they live. They fear that which they see and that which they cannot see. They fear their fellowmen. None of these fears, I hasten to point out, is unfounded. The world is indeed a dangerous and hostile place. People seek out the powers that control this world, and they seek to placate them."

"And can these powers exist as we envision them?" I asked.

"Do you mean, is Jupiter a majestic, middle-aged man attended by eagles? Does Neptune have blue hair and a trident? Is Venus a voluptuous woman of infinite sexual allure?"

He chuckled. "We got that from the Greeks, Decius. For our ancestors, the gods had no form. They were powers of nature. They were worshipped in the fields and in woods and at shrines. But it is difficult to imagine gods without form, and when we saw the images created by the Greeks to represent their gods we adopted them."

"But do we truly influence the gods, with our rituals and ceremonies and sacrifices?"

"We influence ourselves. When we acknowledge these ineffable powers, we see ourselves in a proper perspective, which is one of humility. Our rituals reinforce the ordering of society, from the daily ceremonies conducted by the head of each household to the great rites of state. All are held communally and all emphasize the strict hierarchy of the state in subordination to the gods of the state. As for sacrifice, all men understand the principle of exchange. One gives something of value in exchange for something else. To the common people, sacrifice is just that—the exchange of material objects for less material but nonetheless palpable benefits from the gods. Educated people understand sacrifice as a symbolic act, which brings about the unity of our mortal selves and the higher powers whose supremacy we acknowledge."

"And human sacrifice?"

He gave me a penetrating and half-exasperated look. "Decius, you spoke of an investigation. Might I know where all this is leading?"

"Please bear with me, Marcus Tullius. I would like to hear your thoughts on the matter before I get down to specifics. All shall be made plain. As plain as I can make it, anyway."

"As you wish. Most people, we Romans included, have practiced human sacrifice. It was always the most extreme of offerings. Some societies have been notorious for it, most notably the Carthaginians. We have long since suppressed the practice, not only within Rome, but in all parts of the world where Rome holds sway. If I were a cynic, I might say that this is because there are few things we value less than human life and so we cannot conceive that our gods would want so worthless a sacrifice.

"However, the truth is somewhat different. In a human sacrifice, we offer to the gods that which most resembles ourselves. Identity is a most important factor in religion and in magic. We may despise our fellowman as an economic unit of less worth than a domestic animal, but we recognize the fact that he is a creature very much like ourselves. In fairness to the savage Carthaginians, I must acknowledge that they carried the principle not only of greatest value but of closest identity to its ultimate form, for in their most terrible ceremonies they sacrificed their own children. Toward the end of our last war with them they immolated hundreds to their gods, not that it did them any good.

"Each of us dimly recognizes a life force shared by all of us, and it is the offering of this force that, it is hoped, will please the gods. But it must be done in the proper place, at the proper time, and with the proper ritual. Were it not for these factors, slaughter grounds and battlefields and arenas would be the holiest spots in the world. Now, Decius, why are you asking about human sacrifices?"

I took a deep breath. "Because I witnessed one last night."

He gazed at me steadily. "I see. Please go on."

"The reason I am in Rome right now is that my family recalled me to look into the death of Metellus Celer. You are aware that many people think Clodia poisoned him?"

"Of course. But that is just gossip." He looked at me

sharply. "It has been gossip until now, anyway. What did you find?"

This was sticky. There were rumors, and I had reason to believe that they might have been true, that Cicero had at one time been involved with Clodia. He might still be, which could be delicate. Otherwise, he was just a part of the great Roman brotherhood of men Clodia had made use of then cast aside. The latter seemed most likely, as Clodia was interested mainly in men of current or potential political power, and Cicero's sun looked to be setting at that time. Her only real loyalty was to her brother, anyway. That didn't mean that Cicero wasn't still infatuated with her.

"The first question that arose was: Had Celer been poisoned at all? I consulted with Asklepiodes and he advised me that, in the absence of classic symptoms of well-known poisons, there was very little likelihood of a conclusive analysis."

"Quite logical," Cicero said approvingly.

"But the most likely source of poison, if poison was indeed involved, were the herb women who run a sizable medical and fortune-telling practice out by the Circus Flaminius, since the aediles drove them out of the City."

"A great Italian tradition," he said dryly. "The state cults fail to satisfy some basic needs of the common people. They must forever be bothering the great cosmic powers for details about the future of their petty lives."

"While there I had a rather disturbing interview with a woman named Furia and heard the name Harmodia spoken. Further investigation revealed that this woman had been murdered. The murder had been briefly investigated by the aedile Licinius Murena, but some days later he took the report from the Temple of Ceres and it seems to have disappeared."

"A moment, please," Cicero said sharply.

"When you say 'he took the report,' do you mean that Murena did this personally?"

That stopped me and I had to think about it. "No, now that you mention it, the slave boy at the temple said that a slave came from the court of the *praetor urbanus* and said that the aedile needed it."

"Very well. Go on."

"I went to the Flaminius and there I questioned the watchman who had discovered Harmodia's body. He had little of importance to tell me concerning the incident, but she had been one of the herb women and he was most uneasy in speaking of the subject at all. He was afraid of their powers to curse and cast spells, and he said that the witches had a sacred place out on the Vatican field where there was a *mundus*. He said that the herb women held a great celebration there on the night before Saturnalia."

"That does not greatly surprise me," Cicero said. "These witches, *saga* and *striga* and so forth, are for the most part remnants of the ancient earth cults that once dominated the whole Mediterranean littoral. They were there when the Dorians came down from the north to bring the sky gods to Greece, and they were in Italy when the ancestral Latins migrated here. We acknowledge the underworld gods by holding their rituals in the evening, after sunset. But these remnants of the archaic faith carry out their rites in the ancient fashion, in the dead of night. As for their *mundus*, any hole in the ground will do for a *mundus*, if one is of a frame of mind to believe in such things.

"Everywhere one goes in the world, the greatest festivals are held at the same times of year: the vernal and autumnal equinoxes, and the summer and winter solstices. Saturnalia is our winter solstice celebration. It follows logically that the earth cults would hold their revels at night during those sea-sons."

Cicero could get pedantic at times.

"So it seems. Anyway, last night I went out there to see for myself." Then I told him what had happened in the grove. He listened with great attention and seriousness. When I came to the part about the patrician women I had recognized, he stopped me.

"Fausta? Are you sure it was she?" He seemed alarmed.

"She is a most striking lady. Even without her clothes there is no mistaking her." Why, I wondered, was he disturbed about Fausta? Why not Clodia?

"This is . . . upsetting," Cicero said.

"Not as upsetting as the next part," I assured him. Then I told of the sacrifice. Unlike my father he made no supersti-tious gestures although his expression conveyed a mild dis-taste, probably more at the primitive proceedings than at the killing. No one got to high office in Rome back then without witnessing abundant bloodshed. When I told of how I had bested my captors and made it back to the city, he chuckled and clapped me on the shoulder.

"My congratulations upon your heroic escape, Decius. I have never known a man like you for getting out of incredibly tight spots. You must be a descendant of Ulysses. Someday you must give me a full account of that business in Alexandria. I've had four wildly differing accounts from friends who were there at the time. They all say they don't want to see you back."

Then he resumed his serious tone. "As to this disagree-able business on the Vatican field, it could prove a touchy matter to deal with."

"Why is that? Human sacrifice is specifically forbidden by law, is it not?"

"It is, except under the most pressing circumstances, and it is never to be undertaken without the most solemn state sanction and performed by duly consecrated officials of the state cults. We consider it a remnant of our primitive past and always use a victim who has already been condemned to death for a civil offense.

"But"—he held up a hand, fingers splayed in lawyer fashion while he counted off each objection, like an egg and a dolphin being taken down to mark each lap of a chariot race—"what you witnessed last night took place outside the walls of the City, across the river, in what used to be Tuscia. That alone will greatly reduce the indignation that might have been stirred had it happened within the walls, in some secluded house or garden."

"It's no more than an hour's walk away!" I protested.

He shook his head. "We Romans all but own the world, but mentally we are still the inhabitants of a little city-state situated on one of Italy's less important rivers. It is very difficult for a Roman to feel that something happening outside the walls actually involves him." Another finger went down. "Have you any witnesses?"

"Well, yes, but they were all dancing around the fire and participating."

"In other words, unlikely to support your testimony. You accuse three women from very powerful families." Another finger went down. "Granted, they are women of considerable notoriety, but can you imagine the woe they can bring upon your head? You have Clodius's sister and his betrothed, and you have the betrothed of your good friend Milo, and she is a Cornelia, the daughter of a dictator and the ward of Lucullus, who is still a man of great power and influence. If we were dealing merely with a pack of peasant women and villagers it would be different.

"Then there is the victim." Another finger. "If he were a citizen, especially one of good family, mobs would assault the Curia to get something done. Did you recognize him?"

"No," I admitted.

"In all probability he was a foreign slave. Legally, they are expendable persons, mere property with no rights. The fact of the sacrifice may have been in contravention of the laws, but the victim was of no consequence."

He lowered his hands and placed them upon his spread knees. "But worst of all, Decius, is the time of year. None of the sitting praetors or aediles will want to institute proceedings just a few days before they leave office."

"There are still next year's," I said.

"And which among them will want to take up such a dubious prosecution, one which must drag in the man who will be the uncrowned king of Rome next year?" Then, more gently, "Decius, do you think you can even *find* this place again?"

I thought about it, trying to remember just where I had turned off the Via Aurelia onto the farm road, and where along the farm road I had heard the screech owl and followed its call to the sunken lane. And how far along the lane had that isolated copse stood?

"I think so," I said uncertainly. "The Vatican is a big area, but I think if I looked long enough . . ."

"I thought so. Today being Saturnalia I will bet you my library against your sandals that you couldn't find it by the end of the month. I'll bet further that, even if you could find it, all evidence of the sacrifice is gone. You will find no bones, no sorcerous paraphernalia, no more than a scorched patch of ground. That is not enough to take to court."

"This is most discouraging," I lamented.

"I am sorry that I could not be of more comfort or aid."

"You have been a great help," I protested hastily. "As always, you have clarified matters and put them into perspective. You may also have saved me from making a fool of myself."

He grinned, a welcome expression on his mournful face. "What is life if we can't make fools of ourselves from time to time? I make a regular practice of it. Is there any other way I may be of service?"

"Can you tell me what I should do now?"

"Continue your investigation of Celer's death. Concentrate on the facts involved there and forget about the witches and their repulsive rites. What you have uncovered there is an ancient but deep-rooted cult that will never be fully eradicated and a pack of bored, thrill-seeking women who need something a little more lively than the state religion to get their blood stirring." He stood. "And for now, I return to the festivities. *Io* Saturnalia, Decius."

"*Io* Saturnalia, Marcus Tullius," I said, as he climbed the stair.

When he was gone I sat pondering for a while. Unquestionably, he was right. To institute judicial proceedings at that moment would not only be futile, it would invite ridicule. I took some comfort in the thought that my father and his cronies would be seeking a way to turn my findings to account. Where strict legality failed, perhaps political malice would succeed.

Where to go next? I tried to think where I had been sidetracked and decided it was my interview with Furia. I had let her mountebank's trickery distract me. In the midst of her sorcerous set-dressing, she had given me Harmodia. Forget about Harmodia being one of the witches; Harmodia had been an herb woman. She may have sold somebody the poison that killed Celer, and she had undoubtedly been killed to silence her. If Celer had been murdered because he was about to crack down on the witches, would they have killed one of their own?

With great reluctance, I had from time to time attended classes on philosophy and logic and related subjects. Sometimes, in exile, there is little else to do. Occasionally, these studies coincide with the necessary arts of law and rhetoric, for there are few more distressing things when arguing before the courts than to find yourself tied up in a logical knot because you got some elementary point wrong. A philosopher in Athens had once told me that when you discovered that you were pursuing the wrong course because you had made an incorrect assumption, you should do what a hunter does; you should go back to the last place where you know for certain that you were on the proper track.

I thought this over and decided that I had stepped off the trail when I entered Furia's booth. What I needed to do was to go back and act as if I had never entered it. For purposes of my real investigation anyway. I wasn't about to forget what I had seen, and I wasn't entirely persuaded that the two were unconnected, despite what Cicero had said.

Things began to look a little more clear. What I had to do was find another herb woman, one considerably less formidable than Furia, and question her about Harmodia. They couldn't all belong to the witch cult. It ought to be easy enough to find one I was certain had not been out on the Vatican field the night before. A blind one, perhaps. Nobody without eyes could have danced like that.

Having so decided, I got up and walked from the Senate chamber. I wasn't halfway down the stairs when Julia ran up and grabbed me.

"Decius! I've been looking all over for you! What in the world were you doing inside the Curia?"

"I called my own Senate meeting," I said. "It wasn't well attended." I quailed at the thought of having to go over the previous night's adventures one more time, especially to Julia, who was somewhat more gently bred than her frightening colleagues of the patrician sisterhood who had a taste for human sacrifice. I knew that she would have it out of me though.

"Decius, are you all right?" She held me at arm's length and looked me over. "You've been fighting again!" As if there were something wrong with that. Women are strange.

"Come along, my dear," I said. "It's just that things have taken a new turn, and it is a turn immeasurably for the worse." Arm in arm, we descended the steps. "But before you hear my account, tell me what you've found out. I can tell by the way you're panting and quivering that you have news."

"I am not panting, neither am I quivering," she said. That was true. She had that well-schooled patrician demeanor, which does not leave the breed even during earthquakes and while aboard sinking ships, but the signs were there if you knew where to look.

"My apologies. Please go on."

We walked to a booth and picked up a few items to sustain us through a full day of reveling.

"Are you familiar with the *Balnea Licinia?* Crassus built it last year on the Palatine, and it's become the most fashionable bathhouse in Rome. The appointments are marvelous, far more luxurious than anything we've seen before. Anyway, it has women's hours in the morning, and I've just come from there."

"I thought you smelled especially delectable," I said.

"Better than you," she said sharply, wrinkling her nose. "What have you been *doing?*"

"Never mind that. Just tell me what you've found."

"All right, if you'll just be patient." She took a big bite of flat bread with toasted cheese on top, sprinkled with chopped, spicy sausage. "Anyway, all the most fashionable ladies go there, you know, members of Clodia's set."

"Just a moment," I interrupted. "Was Fausta there or Fulvia?"

"You mean the younger Fulvia?" Her brow wrinkled. "No, I didn't see either of them. Why do you ask?" There was deep suspicion in her voice.

"It's just that they must be in terrible need of a bath this morning."

"Decius! What have you been up to?" she said, spraying crumbs.

"All shall be made clear in time, my dear. Pray continue."

"All right," she said darkly, "but I expect a full explanation. So there I was on a massage table with Cornelia Minor and your cousin Felicia and about five others on other tables in the room . . . they have huge Nubians there, Lydian trained, the best masseurs in the world . . ."

"Men?" I said, shocked.

"No, silly. Eunuchs. It's a wonderful place to pick up the latest gossip and talk about those things women only discuss when there are no men present."

"You must talk rather loudly, I would think," I said, my

mind going into an irrelevant reverie. "All that smacking of flesh, I mean. All those grunts and explosions of breath as the delicate female bodies are pummeled by the dusky hands of brawny masseurs . . ."

"You just wish you'd been there. So I let it be known that I might soon need the services of a *saga* for a condition that must prove embarrassing, since I am unmarried."

"Julia! You shock me!"

"It is not at all an uncommon subject among this crowd. They trade the names of the most fashionable abortionists just as they do those of pearl sellers and perfumers."

"Oh, the degeneracy of the times," I lamented. "Did any familiar names emerge from this colloquy?"

"The first name to be mentioned was Harmodia, but someone said that she had been killed."

"Do you remember who knew about her murder?" I asked.

"I think it was Sicinia, the one called Swan, because she has such a long neck. Is it important?"

"Probably not. She might have wanted to hire Harmodia, asked around the Flaminius, and found out she'd been murdered."

"Furia was also recommended. You mentioned her yesterday, didn't you?"

"Yes, I did," I said.

"But you didn't tell me everything, did you?"

"No, I did not." We had come to the shrine of the *Lares publici*, before which was a low stone railing. I brushed away the dust and we sat. All around us people were carrying on dementedly, having a fine time. A huge man wearing a lion skin and carrying an outsized club performed feats of strength a few steps from us. At the corner of the Sacred Way and the

Clivus Orbius a platform had been erected to display Spanish dancers from Gades who were performing one of the famous dances of their district, which were forbidden by law at other times of year because of their extreme lasciviousness.

"Decius! Stop watching those dancers and pay attention!"

"Eh? Oh, yes. Go on. Did you get anything else out of your langorous companions of the bath?"

"One of them said a woman named Ascylta is very trustworthy and that she has a stall beneath arch number sixteen at the Circus Flaminius."

"Ascylta? At least it doesn't sound like a Marsian name. It's Samnite, isn't it?"

"I think so. And didn't you say Harmodia's stall was at the Flaminius?"

"Urgulus said Harmodia had arch nineteen. There were only two between them. Perhaps this Ascylta is a woman I should question."

"You mean *we*, Decius. *We* should question her."

I sighed. I should have seen this coming. "As always, Julia, I appreciate your help. But I don't see how your being with me will improve matters."

"Decius," she said gently, "I've never said this to you before, but you can be uncommonly dense at times. Especially when you are dealing with women. I think I may be able to speak with this woman and gain her confidence. You would come on like a prosecutor and make her shut up in fear."

"I am not at all intimidating! I am the soul of diplomacy, when I want to be."

"With all those new cuts and bruises, you are even worse than usual. Not only do you lack tact, you are not even truthful. Now tell me about Furia!"

I was not entirely certain where that had come from, nor how her original assertion had led to her ultimate demand. Nonetheless, I knew better than to hold back. So I told her of my upsetting interview in Furia's tent. She sat and glowered as she listened.

"And you thought," she said, when I was finished, "that I would be upset just because you were fondling the udder of that *striga?*"

"I wasn't fondling!" I protested. "The woman took possession of my blood-dripping hand and fastened it to her mammary. 'Udder' is not a properly descriptive term, in any case. Rather an attractive appendage, if you must know."

"Spare me," she said.

"Anyway," I went on, all but squirming like a schoolboy before an unforgiving master, "it wasn't that. It was what she said, about being Pluto's favorite and a hunting dog and a male harpy and all my life being the death of what I love. You know I am not a superstitious man, Julia, but I've dealt with frauds all over the world and I know when I am confronted with something different. The woman left a mark on me."

She took a swallow of the coarse wine and settled down, apparently mollified. "Now tell me the rest of it. What happened last night after you left me?"

The recital didn't take long. It was the third time I had delivered it, and it wasn't even noon yet. I was getting good at it. She listened with equanimity until I got to the part about the sacrifice. Then she turned pale and dropped the honey cake she had been about to nibble. She was no hardened power chaser or decadent aristocratic thrill seeker.

"Oh!" she said when I was finished. "I knew those women were wicked; I never realized they were truly evil!"

"An interesting distinction. I take it you mean the patrician women, not the witches?"

"Exactly. The *strigae* sound no more than primitive, like barbarians or people from the time of Homer. But Clodia and the rest must do this for the perversity of it."

"Cicero said much the same thing just now," I told her.

"Cicero? When did you speak with him?" So I gave her our conversation. Julia loved philosophical things for some reason, and she listened with close attention. Luckily, I had a well-trained memory and was able to repeat him word for word. I was a little put out that she hadn't gone into palpitations over my mortal danger and desperate flight. True, I was right there so she could see that I had survived the experience, but I expected some display of concern. It was not the only disappointment of my life.

"He is right," she said, nodding. "What you witnessed was a ritual of a very ancient religion. It makes those rustic wise women seem rather innocent, in a horrible sort of way."

"Philosophical detachment is an admirable trait," I told her, "but those people wanted to kill me! Put my eyes out anyway."

"Punishments for profanation and sacrilege are always severe. Besides, you got out of it in one piece. You shouldn't make such a great thing of it. You really aren't a hero out of some epic." I could tell she was still angry with me.

"Cicero himself compared me with Ulysses."

"Cicero is sometimes guilty of rhetorical excess. Most politicians are. Now, how do we find Ascylta?"

It was no use. "We may have to wait until she's back beneath her arch at the Flaminius. She is probably out there somewhere"—I gestured grandly to take in the spectacle of the overcrowded Forum—"but it would be futile to try to find her."

"Have you anything better to do?" she asked impatiently.

"Well, it is a holiday, and I had a rough night. I had planned to indulge in a little debauchery . . ."

She pushed off the railing with her hands and landed lightly on her dainty, highborn feet. "Come along, Decius, let's go look for her."

Julia's sprightly energy depressed me. Undoubtedly, she had enjoyed a good night's sleep. Perforce, I concluded that wandering around the city was as good a way as any to spend the day, and we certainly would not lack for distractions. So off we went, peering into booths and tents, pausing to take in some of the innumerable performances or allow a chain of dancing celebrants to wind its mindless way past us.

The fortune-teller's establishments were everywhere. Instead of being concentrated in one area as on ordinary days, they were set up wherever they could find space. And there were far more of them than usual, because the practitioners from all the villages and towns for many miles around Rome had come to town for the holiday. They had come from as far as Luca to the north and Capua to the south.

It seemed as if most of the Italian peninsula had crammed itself into Rome that day. And there was the usual crowd of foreigners, come to the center of the world to gawk, everything from Syrians in long robes to check-trousered Gauls and Egyptians with their eyes outlined in kohl. Somehow, Rome had become a cosmopolitan city. I suppose you can't be the capital of the world without a lot of aliens hanging about.

By early afternoon we had exhausted the possibilities of the Forum Romanum so we decided to try the Forum Boarium, the cattle market. There the relative lack of monuments, platforms, podia, and the like made it easier to explore, as the many small merchants had established a sort of tent city, like a legionary camp, with an almost orderly grid of streets. There were fewer fortune-tellers and more people selling merchandise: ribbons, children's toys, figurines, small oil lamps, and other things of trifling value to be passed along as gifts.

Julia acted as if she were in the great marketplace of Alexandria, exclaiming over every new display of tawdry trash as if she had just discovered the golden fleece hanging in a tree in Colchis. I think it was Colchis.

"Julia, I never knew you had this streak of vulgarity," I said. "I approve. It makes you seem . . . well, you seem more Roman."

"You do have a way with compliments." She picked up a little terra-cotta group: two ladies gossiping with pet dogs in their laps.

I selected a lively little Thracian gladiator, poised to strike and painted in lifelike colors. He held a tiny bronze sword and his helmet sported a crest of real feathers.

"I like this one," I proclaimed.

"You would, being not only vulgar and Roman, but male. Carry these." She handed me her purchases and quickly added a half-dozen others. I thought she had forgotten her mission to locate Ascylta, but Julia had a rare ability to divide her attention. While she was trying to decide between a scarlet scarf and a purple one, she spotted a garish tent covered with floral designs.

"Let's try that one," she said, walking away and leaving me trying to juggle all her junk. I bought the red scarf in order to wrap them all up. I caught up with her at the entrance to the tent. "You stay out here," she said. "If it's the woman we're looking for, I want to speak with her alone for a while. I'll call you when I need you." She pushed the door covering aside and went in.

When Julia didn't come out for several minutes, I decided that we had found our woman. I wasn't used to dancing attendance in such a fashion and I fidgeted uncomfortably, wondering what to do. When I left Hermes this way, he usually sneaked off somewhere for a drink. I always upbraided him for this habit, but now it seemed like an excellent idea. I was looking around for a promising booth when Julia called to me to come inside.

The woman was neither old nor young. She wore a coarse woolen gown about the same shade of brown as her gray-shot hair. She sat amid the usual baskets of dried herbs and jars of unguents.

"Good day to you, sir," she said with a thick Oscan accent.

"Decius, this is Ascylta," Julia told me, although by that time I scarcely needed to be informed. "Ascylta is a wise woman. She is learned in the lore of vegetation and animals."

"Ah, just the lady we have been looking for," I said, unaware of how much Julia had told the woman.

"Yes, but you are not here for my herbs. You are the senator who is asking about Harmodia."

"She guessed," Julia said, smiling sheepishly. "But we've been having a nice talk."

"You people don't need to wear your fine clothes for us to know who you are," Harmodia said. "The way you talk is enough. The highborn people send their slaves when they just want herbs for the household. They come personally only for poisons or abortions. No woman brings her man along when she wants to get rid of a child."

"A wise woman indeed," I said.

"You are not an official from the aedile's office," she said. "Why do you want to know about Harmodia?" To these market people the aediles were the totality of Roman official-dom.

"I think that she sold poison to someone, and I think that the buyer had her killed to silence her. I am looking into the death of a most important man, and I have been warned not to look into her death. My life has been threatened."

She nodded gloomily. I studied her as closely as I could, trying to remember whether I had seen her out on the Campus Vaticanus. I tried to picture her without her clothes, her hair streaming wildly, dancing frantically to the music of pipe and drum. She did not look familiar, but there had been so many.

"It is Furia and the Marsi and the Etruscans who want you to stay away, is that not so?"

"It is," I said. "Was Harmodia one of them? I know that she was from Marsian country, but was she a member of their . . . their cult?"

Her gaze sharpened. "You know about that, do you? Aye, she was one. Some say she was their leader, and now Furia has taken her place as high priestess."

"Do you know whether Harmodia sold poisons?" I asked.

"They all do. The *strigae,* I mean, not honest *saga* like me. It isn't such an uncommon trade. Usually, it is a wife who wants to rid herself of a husband who beats her or a son impatient for his inheritance. Sometimes it is just someone who is tired of life and wants a painless way to die. Everyone knows it is dangerous to sell to the highborn, to the people who talk like you two. That is what brings the aediles down upon us. But many are greedy. Harmodia was greedy."

"How greedy?" Julia asked.

Ascylta seemed puzzled by the question. "Well, everyone knows that the highborn can afford to pay better than others. A seller will charge them ten, twenty, even a hundred times what they would demand from a peasant or a villager. To one who would inherit a great estate or be rid of a rich, old husband to marry a rich, young lover, the money is trifling."

"I understand," Julia said. "What I meant was, do you think Harmodia was greedy enough to be dissatisfied with even an exorbitant price for her wares? Might she have heard of the murder and demanded money for her continued silence?" Once again, my wisdom in bringing Julia along was vindicated. I had not thought of this.

"I cannot say, but I certainly would not put it past her. She was the one who dealt with the aediles, you know." Her mouth twisted in sour distaste. "She was the one who passed along the fees to them. We were all assessed, and no small part of our monthly dues stuck to her fingers."

"Shocking!" Julia muttered. In some ways she was remarkably naïve.

"You have no idea whether the poison buyer was a man or a woman?" I asked her.

"I could not tell you who bought it nor when it was bought. But between the October Horse festival and the night she died, she was spending more freely than before. Her booth had new hangings and her clothes were all new. I heard she had bought a farm up near Fucinus."

So far this wasn't getting us anywhere. "Tell me this, Ascylta. Do you know of a poison that produces death in this way?" And I described the symptoms of Celer's death as they had been described to me by Clodia. Following my recitation, Ascylta thought for a few minutes.

179

"There is a poison we call 'the wife's friend.' It is a combination of herbs carefully blended, and it produces death as you describe, almost impossible to distinguish from a natural passing."

"I would think it would be the most popular poison in the world," I observed.

"It is not an easy one to make. It requires many ingredients and even I know only a few of them. Some of the ingredients are quite rare and costly. It is not easy to administer because it has a most unpleasant taste."

"Does it work swiftly?" I asked.

She shook her head. "Very slowly. And it is cumulative. It must be given in small doses over a period of many months, in constantly increasing doses."

"Why 'the wife's friend'?" I asked. "Why not 'the heir's friend'? I would think it was ideal for someone impatient to come into a legacy."

She looked at me as if I were simple-minded. "Sons do most of the inheriting. How many men take food or drink daily from the hand of a son?"

"Would Harmodia have known how to mix this poison?" Julia asked.

"Oh, yes. It is a specialty of the Marsian *striga* . . ." she cut short, as if a sudden thought had struck her. "Now I think on it, twice last year a Greek-looking man came to my booth for some dried foxglove. It's used in several medicines, but it's also one of the ingredients of that poison. The reason I recall this man is that he came to my stall from Harmodia's. Hers was beneath the next arch but one, and I usually sit outside mine so I saw where he came from."

"And you think she might have been selling him that poison, but was out of foxglove those two times?" I asked.

She shrugged. "It could be. He just stuck in my mind because he didn't look like our usual customers."

"Why so you say that?" Julia asked her. "You've said he was Greek-looking. What was unusual about him?"

"Well, he was very tall and thin, and he wore very expensive clothes in the Greek fashion, three or four gold rings and expensive amulets. And in the front of his mouth, on the bottom, he had a couple of false teeth bound in with gold wire the way they only do in Egypt."

We spoke a while longer, but the woman was able to remember nothing more of any use to us. We thanked her and gave her some money and got out of the cramped little tent.

"What do you think?" Julia asked. "Have we learned anything?"

"We now have a likely poison, if he was poisoned at all. As for the bad taste, Celer was in the habit of taking a cup of *pulsum* every morning. That stuff is so vile someone could mix bat dung in it and you'd never notice."

"So suspicion still points at Clodia. What about the Greek-looking man?"

"Could be a coincidence. Harmodia may have sold that poison to a number of customers, and the foxglove was just one ingredient anyway. As Ascylta said, the ones buying poison usually come personally. Not many want to trust a job like that to a confederate. And if Harmodia was killed because she was extorting the buyer, well, that bothers me too."

"Why?" We were wandering back toward the Forum with no particular aim in mind.

"Urgulus said the woman was nearly beheaded. It takes a strong man to do that with a knife. Somehow I feel that Clodia would have done something more discreet and tidy."

"If she was covering her tracks, she'd deliberately want

181

to direct attention away from herself, wouldn't she? This city is full of thugs who would do such a thing for a handful of coins. If half the stories about her are true, she might have offered him payment in kind."

There was something wrong with what she was saying, but I couldn't quite put my finger on it. Most likely, I was distracted by my craving for something to eat and some wine to wash it down with.

"You are letting your dislike of her color your judgment."

"I think you are trying to find her innocent when that is the most unlikely conclusion possible. So what now?"

"I must talk to a few people: the ex-tribune Furius, with whom Celer had so many colorful rows last year; and Ariston, the family physician who attended him at the time of his death. But I don't think I'll be able to find them today."

When we reached the Forum, a man approached me. He was a dignified individual whom I recognized vaguely as a prominent lawyer and one of my father's clients. He gave me the usual formal salutation.

"Decius, your father instructs you to attend the slave banquet in his house this evening. You may bring your own staff. He says there are important matters to discuss. He couldn't send a slave to fetch you today so I'm the errand boy."

"And a splendid job you've done, my friend. I thank you. *Io* Saturnalia."

He walked off and I grimaced. "His house! I was hoping to have mine at home. Then I could get the disagreeable business over with early."

"It's the oldest tradition of the holiday," Julia chided. "The rest of it is meaningless without the banquet."

"It's all pretty meaningless, if you ask me," I groused.

"All this Golden Age posturing and fake leveling of classes. Who can take it seriously?"

"The gods, one presumes. Now quit whining. Your father probably has some important men to confer with you. This could be useful. I shall be attending at the banquet in the house of the *pontifex maximus* so I may be able to pick something up."

She kissed me and bade me good-bye, and I stood pondering amid the monuments and the riotous crowd. This business had begun with great promise, and now I was awash in a sea of irrelevancies and meaningless complications, with a terrible feeling that I would probably never be able to find out what had happened. In such circumstances I did the only thing possible. I went to look for a drink. When all the other gods fail you, there is always Bacchus.

10

With hermes, cato, and Cassandra, I walked through the streets to my father's house. The slaves were in a good humor because they knew my father was able to set a far better table than I. I was less eager because my father had a lot of slaves. That, I decided, was why he had insisted that I come. He wanted me to help out.

We found the house laid out with the tables and couches set up within the peristyle, since the triclinium was far too small to hold them all. To my great relief father had persuaded some of his freedmen to help out. Most of these were men and women recently manumitted who had no slaves of their own to tend to.

Hermes was already half-drunk and when he crawled onto the couch he wiggled his feet at me insolently until I took his sandals. *Just wait,* I thought to myself. I felt better about serving Cato and Cassandra. They had served my family all their lives and hadn't all that much time left to them. They rated a little indulgence.

For the next couple of hours we brought in the platters, kept the wine cups filled, and generally behaved as slaves. The banqueters, in turn, behaved like aristocrats and ordered us around. They observed certain unspoken limits though, all too aware that they would be slaves again tomorrow.

It was almost worth the bother to see Father, sour-faced old *paterfamilias* that he was, hurrying about, bringing platters from the kitchen, mixing water and wine in the great bowl, keeping a wary eye on the silver lest it wander away.

At last the slaves were replete and betook themselves to the streets to take part in the night-long festivities. I dropped my napkin on the floor and searched among the wreckage for something to eat. I was famished. I was also thirsty and I dipped out a good-sized cup of wine. It was too heavily watered for my taste, but I did not feel like searching out a fresh jug.

"Don't get drunk," Father said. "You are to speak with some important men. They should be here soon." Like me, he was loading a plate from the scattered remnants of the slave banquet. The freedmen were helping themselves as well. Somebody turned up an almost complete tunny fish, and we divided it. There were also some first-rate olives and no shortage of bread. The slaves had gone straight for the meats and exotic fruits, things they seldom got to eat during the rest of the year.

I took a seat and began to munch. "Father," I asked, "do you know where Ariston of Lycia lives? He attended Celer when he died and I have a few questions I want to ask him."

"Never had any dealings with the man," Father said, biting into an apple. "I was never ill in my life. My wounds were all treated by legionary surgeons. Besides, I think you're too late. I heard he was dead."

"Dead?" I said, dropping a piece of long-cold fish.

"That's right, dead. It happens to most people if they live long enough. I heard he was found in the river back"—he paused to remember—"back around the Ides of November, if I recall correctly."

The Ides of November. Harmodia was found dead on the morning of the ninth. I was willing to bet that Ariston had died a few days earlier than the Ides. Had he detected signs of poison? If so, why had he said nothing? Perhaps he was another blackmailer.

"Oh, well," I said, "that's one less to consult."

"There may be no need anyway," Father said. "If what you saw out on the Vatican is sufficient evidence, we may get similar results without having to prove a murder."

"Cicero thinks I have almost no chance of bringing charges." I did not tell him that Clodius wanted me to prove Clodia innocent. Things were complicated enough as it was.

"You told him about it?" Father said, irritated. "I don't know what you hoped to accomplish by that. Cicero is a timid little *novus homo* with dreams larger than his talent. He told you that because he fears that *he* would not be able to secure a conviction in such a case. Cicero is like a man who goes to the races but will bet only on what he conceives to be a sure thing, the problem being that he is a wretched judge of horses."

Much as it nettled me to hear it, there was no little justice in what Father said. I revered Cicero for his brilliance, but he was subject to frequent failures of nerve. His learning was vast, but he could never comprehend his place in the Roman power structure. This I attributed to his obscure origins. Always insecure, he idolized the long-established aristocracy, championed their cause, and thought that made him one of them. In the end, his indecision and self-delusion were to kill him.

I was still brushing crumbs from my tunic when our guests began to arrive. First to appear was the curule aedile Visellius Varro, an undistinguished man, rather advanced in years for the office he held. I read him as a plodding careerist with no great future, and I was right. Next came Calpurnius Bestia whom I already knew and disliked, but I also knew him to be an extremely capable man so I swallowed my distaste. He was wrapped in a tatty robe of off-purple color, probably dyed with sour wine. On his head was a voluminous chaplet of gilt ivy leaves, and his face was painted crimson like that of an Etruscan king or a triumphing general.

"I was chosen King of Fools at a big party on the Palatine," he proclaimed, grinning. I restrained myself from saying that he had to be the only logical choice.

The final arrival came as a surprise.

"Caius Julius," Father said, taking his hand, "how good of you to come. I know how busy you must be with your own preparations."

"If the matter touches upon our religious practice, the *pontifex maximus* must hear of it and rule upon it." Caesar delivered this line without the faintest trace of irony. He could say the most incredibly pompous things and somehow manage never to sound either embarrassed nor overtly hypocritical. I never knew another man who could do this.

Father, like most of the Metelli, detested Caesar's politics and everything else he stood for. On the other hand, Caesar had become one of the most promising contenders for power and might, against all odds, succeed to great prominence. As a family, we Metelli liked to place a bet on every chariot in the race. I had the discomforting suspicion that, as Nepos was the clan's man in Pompey's camp, I would be expected to play the same role with Caesar. My betrothal to Julia was a purely political maneuver as far as my family was concerned.

Father began. "Allow me to preface these proceedings by informing you that my son has been investigating the circumstances surrounding the death of Quintus Caecilius Metellus Celer."

" 'Circumstances surrounding the death,' " I said. "I like that. It sounds much better than just, say, looking into the way the old boy croaked. I may use it myself when I . . ."

"I assure you, my friends and colleagues," Father said, overriding me, "that his peculiar talent is the only reason I had for recalling my son to Rome." He looked pained. Well, he was getting old.

"Tell us, young Decius," Caesar said, "just how did you come to be out there on the Vatican field in the dead of night?"

I gave them a somewhat truncated account of my investigation, leaving Clodius's semipeace treaty out of it. He had probably already told Caesar, but there was no reason for the others to know.

"Clodia!" Varro said. "That woman could destroy the Republic all by herself."

Caesar smiled indulgently. "I don't think the Republic is all that fragile. She is an embarrassment, no more."

"More an embarrassment to you than to the rest of us, Caesar," Bestia put in.

"How can one slightly degenerate patrician woman be an embarrassment to me specifically?" Caesar asked blandly.

"She is the sister of Publius Clodius Pulcher, and Clodius, as all the world knows, is your hound." His smile was malicious and made more so by his paint. As Pompey's lackey he was on the lookout for any way he could discomfit Caesar.

"Clodius is his own man," Caesar said. "He supports me, and by doing so he supports my good friend, Cnaeus Pompeius Magnus. Surely this should be a cause for rejoicing."

Deftly outmaneuvered, Bestia fell silent. He was forced to acknowledge the fiction of the triumvirate formed by Caesar, Pompey, and Crassus.

"This matter of Fausta Cornelia disturbs me," Visellius Varro said. "Granted she is a shameless woman, but she is the daughter of the dictator and, as such, is something of a symbol to the aristocratic party. The Cornelii are a great family, consulars since the founding of the Republic. In these unsettled times the public must have faith in our great families. I think it would be inappropriate to bring her name into this sordid matter."

I tried to remember whether the Vissellii were clients of the Cornelii. They were an extremely obscure family, and I had never heard of any man of distinction with that name, which meant that his father or perhaps grandfather had most likely been a freedman, not that I had any prejudice against the recent descendants of slaves, but such men often had an excessive loyalty to their former owners.

"What about the woman Fulvia?" Father asked. "I've never met her and scarcely know her family. The Fulvii were great once, but they've nearly died out or else removed from the City. There hasn't been a consul of that name for seventy or eighty years."

"This one is from Baiae, I think," said Caesar. "She can be discounted. She's the betrothed of Clodius, but that means nothing. He can always find another."

I cleared my throat rather loudly. "Gentlemen, I hesitate to speak in so distinguished a company, but I thought we were here to discuss what to do about an impious cult practicing forbidden rites on Roman soil, not how to deal with the patrician presence at those rites. I saw quite a few, after all. Those three were only the ones I recognized." Father glared at me but he didn't say anything.

"Quite right," Bestia said. "It might be a mistake to prosecute Fulvia. Who knows whom she might name as her sisters in these unclean rituals?"

"We are dealing with unlawful human sacrifice!" I insisted.

"True," Caesar said. "The law is quite clear on the question. The problem is, I do not know of a single case in which anyone was prosecuted on the charge. If the victim was a slave and the property of one of the participants, the charge of murder is invalid. The censors may expel citizens for immorality, but legal prosecution is another thing."

"Then," I said, "as *pontifex maximus* can you declare these persons and their cult to be enemies of the state and take action against them? Could you not condemn them, level their holy site, and fill in their *mundus?*"

"I could, but what would be the point? Except for the highly placed thrill seekers, these people are mostly aliens, even if they come from places with titular Roman citizenship. The real purpose of driving the more disgusting foreign cults from the City is to preserve public order. These witches practice their rites at a discreet distance from the walls and, as far as we can tell, have been doing so for centuries without causing any public disorder at all."

"But what they are doing is infamous!" I said. "It is an offense to our laws and our gods!"

"I believe," Caesar said, "that I am a better judge of that on both counts. Before I leave for Gaul, I shall appoint an investigative board to look into the matter, and I shall authorize the members to take action by my authority. I shall also speak with Clodius concerning his sister and her friend, Fulvia, who I believe is living with her. I shall speak with Lucullus as well. Fausta is his ward. Her brother, Faustus, is with Lucius Culleolus in Illyricum, and I shall speak with him as well when I get there. I shall urge that all three women be sent away from Rome, not to return, for their own good and for the good of their families. It will, of course, have to be done with discretion to avoid public scandal."

"If you will forgive me, Caius Julius," I broke in, "I think a public scandal is exactly what is needed just now. What I saw . . ."

"What you saw, Decius," Caesar said, in tones like ringing sword steel, "was enough to bring charges against three silly patrician women and exactly one Etruscan peasant woman. I daresay you could harangue the Popular Assemblies and get some sort of action, but it would be mob hysteria and it would be aimed at *all* the market people from the outlying territories, specifically the Marsians. I need hardly remind you that we fought a very bloody war with the Marsians not so long ago, and it wouldn't take a great provocation to make them take arms against us now, the very last thing we need with war facing us in Gaul."

"Very true," Bestia said. "People are on edge just now. A bit of loose talk about witchcraft and human sacrifice would spread through the slums like a fire. One foreign slave sacrificed over a *mundus* would become twenty citizen's children murdered and eaten. I agree, it's too risky."

"I urge moderation also," said Varro. "The offense

scarcely seems to merit the sort of public unrest sure to arise."

"I do not like the idea of alien barbarities practiced right on Rome's doorstep," Father said, "practically beneath the noses of the censors, for all practical purposes. Perhaps we can indict the woman Furia and try her alone. Punish their ringleader or high priestess or whatever she is, and the others will scuttle for their hills."

"An excellent idea at any other time," Caesar said, "but there will be no courts for the balance of December, and with the new year the new magistrates take office. To testify against the woman, your son will have to be in the City while Publius Clodius is tribune."

"That does make it touchy," Father said.

"I'm not afraid of Clodius!" I protested.

"Who needs to be afraid of Clodius?" Father said. "Do you think it will be some sort of Homeric duel between champions? He'll be untouchable, and he'll have a thousand men each eager to curry favor with him by delivering your head."

"Unless," Bestia put in, "it's true what I heard, that you and Clodius have patched things up?"

"What's this?" Father said, frowning.

"Yes, Decius," Caesar said, amused, "tell us all about this prodigy."

"Clodius thinks my investigation will prove his sister innocent," I said, cursing Bestia's big mouth. "I put no stock in his protestations of a truce. Whether I find for or against her, it will be open war again."

"All the more reason to be away from Rome next year," Caesar said. He smiled and cocked an eye at Father. "Cut-Nose, why not send him with me to Gaul? I have plenty of room on my staff for another aide."

This proposal chilled my spine as even the sights out on

the Vatican field had not. I was about to squawk out a horrified protest when the smirks on the faces of Varro and Bestia made me stop.

"I am honored, Caius Julius," I said, managing not to grit my teeth. "I shall, of course, defer to my father's wishes."

"Let me discuss it with the family," said the heartless old villain. "Might do him some good."

Having apparently settled things to their satisfaction, the others took their leave and I saw them all to the door. From outside came the sounds of reveling. The final, frantic night of Saturnalia was well underway.

When they were gone, I turned to Father. "Are you insane?" I cried. "He is marching into a war with a major coalition of Gauls!"

"Of course he is," Father said. "You need a good war. When was the last time you saw any real fighting? Wasn't it that business in Spain against Sertorius? And what year was that?" He thought a bit. "It was during the slave rebellion, in the consulship of Gellius and Clodianus. By Jupiter, that was thirteen years ago! You'll have no future in office if you don't get a few successful campaigns behind you."

"I'll have no future at all if I march off with Caesar! According to Lisas, he's going to end up fighting Germans!"

"So what?" Father said scornfully. "They're just barbarians. They die like anybody else when you stick your sword in them. Why are you so reluctant to spend some time with the legions?"

"It's a foolish war. Most of them are foolish these days. Our wars are just excuses for political adventurers like Caesar and Pompey to win glory and get elected."

"Exactly. And some of them *will* win glory and *will* get elected, and the men who support them in winning that glory will hold the positions of power. Use your head, boy! If they aren't fighting barbarians, they'll fight each other. Then it will be Roman against Roman, just as it was when Marius and Sulla fought it out twenty-odd years ago. Do you want to see those days come again? Let them slaughter Gauls and Germans and Spaniards and Macedonians. Let them march down the Nile and fight the Pygmies, for all I care, so long as they don't shed the blood of citizens here in Rome!"

It was unusual for him to take the trouble to explain himself to me. But then, sending me off to a possibly disastrous war was an unusual circumstance. I choked back my dread and got back to the business at hand.

"They seemed uncommonly passive concerning the doings out on the Vatican. Granted Caesar has bigger things on his mind, but not the other two. A splashy prosecution is just the sort of thing you'd think men like Bestia and Varro would be looking for next year if they plan to stand for the praetorship, and there's no reason to be aedile unless you want to be a praetor."

He rubbed his chin absently. "Yes, it seems odd, but they probably have other plans for advancing themselves. There's nothing we can do about it now. You can get back to your investigation, and try not to be too long about it."

So on that unsatisfactory note I left Father's house and began to make my way back toward my own. The celebrations were in full roar, but I had lost my taste for all the gaiety. Despondent, I trudged on toward the Subura.

It is difficult to explain how I knew I was being followed even in the midst of a raucous crowd, but I knew it nonetheless. I paused to turn around from time to time, which was easy when so many people were jostling me, but I saw no one who looked familiar or especially malevolent; but with so many in masks that would have been difficult in any case. But I had that sensation, and I'd had enough experience of danger in the streets of Rome to know that I had better not ignore my instincts.

In a jammed alleyway I darted through the open gate of an *insula* and into its courtyard, which was as jammed as the alley outside. People were dancing on the pavement and hanging out the windows that looked out over the courtyard from the central air shaft that towered, canyonlike, five stories overhead. Celebrators swayed precariously on the rickety balconies built, most of them in violation of the building codes, outside the windows. Everybody seemed to be roaring drunk and the wine jars were passed promiscuously about.

I took a fast drink from one of them as it flew past, ducked beneath the attempted embrace of a fat, laughing woman, and dashed through an open door. I found myself in a dark apartment where overexcited persons were embracing passionately amid the gloom. I pushed my way through sweaty bodies until I found an outside door and came out onto a street only slightly larger than the alley I had left. I chose a direction at random and followed the street until it turned into a steep stair. I took the stairs at a run, scattering people and pet dogs like grain before a threshing flail.

Celebrators whooped and laughed as I passed. Desperate fugitives are not all that rare during Saturnalia. Despite the general atmosphere of license, there are always a few humorless husbands who grow unreasonably upset upon discovering the wife and the nextdoor neighbor locked in a feverish grapple: and sometimes a slave oversteps the recognized boundaries and finds himself pursued down the street by the master, waving the kitchen cleaver and bawling for blood.

I paused, gasping, at a little square with a fountain in its center and a tiny shrine to Mercury at the corner where a street entered the square. I paused long enough to buy a couple of honey cakes from a vendor and I left them at the feet of the god, hoping that he would lend me speed and invisibility, two of his most salient qualities. I suspected that Mercury, like everybody else, had taken time off from official business, but it never hurts to try.

On such a hectic night it is easy to lose your way in Rome, but I soon had my bearings and was headed for the Subura once more. I slowed to a walk, certain that I had lost my followers. This did not mean I was out of danger. Having lost me, they might easily take a more direct route to my house and wait for me there. The logical course for me was to avoid my house and go put up with friends somewhere or else just stay in the streets and celebrate until daylight.

I was, however, still gripped by the strange mood of self-destruction that had sent me out to spy upon the witches, and playing it safe seemed to be a poor and spiritless way to proceed. Besides, it looked as if I was going to go campaigning in Gaul with Caesar, and the prospect of a horde of snarling Germans made Italian assassins seem a minor danger, relatively speaking.

My flight had gotten me turned around, and I found myself crossing the Forum. The dice games were still going on, and as near as I could tell the very same men were rolling the cubes and the knucklebones. Near the *rostra*, who should I find in the midst of his followers but the very man I most needed at that moment.

"Milo!" I called, waving over the heads of the reeling crowd. In that great multitude he heard and saw me instantly. That dazzling smile spread across his godlike face and he waved me over. I plowed through the mob, and the final cordon of Milo's thugs parted to let me through.

"Decius!" Milo said, grinning. "You look almost sober. What's wrong?" Since becoming a respectable political gang leader, Milo usually wore a formal toga and a senatorial tunic in public (he had served his quaestorship two years before), but for this occasion he was dressed in a brief Greek chiton that came to midthigh and was pinned over one shoulder, leaving the other bare. He looked more than ever like a statue of Apollo.

Less edifying was the sight of his long, muscular arm draped over the shoulders of Fausta. She was dressed almost as minimally as he was, in a hunting tunic like Diana's, girdled up to show off her long, shapely thighs. The upper part was pinned loosely, allowing the neckline to drop perilously low. I would have been more intrigued had I not seen her wearing considerably less the night before. I made a point of ogling her anyway.

"I hope Cato happens by," I said. "I'd like to see him drop in a foaming fit and bark at the moon."

"You sound a little breathless, Decius," Milo said. "Trouble?"

"Some people are trying to kill me. Could you lend me some bullies to escort me home?"

"Of course. Who is it this time?" Milo passed me a fat wine skin, and I took a long pull. Ordinarily he was extremely moderate with food and wine, but he was lowering his limits this night.

"Oh, you know. Just politics." The last thing I wanted was to explain and bring Fausta into it. "It's not Clodius."

"I never knew a man like you for sheer variety of enemies," he said admiringly. "How many are there?"

"Probably no more than two or three. I lost them somewhere near my father's house, but they may be waiting for me in the Subura."

"Castor, Aurius," he called. "Escort Senator Metellus safely to his house." He grinned at me again. "These two can handle any six you're likely to encounter. Are you sure you want to leave the festival so soon? I'm throwing a public banquet for my whole district, and it will go on until dawn."

"Thank you," I said, "but I've had two eventful days and very little sleep, and by now one drunken brawl is pretty much like another. I hate to take your men away from all the fun."

"These fools would rather fight than celebrate any day. Good night, Decius. Tell me all about this when you have the time."

"I shall," I said, knowing that I never would.

I felt much more secure with the two thugs flanking me. Castor, the shorter, had a wiry, compact build and the quick movements of a Thracian gladiator. Aurius had the heavy shoulders and bull neck of a Samnite. Not Samnite by nation, but the type of gladiator we called Samnite back then, who fought with the big shield and straight sword. These days that type is called a *murmillo* if he fights in the old style and a *secutor* if he wears a crestless, visored helmet and fights the netman. The Thracian, with his small shield, curved sword, and griffon-crested helmet, is still with us.

Both men wore heavy leather wrappings around the right forearm and their hair tied in a small topknot at the back of the crown, both trademarks of the practicing gladiator. I saw no edged weapons on them, but each had a wooden truncheon thonged to his broad, bronze-studded belt. They were heavily scarred and looked eminently capable.

"Have no fear, Senator," said Castor, "we won't allow a

single hair of your head to be harmed." He sounded as cheery as a man just come into his inheritance.

"That's right," said Aurius, just as happily, "Milo thinks the world of you. Anyone makes a move for you, just back away and let us handle it." Despite their foreign names and fighting styles, I knew by their accents that both men were City-born. They were also cold sober. Milo had not been joking when he said that they liked to fight. They were bored senseless with the festival and were now all but whistling with glee at the prospect of bloodshed.

I wondered if we were to have a repeat of the little scene of two nights before. As it was, there were similarities and differences. Instead of two Marsian bumpkins stalking me to my gate, we were set upon by no fewer than five men lying in wait, and this time there were no warnings or threats.

The streets of the Subura weren't as crowded as those closer to the Forum. In fact, most of the Suburans were in the Forum and its environs. Those who weren't were mostly celebrating in the guild headquarters, the *insula* courtyards, and on the various temple grounds. We were passing before the huge iron-working shop owned by Crassus, its clanging hammers stilled for the holiday night, when they set upon us.

Three men rushed us from the shadows of the portico fronting the iron factory. This drew our attention to the left. A moment later two more came in from behind a statue of Hercules strangling the Nemean lion that stood on the right side of the street. All of them had bare steel in their hands, and I hoped Milo's boys were as good as he'd said they were.

I had my dagger in my right hand and my *caestus* on my left before they got to us, and I whirled to face the two coming in from behind the statue, trusting the gladiators to protect my back. I heard howls and crunching impacts behind me as I assaulted a man in a dark tunic, who held a wicked, sinuously curved dagger. He seemed surprised that I was taking the offensive and hesitated for a fatal instant, giving me the chance to cut his forearm and smash his jaw with two quick moves of the dagger and *caestus*. The knife fell one way and the daggerman went another and I made a half-turn to face his companion, but that worthy was already crumpling. Castor stood behind him, watching him fall with a look of deep, sensual gratification.

All five of the attackers were on the pavement in the abandoned poses of unconsciousness. Weapons littered the street and a good many drunks were already gathering to gape. Castor and Aurius seemed to be unhurt and were accepting graciously the compliments of a few witnesses.

"Are any of them dead?" I asked.

"We tried not to kill them," Castor said. "It's unlawful even to execute a criminal during Saturnalia. We're law-abiding men, Senator."

"I can see that. Do you recognize any of them?" We rolled over any who needed such treatment and ignored their groans. The one whose jaw I had smashed would be doing no talking for a few days and three of the others would be lucky to survive the head blows they had taken.

"This one's called Leo," Aurius said, picking up the fifth man by the front of his tunic. "He trained at the school of Juventius in Luca. They all did, from the look of them." He gestured toward the others. "See how their topknots are tied with black ribbon? They do that in Luca."

"This was most impressive," I said. "Clubs against steel and outnumbered."

Castor snorted. "We appreciate the thought, sir, but these scum were hardly worth our trouble. Those northern schools don't train 'em as hard as the Roman and Campanian *ludi*. When there's no *munera* in the offing they come down to Rome. A lot of second-rate politicians hire them as body-guards because they work so cheap."

"Milo makes us drill hard with the sticks, Senator," Aurius said. "He says they're as good as a sword in a street fight and they're legal inside the City." He whirled his with a snap of the wrist and something flew off it to strike a nearby wall with a moist splat.

"Speaking of which," Castor said, "if I was you I'd get that blade and those bronze knuckles out of sight, Senator. This may be the Subura, but you never know when you'll run into some stickler for the fine points of law."

"Good idea," I said, stashing my weapons inside my tunic. "Can our friend Leo speak?"

"Let's find out." Aurius hauled the man over to a quench-ing bath that stood just outside one of the furnace rooms of the iron works. He plunged Leo's head beneath the dirty water and held it there for a while, but the man didn't struggle. When he pulled him out, Leo muttered a few words in a rhyth-mic manner. I realized that he was singing something in a northern dialect.

"Afraid I tapped him a bit too hard, Senator," Aurius said, dropping the man in a heap next to the trough. "Poor old Leo won't be talking sense for a few days. Maybe never, if he starts to rattle."

"Ah, well," I said, "it would have been nice to know who hired them, but one can't have everything. I'll just have to be satisfied with getting home in one piece."

We walked away from the scene of the little battle, and behind us the reeling celebrants were already stepping over the bodies as if they were just others who had imbibed too

202

deeply. Even as I glanced back, boys darted in and confiscated the dropped weapons. Nothing of any value stays on the ground long in the Subura.

When we came to my gate I turned to thank the men and send them on their way, but they pushed past me and went in.

"Let us check out your house, Senator," Castor said. "They could have men hiding here in case you got past the others or took another way home."

"Many a man's been killed in his home because he thought he was safe after he locked the door," Aurius affirmed. This seemed like eminently sensible advice so I waited while they went through the house room by room, explored the roof, and even looked over the walls into the yards and rooftops of the adjoining buildings. When they were satisfied, I bade them good-bye and tipped them a few denarii. I really needn't have. It was probably the most fun they'd had that holiday.

There was no sign of my slaves. Hermes I could understand, but I wondered what two as old as Cato and Cassandra could find to do so late. Once again I washed the blood off my weapons and dried them; then I threw off my tunic and collapsed into my bed and was asleep before I closed my eyes.

It had been another long day.

11

Rome awoke to the great, collective hangover of the day after Saturnalia. All over the city hundreds of thousands of bleary eyes opened, the merciless light of morning pierced through them, and a vast groan ascended unto Olympus. Patrician and plebeian, slave and freedman, citizen and foreigner, all were afflicted and were half certain that Pluto had them by the ankle and was dragging them toward the yawning abyss; and, on the whole, they viewed the oblivion of the trans-Stygian world as not such a bad prospect after all. Even Stoic philosophers were retching into the chamberpot that morning.

But not me. I felt fine. For once I had been moderate in my intake and what little I had imbibed I had sweated out in my flight through the city the night before. For the first time since leaving Rhodes I'd had a decent night's sleep. I awoke clear-eyed, clear-headed, and ravenously hungry. The sun was high and it flooded through my window as though Phoebus Apollo were especially pleased with me.

"Hermes!" I bellowed. "Cato! Get up, you lazy rogues! The world is back to normal now!"

I got up and went into the little sitting room I use for an office. I threw open the latticed shutters and breathed in the clear air and listened to the songs of the birds and did all those things that I ordinarily despise. As a rule, morning is not my favorite time of day. I heard a slow shuffling behind me and Cato pushed the curtain aside.

"What do you want?" he asked grumpily. I'd seen livelier looking mummies in Egypt.

"Bring me some breakfast," I ordered. "Where's Hermes?"

"No sense calling for that wretch. He won't be finished vomiting until noon. Those young ones don't have the head or the stomach for proper celebrating." He shuffled off chuckling, then moaning.

I unwrapped my bandaged hand and was pleased to see that the cut was almost healed. Everything seemed to be going well that morning. I took out one of my better tunics and my best pair of black, senatorial sandals. To these I added my second-best toga, since I was likely to be calling on some official people that day.

Cato brought in bread, cheese, and sliced fruit, and as I fueled myself for the day ahead I planned out my itinerary. In a city as sprawling as Rome, geography is the most important consideration. The idea is to avoid backtracking and, above all, climbing the same hill twice. In a city as hilly as Rome, this last is difficult. I dipped a piece of bread in garlic-flavored olive oil and thought about it.

I decided to try Asklepiodes first. He would be in the

Transtiber, and I could stop at the Temple of Ceres on the way back into the City. Besides, as a man of moderate habits the Greek was unlikely to be in a homicidal mood this morning. I called for hot water and went through the unfamiliar act of shaving myself. It would not be a good day to entrust myself to the shaky hand of a public barber.

Dressed and freshly, if inexpertly, shaved, I went out into the uncommonly subdued streets of the City. Rome seemed to be half-deserted and looked as if it had been defeated in a major war. It was something of a miracle that no destructive fires had started during the uproarious celebrations. Everywhere people lay like the corpses of slain defenders, only snoring much more loudly. Discarded masks, chaplets, and wreaths littered the streets and public buildings.

On a hunch I took the Fabrician Bridge to Tiber Island. On a good many mornings Asklepiodes was to be found in the Temple of Aesculapius, and if he was there I would be spared the walk to the *ludus* where he had his surgery. The splendid bridge had been built four years earlier by the tribune Fabricius, who never did anything else, but who ensured the immortality of his name with this gift to the city. Relative immortality, anyway. I suppose in a hundred years another bridge will stand there bearing another politician's name, and poor old Fabricius will be forgotten. For once, the beggars who ordinarily throng all the bridges of Rome were absent, sleeping it off with the rest.

The morning was unseasonably warm and children crowded the bridge's abutments and supports, diving into the chilly water, screaming in delight, or more sedately fishing with long poles. While their elders slept off the excesses of the night before, the children of Rome had an extra holiday, free from supervision.

207

I paused in the middle of the bridge and savored the sight. To the east and south the City bulked behind its ancient walls, the gleaming temples atop the hills lending it the semblance of the home of the gods. The play of the children below me made the scene as idyllic as something from a pastoral poem. How deceptive it all was. But I could remember playing here myself as a child on the day after Saturnalia. The bridge was wooden then, but otherwise things were unchanged. There in the water had been the real holiday, when noble and common and slave and free and foreigner were all the same. We had yet to acquire the hard and bitter perspectives of adulthood.

Or maybe I was idealizing the memory. Children have their own cruelties to go with their own terrors. I continued my walk, knowing I was not made to be a poet.

The Temple of Aesculapius had the serenity possible only to a temple that is built upon an island. The majestic, dignified temple towered above the curiously ship-shaped walls that enclosed the long and tapering island, complete with ram and rudder, all of stone. The plantings of the temple grounds were among the finest to be seen anywhere in or near the City. The cedars, imported all the way from the Levant, were especially stately.

I arrived just as the priests and staff were finishing a morning ceremony that included the sacrifice of the traditional cock. The ceremony was in the Greek fashion and was conducted entirely in Greek, in the dialect of Epidaurus, whence the god had come to Rome. I spotted Asklepiodes among those attending and waited until the ritual was over.

"Ah, Decius," he said, when I caught his eye, "I suppose you are in need of a morning-after remedy?"

"Not at all," I said proudly.

"At last you learn moderation. That stay on Rhodes must have done you some good."

"All the gods forbid it. No, I was just too busy last night to indulge. I came to speak with you about my investigation."

"Wonderful. It was beginning to look like a boring day. Come with me." We went outside and found a bench beneath one of the cypresses. Asklepiodes brushed a few leaves from it and we sat. "Now tell me all about it."

I gave him Clodia's description of the symptoms Celer had evinced prior to his demise, and he listened attentively.

"This tells me very little, I fear. I wish I could confer with Ariston of Lycia, but as you may have heard he is unavailable."

"All too true. I had hoped to question him closely. Not only about the events surrounding Celer's death but whether he had been treating him for any other condition. Clodia wouldn't necessarily know."

"They were not close?"

"It would be fair to say that."

"I had little liking for Ariston. He was over fond of money and may have strayed from the strict Hippocratic path in his pursuit of it."

"I have my suspicions of the man as well." I told him of Harmodia's murder and its uneasy propinquity to the supposed drowning of Ariston. "Did you happen to examine his body after it was found?"

"No. I attended his funeral, but there was no suspicion of foul play so we all assumed it to be an ordinary drowning. He had an injury on the side of his head, but it was assumed that he had fallen over the parapet and struck his head on one of the bridge supports before landing in the water. It was after a banquet, and if he had imbibed too much, such a fate is hardly a matter for suspicion."

"He was our family physician, but I don't think I ever saw him. He probably attended my mother in her final illness, but I was in Spain at the time."

"You would have remembered him if you had seen him. He was a striking man, very tall and thin. He smiled more often than necessary to show off his expensive Egyptian dental work."

My spine sang like a plucked bowstring. "Egyptian dental work?"

"Yes. Right here"—he pulled down his lower lip with one finger—"he had two false teeth bound in with gold wire. Excellent work, I might add. There is no one in Rome skilled in that craft. You have to go to Egypt, and Ariston was always fond of reminding people that he had lectured at the Museum of Alexandria. As," he added complacently, "have I."

But I wasn't listening. I silenced him with a raised hand and told him what I had learned from Ascylta, and he all but clapped his hands and rubbed his palms together with glee. Then, of course, he had to have the rest of the story out of me, and he chuckled with each horrible new revelation. Sometimes I wondered about Asklepiodes.

"This is marvelous!" he proclaimed. "Not a mere sordid poisoning but an ancient cult of human sacrifice and filthy politics as well!"

"Not to mention," I pointed out stiffly, "what now looks like the involvement of the medical profession."

That soured his face. "Yes, well, that is rather scandalous. It is a greater straying from the path of Hippocrates than I ever suspected Ariston of undertaking."

"What about this poison, the one Ascylta called 'the wife's friend'?"

"I have never heard of it, but there is no medical reason why it cannot exist. The presence of foxglove alone would make it potent."

"Did Ariston have assistants, students or others familiar with his practice?"

"Assuredly. I usually saw him with a freedman named Narcissus. Ariston's offices were near the Temple of Portunus. If Narcissus plans to assume Ariston's practice, he may still be there."

"Will you accompany me?" I asked as I stood.

"Decidedly." He grinned. We left the island and walked back into the city through the Flumentana Gate. The district was not one of Rome's better ones, despite the presence of some of Rome's most ancient and beautiful temples. The dwellers there were involved mainly in the port trade: wharfage, warehousing, barge hauling, and so forth. More foreigners lived there than in any other district within the walls of Rome. Worst of all, the district was directly adjacent to the outlets of Rome's two largest sewers, including the venerable *cloaca maxima*. The smell that morning was dreadful, although not as lethal as on a hot summer day.

Ariston's surgery was located on the upper floor of a two-story building that faced the *Forum Boarium*. The ground floor was a shop selling imported bronze furniture. The stairway was external, running up the side of the building to an open terrace surrounded on three sides by planter boxes full of ivy and other pleasant greenery. The railing of the stair and the corners of the parapet around the terrace were decorated with sculptured symbols of the medical profession: serpents, the caduceus, and so forth.

We found Narcissus on the terrace, examining a patient in the bright light of morning. He looked up with surprise at out arrival.

"Please, do not let us intrude," Asklepiodes said.

"Master Asklepiodes!" said Narcissus. "By no means. In fact, if you would do me the courtesy, I would greatly appreciate a consultation."

"Of a certainty," Asklepiodes said.

"Good day, Senator . . . my apologies, but I feel that I should know you." Narcissus was a handsome, serious-looking young man with dark hair and eyes. Around his brows he wore the narrow hair fillet of his profession, tied at back in an elaborate bow.

"You have treated members of his family," Asklepiodes said. "This is the senator Decius Caecilius Metellus the Younger."

"Ah! The facial features of the Metelli are indeed distinctive. Welcome, Senator Metellus. Are my services required by your family?"

"I take it then that you've assumed the practice of the late Ariston?"

"I have."

"No, I have some questions about your former patron and mentor. But please attend to your patient first."

Narcissus turned and clapped his hands. A hungover slave appeared from the penthouse that formed the fourth side of the terrace. "Bring a chair and refreshment for the senator," the physician ordered.

The man in the examining chair was a stout specimen in his thirties, whose head was a bit malformed on one side. He wore a somewhat sleepy, dazed expression.

"This is Marcus Celsius," Narcissus said. "He is a regular patient of mine. Last night, during the celebrations, he passed by a tenement where a party was being held on the roof. A tile was dislodged from the parapet and fell four stories, striking him on the head."

The slave brought me a chair and a cup of warmed wine, and I sat down to watch the proceedings with interest.

"I see," Asklepiodes said. "Was he carried here or did he walk?"

"He walked and he can speak, although his words grow disjointed after a while."

"So far, so good then," Asklepiodes said. He went to the patient and felt the man's skull with long, sensitive fingers. He probed and poked for a few minutes, during which the patient winced slightly, and only when he touched the minor lacerations of the scalp. Satisfied, Asklepiodes stepped back.

"You are of course familiar with the *On Injuries of the Skull* of Hippocrates?" Asklepiodes said. He had switched to Greek, a language in which I was tolerably fluent.

"I am, but like my former patron I commonly deal with illnesses rather than injuries."

"What we have here is a fairly simple depressed skull fracture. The detached cranial fragment moves rather freely and should only need to be lifted back into place and perhaps set with silver wire. I cannot say until I see the fracture exposed, but it may be possible to raise the fragment with a simple probe. Otherwise, it may be done with a screw. My Egyptian slaves are very skilled in both procedures."

Actually, Asklepiodes did much of his own cutting and stitching, but that was not considered respectable by the medical community, so in public he pretended that his slaves did it all. "The injury is common among the boxers who wear the

213

caestus, so we have a few such cases after almost every set of games that feature athletic contests.

"It is of course impossible to predict these things with certainty," he went on, "but I see no reason why a complete recovery may not be effected. Have him carried to my surgery at the Statilian *ludus* and we shall operate this afternoon."

"I am most grateful."

Narcissus called in a pair of muscular assistants and they bore off the unfortunate Marcus Celsius. No mention was made of fees, such things being forbidden. But physicians, like politicians, have their own ways of arranging favor for favor.

"Now, Senator," Narcissus said, "how may I be of service?"

"Your former patron, Ariston of Lycia, attended my kinsman, the consul Quintus Caecilius Metellus Celer, in his final illness. Did you accompany him on that occasion?"

He nodded gravely. "I did. He was a most distinguished man. His passing was a great misfortune to Rome."

"Indeed. Did Ariston remark at the time upon, oh . . . any irregularities in the manner of Celer's passing?"

"No, in fact he stated rather emphatically that the symptoms were those common to death from natural, internal disorders such as attend a great many common deaths. This time, he declared, the only unusual circumstance was the seemingly robust health enjoyed by the deceased."

"You said 'seemingly robust health,' " I pointed out. "May I know why you qualify it thus?"

"Well, first of all, he was dead. This alone means that he was not as healthy as he had seemed."

"Clearly, unless said good health was terminated by an outside agent. Poisoning has been freely conjectured."

Narcissus nodded, a puzzled expression on his fine, serious features. "I know. It made me wonder why Ariston never told the widow or the close relatives about Celer's previous visits."

My scalp prickled. "Previous visits?"

"Yes. I said nothing at the time because that would have been in violation of the confidentiality that must always exist between physician and patient. But since both Celer and Ariston have passed on, I see no reason why I should withhold evidence that should lay to rest these rumors of poison."

"None indeed," I said encouragingly. "Please, do go on."

"Well, you see, the distinguished consul came here about a month before the termination of his period in office, needing urgently to confer with my patron."

"Wait," I said, "he came *here?*"

"Oh, yes. Ordinarily, of course, a physician is summoned to attend upon so prominent a client. But in this instance, the consul called after dark, dressed as an ordinary citizen. Truly, this is not a terribly uncommon occurrence. You must understand," he glanced back and forth between Asklepiodes and myself, "that the confidentiality I mentioned sometimes calls for clandestine meetings between physician and patient."

"To be sure," I affirmed. More than once I had called upon Asklepiodes to patch me up after some extra-legal encounters.

"So it was in this instance. The consul had been suffering severe pains in the chest and abdomen. He was a strong and soldierly man and was able to conceal this infirmity from even his closest companions. Apparently even his wife was unaware of it."

"Not a difficult bit of deception considering how much they saw of each other," I commented.

215

"And you must understand why he did not want his condition to become known?"

I nodded, much becoming clear. "Exactly. He had been given the proconsular command everyone has been drooling over for the last year or two: Gaul. He couldn't afford to appear unfit for the command."

"It was not the first time a man of great public importance came to Ariston for confidential treatment of a condition potentially injurious to a career, rather as women often resort to the clandestine treatment of a *saga* for the well-known condition so injurious to marriage."

"And did Ariston provide a satisfactory treatment for the consul's condition?" Asklepiodes asked.

"As you know, Master Asklepiodes, the symptoms evinced in this case are the classic signs preceding death from apoplexy, although men may suffer them for many years before the inevitable happens. However, Ariston provided a medication sufficient to suppress the painful symptoms."

"I see," Asklepiodes said, apparently full of professional interest. "Do you know what the contents of this prescription might have been?"

Narcissus frowned slightly. "No, Ariston insisted that I was not yet advanced enough in my studies to entrust with that particular formula." That flicker of disloyalty told me why Narcissus was willing to discuss Ariston's questionable behavior. "I do know that each time Celer was given a supply sufficient to last for a matter of weeks."

"He had some on hand at the time of the first visit?" I asked.

"Yes. I heard him instruct the consul to take it each morning. Celer said that he would mix it with his morning *pulsum*."

"I see. This way the vinegar would disguise the taste of the medicine?"

He looked puzzled. "No. He told Celer that the medicine was nearly tasteless. But the consul was a man of regular habits, and the *pulsum* would ensure that he took it regularly every morning."

I glanced at Asklepiodes and he raised his eyebrows quizzically.

"How many times did Celer call here?" I asked.

"Three times that I am aware of. The last time was about half a month before his death."

I stood. "You have been most helpful, Narcissus. I am grateful."

He stood as well. "It is nothing. Consider it a part of my service to the illustrious Metelli." Reminding me that he, and he alone, would follow in the footsteps of Ariston of Lycia as physician to the Metelli. Asklepiodes and I made our way down the stairs.

"What do you think?" I asked when we were out on the street. Before us lay the cattle market, where even the livestock looked hung over.

"Much is now made plain, but much is obscure. In the first place, Celer may not have had a fatal condition at all. Narcissus is correct in naming the symptoms as those of a preapoplectic condition, but they could as easily reveal ulceration of the stomach or esophagus, not uncommon conditions among men who spend their careers arguing with people."

"The condition is hardly material. What is important is that it provided an excuse to introduce poison into the daily ingestion of a man who rarely needed medication. I think there is no doubt that we have our poisoner here."

217

"The question is one of motive," Asklepiodes said. "Why would a man like Ariston want to poison Celer? He was unscrupulous, I admit, but this is rather extreme."

We were walking along the street, our heads down and our hands behind our backs, like two academic philosophers conferring on abstruse points of logic. Or was it the peripatetics who walked around like that?

"Cicero has expounded to me upon a very basic principle of criminal law, a question the investigator must ask himself and a prosecutor expound to the jury in every case of anomalous wrongdoing: *Cui bono?* Who stands to benefit from this?"

"As you have said, Celer was not a man without enemies."

"Envious enemies. Noisiest and most colorful among them being the tribune Flavius."

"Their public rows were the talk of Rome last year," Asklepiodes said. "But Roman politics are usually boisterous. And yet it seems to me that Flavius accomplished his ends without resorting to poison."

"Not for certain. The very day he dropped, Celer was going to court to sue for the return of his Gallic command. Flavius still stood to lose."

"But by that time Flavius was out of office," Asklepiodes pointed out.

"Out of the office of tribune. But he was standing for the office of praetor for next year, and it wouldn't have looked good if his coup against Celer failed. Besides, their conflict went far beyond ordinary partisan politics and into the realm of personal insult and violence. Plain revenge could play a part here."

"That much makes sense," Asklepiodes admitted. "But

how would he have known that Celer would need to be treated by Ariston?" Learned as Asklepiodes was, he did not extrapolate very well, probably the result of receiving wisdom from long-dead Greeks.

"Ariston told him. You heard Narcissus say that the medication was supposed to be tasteless?"

"And was puzzled by the statement. It scarcely agrees with what the woman Ascylta said."

"That is because the first time Celer visited he was given a legitimate medication, at least one that was not harmful. Once Ariston realized the possibilities, he went shopping for someone needing his services. In the case of Celer, there was probably no shortage of buyers."

"That was extraordinarily cold-blooded."

"I suspect that it was not the first time. He knew exactly where to go to find the poison he needed. He may have been a regular patron of Harmodia's little stall. A list of Ariston's late patients might make for some interesting reading. Who is in a better position than a physician to surreptitiously hasten one's transport to the realm of shades?"

"Assuredly," he murmured, "this is a most exceptional case."

"I don't doubt it a bit. Still, from now on I shall be very careful in my choice of physicians. I am, of course, more than fortunate in having a friend such as you to patch me up while I am in Rome."

"Will your stay be a lengthy one this time?" he asked.

"No, everyone wants me away while Clodius is tribune. My father wants to pack me off to Gaul with Caesar." An involuntary shudder ran down my spine. "I must find some way out of it."

"If I may make so bold, certain men have come to me

desirous of avoiding hazardous service. The usual expedient is to amputate the thumb of the right hand and pretend that it occurred in an accident. I am quite skilled at the operation, should you . . ."

"Asklepiodes!" I said. "How utterly unethical!"

"This presents a problem?"

"No, I'd just rather not lose my thumb." I held up that unique digit and exercised it. "It comes in handy. Nothing like it for jabbing a man's eye in a street fight. No, I'd feel incomplete without it. Besides, nobody would believe it was accidental. I'd be accused of cowardice and barred from public office."

"Even heroes resort to stratagems to avoid particularly onerous or foolhardy military adventures. Odysseus feigned madness, and Achilles dressed as a woman."

"People already think I'm insane. Anyway, if I dressed like a woman, everyone would think I was just one of Clodia's odd friends."

"Then I fear I run short of suggestions. Why not go? You might find it amusing, and a countryside filled with howling savages is no more dangerous than Rome in unsettled times."

"Yes, why not? Shall I suggest to Caesar that you accompany the expedition as army surgeon?"

"And here I must leave you," he said, turning abruptly. "I must go prepare to operate on the unfortunate Marcus Celsius." He walked off in the direction of the Sublician Bridge.

I proceeded to the Forum, where Rome was beginning to come shakily to life. Most of the drunks had risen like animated corpses to totter off and seek dark corners to continue their recovery. The business of the City was resuming, after a somewhat late start. Everywhere, state slaves were listlessly but steadily plying their brooms and mops, repairing the wreckage of Saturnalia.

I went to the basilicas and asked questions and eventually ended up in the Basilica Opimia, where several of the praetors-elect were conferring, making their final arrangements for the ordering of their courts. Some of them had already assumed the purple-bordered toga of curule office; others were waiting until the beginning of the new year.

A slave pointed out the man I was seeking. He was one of the stripe wearers, tall and craggy-featured, with unruly, graying hair that stuck out from his scalp in stiff waves. His beak of a nose was flanked by the sort of cold, blue eyes you don't want to see looking at you over the top of a shield. I walked up and presented myself for his attention.

"Lucius Flavius?" I asked, not bothering with his title since he had yet to assume office.

"That is correct," he said. "I don't believe we've met."

"I am Decius Caecilius Metellus the Younger."

"Then you are a man of distinguished lineage." Clearly, his warmth toward the Metelli was limited.

"I am looking into the circumstances surrounding the death of Metellus Celer. I understand you had some rather notable run-ins with him."

"That was last year. I am busy preparing for next. By whom have you been commissioned to investigate?"

"By the tribune Metellus Pius Scipio Nasica and . . ."

"A tribune is not a curule officer," he snapped. "He cannot appoint an *iudex*."

"This is an informal investigation requested by my family," I told him. "Including Metellus Nepos, who would appreciate your cooperation."

That gave him pause. "I know Nepos. He's a good man."

As long as both supported Pompey, they would be colleagues. Flavius put a hand on my shoulder and guided me to a relatively uncrowded alcove of the vast, echoing building. "Is it true that Nepos will stand for next year's consular election?"

"It is."

He rubbed his stubbly chin. He hadn't dared to trust a barber that morning either. "It will be an important year to have such a man in office, if he wins."

"He will win," I said. "When a Metellus stands for consul, he usually gets the office. It's been that way for more than two centuries."

"All too true," he mused. "Very well, what do you want to know?"

"I understand that your disputes with Celer were occasions of public violence."

"Not all of them, but a few times. What's unusual about that? If our debates didn't involve a little blood on the pavement from time to time, we'd all turn into a pack of effeminate, philosophy-spouting Greeks."

"We certainly wouldn't want that. Do I understand correctly that the gist of your dispute was the land settlement for Pompey's veterans?"

"You do. And a more just and politically wise policy could hardly be imagined. Celer was the leader of the loony end of the aristocratic party. They'd rather face civil war than give public land to hungry veterans who've earned it. And for all their protestations, it's because they've been using that land themselves at a nominal rent or wanted to buy it up cheap. They . . ."

I held up a hand. "I know the argument, and I am fully in sympathy with the land settlements."

He settled his ruffled feathers. "Well, even Cicero supported the settlement, once he'd added some amendments concerning compensation for former owners, and Cicero is a notorious supporter of the aristocrats." He shook his head and snorted through his formidable nose. "Those last weeks in office Celer seemed scarcely in control of himself once he got angry."

His last month in office Celer had been taking Ariston's medication. I wondered whether this might have affected his judgment and self-control.

"He was especially indignant over your depriving him of the proconsulship of Gaul?"

"Who wouldn't be? But I considered his behavior in office disgraceful and urged the Popular Assemblies to overrule the Senate and that was that."

"Except that he was suing to get the command returned to him," I commented.

"Yes. But he died before he could win his case. What difference does it make? If he hadn't died in Rome he'd have died in Gaul, and it would be some legate tidying up the paperwork to hand it over to Caesar right now." The way he pronounced Caesar's name told me what he thought of him.

"I think Celer would not have died if he had gone to Gaul."

"Why should that be?"

"I now know for a fact that Celer was poisoned."

"That's unfortunate, but he never should have married that slut."

"No, I am nearly certain that Clodia is entirely innocent, for once."

"Then what is this all about?" he asked suspiciously.

"When you urged the assemblies to strip Celer of his

imperium in Gaul, did you also try to get it transferred to Pompey?"

"Of course I did! Pompey is the most capable general of our age. He would settle that Gallic business quickly, efficiently, and at the minimum cost to Rome."

I knew better than to argue Pompey's merits, or rather lack of them, with one of his rabid supporters.

"So Pompey was the man with the most to lose if Celer was given back Gaul," I said.

"What are you implying?" His face went dark. "Pomptinus was continued in command in Gaul until the matter could be settled, so he gains. Caesar is to have the whole place for five years, so he gains. Pompey is serving here in Italy on special civilian commissions and has made no move at all to take Gaul from Caesar. If you are looking for a poisoner, Senator Metellus, you are looking in the wrong place! Go look into Caesar's doings! Good day to you, sir, and if you come to me again with unfounded allegations I shall have my lictors drag you into court!" He whirled and stalked off.

I sighed. One more powerful man in Rome disliked me. I would just have to live with it. I had borne up beneath such burdens before. I walked out into the sunlight and went to provoke somebody else. Back across the Forum and past the Circus Maximus and up the slope of the Aventine to the Temple of Ceres. The elderly freedman and the slave boy I had encountered two days before were still there, but there were no aediles present. I asked after Murena, fearing that he would still be home in bed, nursing an aching head like much of the City.

"The aedile Caius Licinius Murena," the freedman said importantly, "is in the jeweler's market this morning."

So I went to find him. Outside, on the temple steps, I

paused in case the slave boy should run out with more information to sell. After a reasonable interval I set off for another trudge: back past the circus, back past the cattle market, and through the Forum. No matter how I tried to plan, I always seemed to be retracing my steps.

The jeweler's market sold a great deal more than jewelry, but all of the wares displayed there were expensive luxury goods: silks, perfumes, rare vases, furniture of exquisite workmanship, and a great many other things I couldn't afford. There the merchants did not operate from tiny booths and tents that they set up and took down every day. The jeweler's market was a spacious, shady portico where the dealers could display their wares to wealthy patrons in gracious ease. No raucous-voiced vendors cried their wares, and even the most elegant ladies could descend from their litters and browse through the great arcade without being jostled or forced into proximity with the unwashed. The splendid portico was owned by the state, and the merchants secured their enviable accommodations through payment of regular fees, some small part of which usually stuck to aedilician fingers.

Murena was easy to spot in the rather thin crowd that morning. As a curule aedile he was entitled to wear the purple-bordered toga, and when I came upon him he was speaking with a Syrian who displayed a dazzling assortment of golden chains, from hair-thin specimens for a lady's neck to massive links suitable for shackling a captive king. Doubtless, I thought, Murena was squeezing out a few more bribes before having to fold up his curule chair and doff his toga *praetexta*.

"May I have a moment of your time, Aedile?" I asked.

He turned, smiling. Murena was a man a few years older

than I, with an engagingly ugly face. "How may I help you, Senator?"

I went through the usual introduction and explained the bare bones of my mission. "In my inquiries concerning possible vendors of poison I came across the name of Harmodia, a Marsian woman who had a stall beneath the arches of the Circus Flaminius. She was discovered on the morning of the ninth of November, murdered. A watchman from the circus reported the killing at the Temple of Ceres, and you went out to investigate. Upon your return you dictated a report to a secretary and it was filed. Is this correct so far?"

"I remember the incident. Yes, you are correct so far as my part in it goes. Why is the woman significant?"

"I have strong evidence that the woman sold the poison used in the murder I am investigating, and I believe she was killed to silence her."

"Those people are notorious. The City would be improved if they were all driven off."

"Perhaps so. Now," I went on, getting to the heart of the matter, "about two or three days after the murder, you sent a slave to the Temple of Ceres to fetch your report of the woman's death for a presentation to the *praetor urbanus,* is this correct?"

Murena frowned. "No, I made no such report."

"You didn't?" Another unexpected twist in a case already full of them.

"No, it was the last full month of the year for official business and the courts were extremely busy. Nobody was interested in a dead woman from the mountains."

"And yet the report is missing."

"Then it was misfiled, as often happens at the temple, or

else the slave picked up the wrong report, as also happens rather commonly."

"Possibly. Could you give me the gist of your report? It might have some bearing not only upon the murder but upon the reason for the report's disappearance."

"Inefficiency requires no reason, Senator Metellus," he pointed out.

"Profoundly put. But, if you will humor me . . ."

"Very well. Let me see . . ." He concentrated for a while. "This was several weeks ago, and the incident was a trifling one, so please bear with me if my memory lacks its usual keenness."

"Quite understandable. A mere murder, after all." It was a pretty fair assessment of a homicide in Rome in those days, at least when the victim was a person of no importance. At the moment, though, I could feel little sorrow over the death of Harmodia. She was a seller of poisons. Ariston had been equally despicable. As far as I was concerned, their murders were just an impediment to my investigation. As, of course, they were intended to be.

"The murder was reported by one Urgulus . . ."

"I have spoken with him," I said.

"Then you know the circumstances under which she was found and I was summoned. I went to the Flaminius and found the body of a fairly stout woman in her thirties or forties lying in a large pool of blood. The cause of death was a deep knife wound to the throat, nearly severing the head. Questioning revealed no witnesses to the deed, which had occurred several hours before, judging by the condition of the body."

"Were there any other wounds?" I asked. "Urgulus was unsure."

"While I was asking questions, the Marsian women prepared her for transport to her home for burial. They took off her bloody gown, washed her body, and wrapped her in a shroud. I saw no other wounds, but I suppose if she'd been knocked on the back of the head with a club there might have been no obvious sign of it."

"No evidence found nearby? The murder weapon, that sort of thing?"

"In that district? Thieves would have stolen the blood if they could have gotten anything for it."

"That is so. Anything else?"

He thought for a moment. "No, that is what I reported. As I said, there was very little to report. When I went to court that morning I made a brief mention of it for the morning report."

"Yes, I found that at the *tabularium*. Tell me, Caius Licinius, weren't you in Gaul a few years back?"

"Yes, it was four years ago, when Cicero and Antonius were consuls. I was legate to my brother, Lucius. I was left in charge when he returned to Rome for the elections. Why, were you there at the time?"

"No, it's just that Gaul is on everybodies' minds these days."

"It may be on everybodies' minds, but it's in Caesar's hands now, though he may come to regret that, and serve him right."

"You favor Pompey then?"

"Pompey!" he expressed utter scorn. "Pompey is a jumped-up nobody, who earned his reputation over the bodies of better men. And before you ask, Crassus is a fat sack of money and wind who once, with help, beat an army of slaves. Is that satisfactory?"

"Eminently."

"Those men want to be kings. We threw out our foreign kings more than four hundred years ago. Why should we want a home-grown variety?"

"You are a man after my own heart," I told him. Indeed he was, if his sentiments were sincere. I took my leave of him and walked away, pondering. He was not what I had expected, but it is always foolish to expect people to fall into one's pre-conceived notions. He certainly seemed plausible, even likable. But Rome was full of plausible, likable villains.

Flavius had been more the sort of man I expected to find involved in this: the kind of brutally aggressive tribune who made the lives of the senior magistrates such a torment. That made me want to believe that he was a part of the plot to poison Celer, and that, too, was a foolish line of thought. The will to believe is mankind's greatest source of error. A philosopher told me that once.

I felt that I had come to a dead end and had learned all I was going to by asking questions. The year was dwindling, and I had satisfied no one. All I had really determined was that Celer had indeed been poisoned. Clodia's guilt or innocence was unproven. Clodius would be growing impatient. So would the leaders of my family. Gaul was looking better all the time.

"Up so early?" A small, veiled figure stood at my side.

"Julia! I'll have you know I was up before dawn . . . well, not long after dawn, anyway, and working diligently. How did you get away from Aurelia?"

"Grandmother is never quite well on the day after Saturnalia. Waiting on slaves upsets her."

"How very un-Roman. I expect greater respect for our traditions from our distinguished matrons."

"I'll be sure to tell her that. Where can we talk?"

"There is no shortage of places. The Forum isn't exactly thronged this morning."

We ended up on the portico of the beautiful little Temple of Venus on the Via Sacra near the Temple of Janus. Like that of Vesta, Venus's temple was round, in the shape of the huts in which our ancestors had lived. The place was deserted, for the goddess had no rites at that time of year. The portico was newer than the rest of the building and featured a long bench against the wall of the temple, where citizens could sit and enjoy the shade on hot days, which are numerous in Rome.

From where we sat, we could see the doors of the Temple of Janus. We could see one set of doors, I should say, for that temple has doors at each end. The doors were open, as usual. They were only closed in times of peace, when Roman soldiers were nowhere engaged in hostilities. This is to say that they were never closed.

"Now tell me what you've been up to," Julia said. It seemed to me that she was growing all too accustomed to making such demands.

"The hours since we parted yesterday evening have been eventful and more than a little puzzling," I informed her.

"Tell me. I can probably make more sense of it than you."

I began with the meeting in my father's house after the slave banquet. Julia frowned as I described the proceedings.

"You mean they treated that . . . that atrocity as if it were just another little political embarrassment?"

"These men look at everything that way," I affirmed.

"But my uncle is *pontifex maximus!* How can he treat this flouting of our sacred laws so lightly?"

"My dear, the supreme pontificate has become just another political office. Caius Julius is widely known to have secured it through a campaign of bribery such as has seldom been seen in Rome, even in this decadent era."

"I cannot believe that. But I confess to being shocked at his cavalier treatment of the matter. It must be that the Gaulish campaign weighs so heavily on his mind. I know what a burden it is, spending as much time in his house as I do. Lately he has been agitated and busy from long before dawn to long after dark. He just calls for lamps and keeps on working, interviewing prospective officers, dispatching letters all over . . . he has become distracted with work."

"I can imagine the shock," I said. Caesar had long been famed for his indolence. The sight of him actually working had to be a worthy spectacle. "It seems that I may be one of those lucky men who shall go out and win undying glory for him."

"What?" Now she had to hear all about that.

"It's true. He asked for my services and my father thinks it's a good idea and now I'm cornered. I may spend the next few years among the barbarians, constantly under attack and eating the worst food in the world."

"This is disturbing news," she said. From somewhere within her mantle she produced a palm frond and fanned herself with it. In December. She had probably overdone it in disguising herself with cloaks and veils. "But surely he will assign you to administrative duties . . . embassies, payrolls, that sort of thing."

"He'll have quaestors for the payrolls," I told her, "and embassy or envoy duty can be dangerous in that part of the world. Nations wishing to join a rebellion usually declare their loyalty by killing their Roman ambassadors. Envoys who deliver terms the Gauls don't like are often slaughtered. The Germans are rumored to be even worse."

"Well, I am certain that my uncle will keep you well away from danger. Your reputation has never been that of a soldier, after all."

"I am touched by your faith."

"Anyway, that is next year. What happened after the conference?" This time she got the story of my flight from my father's house and the little battle near my house.

"It's a good thing Milo assigned you such capable men," she commented.

"I did pretty well for myself," I said. "I settled for one and was about . . ."

"You would have been killed had you been alone," she said flatly. "Do you think the men were Clodia's?"

"No, and that is a part of all the things that have bothered me about this case. It's not Clodia's style."

"Have you forgotten?" she said crossly. "I told you that she might do just such a thing to divert attention from herself."

"I remember quite well. No, it's the quality of the men. I've been in Clodia's house quite a bit"—I caught her look and added hastily—"in the line of duty, of course. Everything Clodia owns, buys, hires, or in any way whatever associates with, is first class. Her clothes, her furniture, her collection of art, even her slaves all are of the very highest quality."

"I'd like to get a look at her house some time," Julia said wistfully.

"But Milo's thugs said that the attackers were very inferior fighters from an inferior school. Even allowing for the customary school rivalry, they did seem less than adept. They were not very pretty either. If Clodia had hired assassins, she would have hired only the best."

"No pursuit is so low that good taste cannot be observed,"

Julia said. "I still think you're trying to find her innocent in spite of all evidence."

"Then listen to this." I told her about the interview with Narcissus. She was enthralled by, of all things, Asklepiodes's diagnosis of the injury caused by the falling roof tile.

"And he can actually open up a man's head and heal so terrible an injury!" she said, dropping her fan and clasping her hands in delight. "Such a skill must truly be a gift from the gods."

"Well, if anyone can do it, it must be Asklepiodes. Now pay attention. That is nothing."

"Nothing!" she said before I could continue. "All you men spend your days scheming about how to injure people and you idolize the worst butchers, but you think it is nothing that someone can draw an injured man back from death like that!"

"I don't go around injuring people," I protested. "And I don't admire people who do. Besides, we don't know that he will pull through. Marcus Celsius may have the Styx lapping about his ankles this very moment." How had we gotten off onto this? "Enough. Let me tell you about a less admirable physician."

Julia listened open-mouthed as I described the activities of the late Ariston of Lycia.

"Oh, this is infamous!" she cried. "A physician, sworn to the gods by the oath of Hippocrates, deliberately poisoning his patients!"

"You think you're shocked?" I said. "He was *my* family's physician. Suppose I'd fallen ill?"

"Do you think you are important enough to poison?"

"Some people have deemed me quite worthy of homicide."

"They might have stabbed you to death in the street, perhaps. That usually calls for a temporary exile. Poisoning brings a terrible punishment."

"It is a puzzler, and that brings up another question. With all the suspicions about her, why would Clodia poison Celer? She had to know that she would be the most prominent suspect. If she, as you suggested, might wish to divert suspicion from herself, would she not have hired an assassin to strike him down in the city? Everyone would have automatically assumed that he had been killed by one of his multitude of political enemies."

That gave her something to think about. "It does confuse things."

"So, having determined that the poison originated with Harmodia and that Ariston was the vector, as it were, by which it was transmitted to the victim, I have to sift through the rather numerous suspects to determine which one hired Ariston."

"Must it be only one?" she asked.

"What do you mean?"

"As you've said, Celer had no dearth of enemies. Might Ariston not have shopped his services around to a number of them? He might have taken pay from more than one, and each would think that he was the only one who had hired Ariston."

"I hadn't thought of that," I admitted, intrigued by the idea. "It would present some interesting judicial problems in assigning guilt, wouldn't it? I mean, if it wasn't, technically, a conspiracy, how would the courts go about punishing them? Give each a portion of a death sentence? Find extremely tiny islands for them all?"

"Rein in your imagination," she said. "Probably only the *saga* would get the full sentence of the law; perhaps the Greek physician as well. Those who hired him might get off with exile, since they were probably of the nobility. They would at least be given the option of honorable suicide."

"Probably," I mused. Then I shook my head. "It wouldn't work anyway. The more people Ariston involved, the greater the chance of discovery. He was a cautious man, and poison is notoriously the weapon of a coward. I can't imagine him being so bold as to dupe a number of murderously inclined men that way. I think he sold his services to one of them and deemed himself safe."

"It is worth considering. Anything else?"

"Yes, I conferred with Flavius, the fire-eating tribune of last year." I told her of my interview. "He was everything I'd hoped: violent, abrasive, obnoxious, and a firm supporter of Pompey."

"So what is wrong?"

"He's too good to be true. Besides, everything about him proclaims a willingness, even an eagerness, to shed his enemy's blood with his own hands. I just don't think poison is his style, although Celer's death was awfully convenient for him, coming when it did. His anger when I brought up the subject of poisoning was too convincing. If he'd been expecting the accusation, I doubt he'd have been able to summon up that extravagant facial color on cue."

"I am not convinced that your judgment of men is as accurate as you think, but where does that leave us?"

"It leaves us with the curule aedile Murena, who reported upon the death of Harmodia and then sent for the report, which has subsequently disappeared."

"Have you found him?"

"I have. I told you I haven't been wasting my time today."

She patted my hand. "Yes, dear, I didn't mean to imply

that you are an irresponsible overgrown boy who drinks too much. Now proceed."

I told her of my interview with Murena in the jeweler's market, finishing with: "And then I walked out into the Forum and you found me."

"Politically, he sounds just like you," she observed.

"That's the problem. I rather liked the man. But I won't deny that I have been fooled before."

"There are too many things that don't fit together," she said. "There has to be something we are overlooking."

"Undoubtedly," I said, gloomily. "I am sure it will come to me in time, but time is just what we're short of. It's going to do us little good if, six months from now, I wake up in a leaky tent in Gaul while the savages beat their drums and toot their horns all around the camp in their massed thousands and I cry, 'Eureka!' "

"Yes, that would do us little good," she agreed.

"Did you hear anything last night?"

"I may have. After the banquet was over and the slaves had departed for the festivities, we cleaned up the triclinium and the ladies of the various households visited among themselves, bringing gifts. It's traditional."

"I'm familiar with the custom," I told her. "My father's house has been without a lady since my mother died and my sisters married, but I remember them all flocking about on Saturnalia."

"Since my uncle is *pontifex maximus*, we went nowhere. Everyone came to us. Only the family of the *Flamen Dialis* has as much prestige, and there hasn't been one of those in almost thirty years." The high priest of Jupiter was so bound by ritual and taboo that it was increasingly difficult to find anyone who wanted to assume the position, prestigious as it was.

"I know why Caesar wanted to be *pontifex maximus*," I said. "His mother put him up to it. Aurelia just wanted to have every woman in Rome, even the ladies of the highest-ranking households, come to her and abase themselves."

She punched me in the ribs. "Stop that! As usual, there was gossip. People speak more freely at Saturnalia than at other times. A lot of it was about Clodia."

"Everyone assumes she poisoned Celer?"

"Of course. But there was more. It seems to be common knowledge that she is the brains behind her brother's rise to political power. They are wildly devoted to one another; everyone knows that. She may do most of his thinking for him as well."

"It wouldn't surprise me," I said. "Clodius certainly isn't the brightest star in the Roman firmament."

"Then," she said, leaning close and being conspiratotial, "if someone wanted to eliminate Clodius without bringing the wrath of Clodius's mob down upon him, wouldn't it make sense to get rid of Clodia?"

"I thought you were of the opinion she is guilty," I said.

"I'm trying to think like you, dolt!" Another punch in the ribs. "Now pay attention. By poisoning Celer, somebody hoped not only to eliminate him as an enemy, but to bring Clodius into disgrace as well, possibly to eliminate him entirely by getting the sister upon whom he depends sentenced to death by the state as a *venefica*. Even if Clodius is capable of handling his own career, the disgrace would be devastating. Does this plan eliminate a few suspects from your list?"

"It does that," I admitted. "If Clodius was one of the real targets, then somebody wants to cut Caesar's support in the

City out from under him while he's in Gaul." I glanced at her suspiciously. "You didn't brew this up just to make your uncle look innocent, did you?"

"I only search for truth and justice," she said, with lamb-like innocence. Then her eyes went wide with alarm. "Those men over there!"

I looked around, expecting assassins. "Where? Is some-one after us? Me, I mean?" I reached into my tunic and grasped the hilt of my dagger. I could see no northern thugs or Marsian louts.

"No, idiot! Those two old slaves over there. They belong to my grandmother, and they're looking for me." She drew her veil aside and kissed me swiftly. "I have to run back. Be careful." Then she was up and away, around a corner of the temple.

12

For a few minutes longer I sat on the portico of the temple, basking in the light of the sunny morning. With most of the litter of the holiday swept up and carted away, the Forum was almost back to its customary state of majestic beauty, and the eye was not distracted by the usual swarming crowds. Rome at its most beautiful, though, can be a strange and dangerous place.

I decided that there was one person I ought to talk to, although I dreaded the prospect. I had no excuse to procrastinate, save my own cowardice. On the other hand, I consider cowardice to be an excellent reason to avoid danger. It has saved my life many times. But time was pressing and this was one thin possibility and it had to be pursued. With a sigh of resignation I got up from the bench, descended the steps of the little temple, and began the walk around the base of the Capitol to the Field of Mars and the Circus Flaminius.

It was just about noon when I reached the warren of stalls and tents. There were not as many as there had been three days before. Could it really have been only three days? It hardly seemed possible. Many of the vendors had disposed of all their wares during the holiday and had returned home for more. Others had ended their business season and would not be back until spring.

I half-hoped that Furia would not be there either. On the lengthy walk I was forced to face my fear. It wasn't just that she was a woman of great presence who was a little too handy with a knife—I had confronted murderous females before without trepidation—no, I was forced to admit it was because she was a *striga*. Educated, aristocratic Roman I might be, but my roots were buried deep in the soil of Italy, like those of an ancient olive tree. My peasant ancestors had cowered in fear of such women, and their blood was more powerful in my heart and veins than the mishmash of Latin and Greek learning in my brain.

I saw the tent of Ascylta but I walked past it without a glance. For all I knew I might put the woman in danger by speaking with her out here. I had the uncomfortable but familiar feeling of being watched from every booth and tent entrance I passed. Among these people, I was a marked man.

Then I stood before the arch curtained by Furia's familiar hangings. I took a deep breath, summoned up an expression of fake courage, pushed the curtains aside, and strode in.

Furia glared up at me beneath the brim of her odd headdress. "I didn't expect to see you snooping around here again."

"So you did not. You did not expect to see me alive at all, at least not with eyes in my head."

"Those incompetent fools!" She calmed herself and put on a faint smile. "Still, I notice that you aren't here with a crowd of lictors to arrest me. Not having much luck with your law-enforcing peers, are you?"

I crouched so that our eyes were on the same level. "Furia, I want some answers, and I won't leave this booth until I have them."

"Do you really believe I will betray my religion?" she said.

"I won't ask you to. I need to catch a murderer. It is the death of Quintus Caecilius Metellus Celer I am investigating, but the same killer murdered Harmodia. She was the leader of your cult, was she not? Don't you want to see her avenged?"

"She has been!" Her eyes were as steady on mine as those of a bronze statue, and about as informative.

"I don't understand."

"There is much you don't understand, Senator."

"Then let's talk about what I know. I know that Harmodia was selling poison to a Greek physician named Ariston of Lycia. Some months back she sold him a slow-working concoction you *veneficae* call 'the wife's friend.' " At the name her eyes widened fractionally. I had managed to surprise her. "It was this poison that killed Celer. Not long after he died, Harmodia was murdered by a killer who wanted to hide his tracks. Within a very few days the physician was dead as well, supposedly by accident; but we know better, don't we, Furia?"

"Harmodia was foolish!" she said. "She dealt too much with that Greek. It is one thing to sell a woman the means to get rid of a husband who beats her or a son an easy way to dispose of the rich father who takes too long to die. What are such people to us? But the Greek was an evil man. He killed those who entrusted themselves to his care. Even worse, he sold his murdering services to others."

It seemed that even poisoners had their own code of

241

ethics, and Ariston had overstepped the boundaries.

"Why do you say that Harmodia has already been avenged?" I asked her.

"The Greek killed her."

"Are you certain of that?"

"Of course. He was a great and respectable man." These words were spoken with the withering sarcasm possible only to an Italian peasant or Cicero on one of his best days. "He could not afford to let Harmodia expose him, so he killed her."

"Was Harmodia blackmailing Ariston? Did she demand money in return for her silence?"

Furia stared at me for a long time. "Yes, she did. I told you she was foolish. And she was greedy."

"How did she expect to expose him without attracting the awful punishment meted out to a *venefica?*"

Furia actually chuckled. "She was no Roman politician. She did not threaten to accuse him in the assemblies. She would simply let his deeds be known to many people in many places. He never told her who he was poisoning, but we have our ways of learning such things. She would be far away before he could implicate her."

"A friend of mine, also a Greek physician but an honest one, told me that the deadliest weapon in Rome today is the spoken word."

"Then your friend is a wise man. Some things are best not spoken of."

"Tell me, Furia," I said, "about your cult. . . ."

"My religion!" she corrected vehemently. "Your spying was a profanation, and you should have died for it."

"That," I said, "is something that has me puzzled. While I abhor your rites, I recognize that yours is an ancient religion and one native to Italy."

"It is that. My foremothers practiced our rituals long before you Romans arrived. Even you adopted them before you began to imitate the Greeks from the south. You Romans call human sacrifice evil, yet you allow men to fight to the death in your funeral games."

"That is different," I told her. "It is for another purpose, and the men aren't always killed. You must understand the distinction between . . ."

"I spit on your distinctions! On the eve of the Feast of Saturnus you saw us sacrifice a slave. In the old days, before your censors made it a criminal offence, the sacrifice was a free volunteer. In times of terrible crisis, a prince of our people would willingly pour his blood into the *mundus* for the good of the people. What are your slaughters of bulls and rams and boars to a sacrifice like that?"

"Be that as it may, venerable and hallowed as your religion is, why do you allow the likes of those patrician women to attend? You must know that they come only for the excitement, for the decadent thrill of doing something forbidden. I know that you practice your sacrifice as a holy rite pleasing to your gods. Why then do you allow your religion to be defiled by a foreign people who enjoy it as something evil?"

"Isn't it obvious, Senator?" She smiled knowingly. "They are our protection. I observed before that you bring no officers to arrest me and throw me into prison. Is it not exactly because of those loathsome ladies? They are most highly placed. This, too, is an ancient tradition, Roman. You have your King of Fools on Saturnalia. These women play the same role, although we don't tell them that. And being women, their presence does not pollute our rites, as yours did."

"There were other men there," I said. "At least one of them was a Roman."

"There were no *men* there save yourself, Senator. There were masked creatures somewhat manlike in shape to make the music and stand watch over our solemnities."

"Who was the masked Roman who volunteered to kill me, Furia? I knew his voice. He was not one of your *strigae*, and he was not one of your people."

"He is one of us nonetheless. It was he who avenged Harmodia."

Glimmerings of light began to sift through the gloom that enshrouded this tangled, demon-ridden affair.

"It was he who killed Ariston?"

"He did. He said he'd do it the Roman way and sacrifice him to the river god."

That gave me pause. "You mean he was thrown from the Sublician Bridge?" I had assumed that he had been crossing the Fabrician to the island where many of the physicians of Rome had their living quarters.

"Yes, that was the one. Why should I give him to you? He may be a Roman, but he avenged our sister."

I leaned close. "I don't think he did, Furia. I think he is the one who hired Ariston to poison Celer. I furthermore think that he killed Harmodia himself to cover up his tracks. Ariston was a coward who liked to use poison and keep his own hands clean. Your Roman enjoys spilling blood. He killed Harmodia, then he killed Ariston to destroy the last link between himself and the poisoning, and in doing it he further ingratiated himself with you. He is a clever man, Furia, cleverer than you and almost as clever as I. I am going to find him and I will see justice done, if I have to mete it out myself."

She regarded me for a long time with cool, steady eyes. "Even if I believed you, I could not reveal his name. I am bound by sacred oath and cannot reveal an initiate to an outsider even if one of them sins against the gods."

I knew better than to try to break that sort of determination. I stood. "Good day to you, then, *striga*. I think that I will know my man before the sun sets. I can feel it now just as you read my future in my palm and my blood."

"A moment, Senator."

I waited.

"It was the blood of both of us. Tell me one thing: Since I first saw you, you have been as grim and determined as a hound on a scent. You were that way when you came in here just a little while ago, although I could tell that you were in fear of me as well. But now you are angry. Why is that?"

I examined my feelings for a few seconds. "I was determined to find out who killed Celer because he was a member of my family and a citizen. But Romans of my class have been murdering each other for centuries, and sometimes it is as if we've asked to be killed. Anger in such cases is as futile as anger against an enemy soldier who kills from duty and habit. Also, I wanted to make sure that a woman was not accused unjustly, although she has plenty of blood on her hands and her brother is my deadly enemy." I paused, thinking of the thing that stirred anger within me.

"Your masked drum beater, this Roman swine, killed a worthless man. But he did it in mockery of one of our most ancient rituals, the sacrifice of the Ides of May, when the sacred *argei,* the puppets of straw, are cast from the Sublician Bridge into the Tiber. Politics is one thing; sacrilege is another."

She turned and rummaged through one of her baskets. "Roman, you are no friend of mine or my people. But I think you are a good man, and those are rare in Rome. And your gods watch over you; this I saw when you were here before.

Take this." She held something out to me. It was a thin disk of bronze, pierced at one edge and hanging from a leather thong. I took it and examined it in the dim light. On one side was writing in a language I had never seen before. On the other was a stylized eye surrounded by lines like rays.

"It will protect you and help you spy out evil."

I took it and placed it around my neck. "Thank you, Furia."

"Now forget about us. Some day you may be a high magistrate and may feel you should try to wipe us out. It has been tried before, many, many times. It is useless. You will never be able to find our *mundus* again, I promise you, scour the Vatican as you will. It was the gods who led you there in the first place for their own reasons, but their purpose has been accomplished. Go now. I have called off my dogs; they'll not bother you again." She lowered her gaze and her face was hidden by the stiff, black brim of her hat. I turned and walked out.

It was well past noon as I walked back from the Campus Martius and through the Porta Flumentata into the City. For the first time since returning to Rome I felt confident. I felt that luck was with me and maybe even the gods. Maybe Furia's eye amulet was helping as well. I felt that, in some inexplicable way, I saw everything more clearly, not just their appearance, but their hidden meaning.

As I crossed the cattle market I glanced up and to my right and saw the beautiful Temple of Ceres low on the slope of the Aventine, glowing as by an inner light and looming, in some fashion, larger than was normal. I stood as one struck by a vision, jaw gaping, causing passersby to stare and point.

I knew what I had overlooked, what Julia and I had been discussing no more than two hours before. Had the investigation been a simple one, it would never have escaped me. It had been all those witches and their horrible rites and the presence of outlandish patricians and all the other anomalies that had cluttered up the case that caused me to overlook it. Or maybe Julia was right and I was sometimes dense.

Toga rippling in my self-made breeze, I ran all the way up to the temple and practically leapt down the stairs into the offices of the aediles. The aged freedman looked up in consternation.

"I need to borrow your boy!" I said.

"You'll do no such thing!" the old man informed me. "He has work to do."

"I am Senator Decius Caecilius Metellus the Younger, son of Metellus the Censor. I am an important man, and I demand that you give me the use of that boy for an hour."

"Bugger that," the old man said. "I am a client of the state and in charge here, and you are just a senator with no stripe on your toga. Get elected aedile and you can order me around, not before."

"All right," I grumbled, rummaging around in my rapidly flattening purse. "How much?" We reached an accommodation.

Outside, the boy walked beside me, unhappy about the whole situation. "What do you want me for?"

"You said a slave came and requisitioned the report on the murder of Harmodia. Would you recognize that slave if you saw him again?"

He shrugged. "I don't know. He was just a state slave. They all look alike. I'm a temple slave."

"There's another silver denarius in it for you if you guide me to the right man."

He brightened. "I'll give it a try."

We trudged around the basilicas, and the boy squinted at the slaves who stood around waiting for somebody to tell them what to do. Since the courts were not in session, this was not a great deal. That is one of the problems with Rome: too many slaves, not enough for them to do.

We started at the Basilica Opimia and the boy saw nobody he recognized. It was the same with the Basilica Sempronia. Finally, we went to the Basilica Aemilia and it looked as if that was going to be a dead end as well. I was beginning to doubt my new, god-bestowed vision when the boy tugged at my sleeve, pointing.

"There, that's him!" The man indicated was short, balding, and middle-aged, dressed in a dark tunic like most slaves. He held a wax tablet and was taking notes, apparently enumerating some great rolls of heavy cloth at his feet, probably intended to make an awning for the outdoor courts.

"Are you sure?"

"I remember now. Come on." We walked over to him, and the man looked up from his task.

"May I help you, Senator?"

"I hope so. Do you run errands for the law courts?"

"Nearly every day they are in session," he said. "I've been doing it for twenty years."

"Excellent. Around the Ides of November, did you go to the Temple of Ceres to fetch a report for the aedile Murena? It was for a report he was to make to one of the praetors, probably the *urbanus.*"

The slave tucked his stylus behind his ear and used the hand thus freed to scratch his hairless scalp. "I do so many things like that, and that's awhile back. I don't recall . . ."

"Sure you remember!" the temple boy urged. "You asked about the trials going on in the circus that day, and I told you the new Spanish horses the Blues had were the best ever seen in Rome and I'd been watching them all week. I remembered that when I saw you just now because I recognized that birthmark on your face." There was a small, wine-colored patch just in front of the man's left ear.

The state slave smiled a bit, the light dawning. "And you told me the two Blacks called Damian and Pythias were pulling trace and they were better than the Reds' Lark and Sparrow. I won some money on that tip at the next races. Yes, I remember now."

Trust a Roman, whatever his station in life, to remember the names of horses when he's forgotten the names of his parents or the gods.

"Do you remember the report then?" I said, elated and at the same time wanting to throttle them both.

"Well, yes, but . . ." he tapered off as if something was impeding his rather limited powers of reasoning.

"But what?" I asked impatiently.

"Well, it wasn't for the curule aedile Caius Licinius Murena, it was for the plebeian aedile Lucius Calpurnius Bestia."

I could have kissed him. "So you delivered it to him, and he took it into the praetor's court?"

"I delivered it all right, but he just took it and walked away, toward the cattle market. It was nothing to me. My job was to fetch it."

I tipped them both and bade them be about their business. My soles barely touched the pavement as I walked, once again, back around the base of the Capitol, skirting the northern edge of the cattle market, until I was once again in the precincts of the Temple of Portunus, amid the dense smells of our wonderful but all too fragrant sewers.

For the second time that day I ascended the stairs with

their medical symbols and, upon the terrace, found the freed-man Narcissus seated at a small table, eating a late lunch or early dinner. He was surprised to see me.

"Good day, esteemed physician Narcissus," I said, all good cheer.

"Senator! I did not expect to see you again so soon. Will you join me?"

"Are you certain it is no imposition?" I suddenly realized how long ago breakfast had been.

"A distinguished guest is never an imposition." He turned to a slave. "A plate and goblet for the senator." The man was back before I had arranged my toga to sit. For a few minutes we munched in silence, observing the proprieties; then I sat back as the slave refilled my cup.

"How went the operation?" I asked.

His face brightened. "It was perfect! Asklepiodes is the most marvelous physician. Marcus Celsius should make a complete recovery if infection does not set in. Asklepiodes actually lifted out the detached piece of bone and cleaned out clotted blood and some small bone splinters from the brain itself before replacing it and securing it with silver wire."

"He is a god among healers," I said, pouring a bit of wine onto the pavement as a libation so the gods should not take my words as a challenge and grow jealous of my friend Asklepiodes.

"And," Narcissus said, leaning forward confidentially, "he actually did much of it with his own hands, instead of just directing his slaves. I only say this because I know you are his friend."

"It will be our secret," I assured him. "Now, my friend Narcissus, it occurred to me just now that I neglected to ask you something this morning touching upon the demise of your late patron."

"What may I tell you?"

"I understand that he fell from a bridge and was drowned. Do you happen to know where the banquet was held where he imbibed too much?"

"Why, yes. He dined out most evenings, often at the house of someone distinguished. That afternoon, just before he left, he said, should he be needed for an emergency, by which he meant a sudden illness in a *very* rich and prominent family, he was to be found at the house of the aedile Lucius Calpurnius Bestia."

"Calpurnius Bestia," I said, all but purring.

"Yes," he said, a little puzzled at my tone. He pointed to the south. "It's up there someplace on the Aventine. He must have come down late, long after dark, and didn't think to ask the aedile for a slave to accompany him. He was usually a moderate man, but most people drink too much at a banquet."

"A common failing," I noted.

"Yes. Well, when he came down onto the level area, instead of walking straight home, he must have accidentally turned left and not realized it until he found himself on the Sublician Bridge. It was a very dark night, I remember that. It is easy to lose one's way, even near home. He probably went to the parapet to get his bearings, or perhaps he had to vomit. In any case, he leaned too far over and fell in, striking his head. He was found just a few paces downstream on the bank."

I stood and took his hand in both of mine, cheered by both the wine and the recitation. "Thank you, my friend Narcissus, thank you. You have been of inestimable help, and I shall recommend you most heartily to my family."

He beamed. "Any service I may render to the illustrious Metelli, I am overjoyed to provide."

I left his terrace, chuckling and whistling. I must have looked a perfect loon, but I was past caring about my appearance. I walked back toward my house, not feeling the many miles my feet had carried me that long day. I would have more walking to do before I went to my well-earned sleep.

As I walked I thought about Bestia. Bestia, Pompey's cunning spy in Catilina's conspiracy. Bestia, who would do anything to advance himself with Pompey. And how better than to eliminate Pompey's rival for the Gallic command, Celer? Bestia hadn't known that Pompey and Caesar had already reached an agreement on that. But perhaps not. Pompey might have wanted Caesar to go and fail and thus secure the command after the enemy had been softened up by his fellow triumvir. In any case the neat framing of Clodius through his sister could only help Pompey's position in the city, while cutting down Caesar's by destroying his henchman.

Ah, yes, Bestia. Bestia, whose voice I had recognized out on the Vatican field, muffled though it had been by his mask. I might have caught it sooner had I not been so terrified at the time. Bestia, whom I had seen only the night before, his face painted crimson, not because he had been elected King of Fools, but to hide the marks left by my *caestus.*

I had to marvel at the man's slyness and his audacity. He had accomplished his ends through indirection and covered his tracks neatly. He had slipped only twice: He'd neglected to appropriate the brief mention of Harmodia's murder in the *tabularia,* and he had not eliminated the slave he sent to the Temple of Ceres. Make that three times. He had failed to kill me. It was that last one he was going to regret.

13

It was late afternoon when I finished the letter, rolled it up, and sealed it. "Hermes!"

The boy came to my desk. He was nearly recovered from his excesses of the night before. I handed him the letter.

"Take this to the house of the aedile Lucius Calpurnius Bestia. It is on the Aventine somewhere."

"The Aventine!" He groaned. "Can't it wait until tomorrow?"

"No, it can't. Give this letter to his doorkeeper and tell him that it is a matter of utmost urgency. Don't wait for a reply; just leave and come straight back here. Waste no time." Something in my tone cut through the fog of his hangover, and he lost his customary insolence. He nodded and left.

I opened my arms chest and took out my swords. My military sword was a bit bulky for my purposes, so I selected a smaller *gladius* of the sort that is used in the arenas. It was wasp-waisted, its swelling edges honed to razor keenness, its long, tapering point apt for stabbing. I tested the edges, found a couple of spots that felt slightly dull, and stroked them lightly with a small whetstone. Then I did the same with my dagger.

When all was in order I sat back and looked out my window to the west. Storm clouds were piling up beyond the Capitol, black and ominous. I lay down for a while, hoarding my strength. Despite my tension, I slept.

I woke when Hermes got back. A little twilight lingered in the sky, and I heard distant thunder. I rose, feeling greatly refreshed and oddly at peace with myself. I had determined upon a course of action, and I would see it through, whatever the cost.

"He got it," Hermes reported. "The doorkeeper said he was home and he'd deliver it right away." He glanced at the weapons laid out on my bedside table. "What are you going to do?"

"Nothing you need concern yourself about," I told him, fastening on my hunting boots. "Get my dark cloak." I put on my military belt and hooked the sheathed blades to their suspension rings. Then I tucked my *caestus* beneath my belt. Hermes handed me my cloak and I draped it over my shoulders, hiding my weaponry. He fastened it at the left shoulder with a Gallic fibula.

"You'd better let me go with you," Hermes said.

"There would be no point. Stay here and be ready to open the door for me later on tonight."

"And if you don't come back?" He was most solemn, a rare thing in Hermes.

"You'll be taken care of," I told him.

"Let me carry your other sword," he urged.

"I am touched by your loyalty, Hermes, but I haven't yet sent you to the *ludus* to be trained. Either matters tonight will work out as I hope or they won't. In neither case will your presence help, and it would only expose you to needless danger. Now I must be going."

Hermes was a little teary-eyed as he opened the door for me. He really wasn't such a bad boy after all, on his better days. The door shut behind me with great finality.

So I set off on yet another long walk through the streets of Rome, perhaps to be my last. The light was dimming fast and soon would be inky black. The ugly clouds now piled high over the Capitol and through them snaked fitful lightning. We Romans love omens and it was altogether just and fitting that these should be such evil ones. Something bad was going to happen to someone that night.

I came into the northeastern end of the Forum and turned onto the Sacred Way. The darkness was so complete that even the whitest buildings were all but invisible, and I had to pause from time to time and wait for a lightning flash to give me my direction again. Then I was on the winding street that climbs the Capitol. The rising wind tugged at my cloak, but there was as yet no rain.

Roman law and Roman courts are the best in the world, but sometimes they fail. Very clever and ruthless men know how to circumvent the laws, how to use the courts to their own advantage, how to suborn juries and use the power of ambitious faction leaders to secure their own protection. Some of the worst men in Rome were our public officials, and they were the men best-trained in the law. At such times a man who loves the laws and customs of Rome must violate them if justice is to be served.

At the apex of the Capitol I walked up the steps of the

great Temple of Jupiter. A low, smoky fire burned atop the altar that stood before the doorway of the temple. Inside, the awesome statue of the god was dimly illuminated by a multitude of oil lamps. I drew my sword and cut off a small lock of my hair, which I dropped onto the altar coals. As it sizzled and smoked, I called upon the god by one of his many names.

"Jupiter Tarpeius, punisher of perjurers, oath-breakers, and traitors, hear me! The laws of man and of the community of your sacred city fail, and I must take action in your name. If my deeds are displeasing to you, punish me as you will."

I had done all I could do. I went down the steps and crossed the broad pavement to the precipitous southern edge of the Capitoline, overlooking the triumphal path. There I waited. I knew there had to be at least one attendant inside the temple to see to the lamps, but otherwise I seemed to have the whole hilltop to myself.

Then a lightning flash revealed a lone figure trudging up the path. When he reached the top and came out onto the plaza before the temple, he stopped and looked around.

"Over here, Lucius," I said. He turned and I saw the gleam of his teeth when he grinned. He walked slowly toward me. Like me he wore a dark cloak, and within it he bulked larger than I remembered. His cowl was drawn up, so I saw little more than eyes and teeth.

"I am amazed that you really came alone," I said.

"I know you to be a man of your word, Metellus, and I don't expect to need help. It was the strangest letter I ever received: *Murder, poisoning, treason, sacrilege. Tonight I will be atop the Capitoline, alone. Meet me there, alone, or see me in court.* Admirably succinct."

"I've always prided myself on a fine prose style. Would you mind answering a few questions before we start?"

He glanced up. "You won't be long, will you? It's starting to rain and I hate to get wet."

"I shall be brief. Was all this Pompey's doing?"

"Certainly not. You know how one serves great men, Decius: Try to do what they want, especially the less savory tasks, without waiting for them to tell you to. That way their hands stay clean, but they are aware of how much they owe you."

"And your disgusting witch cult? How did you get involved in such a thing?"

"Decius, there are many such clandestine religions in Italy, and I am an initiate in several of them. The dark gods are far more interesting than the Olympian crew. Their worship provides a genuine personal experience instead of the collective civic event provided by the state religion."

"I could tell you had little respect for the gods," I said. "Throwing Ariston from the Sublician Bridge like that. And I take it especially ill that you sent men to kill me on Saturnalia when even condemned men can't be executed. And why such inferior thugs?"

He shrugged. "I'm not a wealthy man. All the really good thugs work for Milo or Clodius, so I couldn't hire them. And I had to use out-of-towners who wouldn't know me by sight. Now answer me something: How did you figure it all out?"

So I told him where he had slipped up.

"Let that be a lesson to me," he said, shaking his head ruefully, "always make a clean sweep. even if it means another few killings."

The storm was coming on quickly. The lightning flashes were almost continuous, and the wind whipped dry leaves around so hard that they stung when they hit. I unpinned my cloak and let it fall.

"Let's finish this," I said, drawing my sword. I had to raise my voice to be heard above the wind.

He grinned again. "So we're to have our own little *munera?* Here, on sacred ground? Aren't you afraid Jupiter will be displeased?"

"If so, he can strike us both down. He has plenty of ammunition ready."

"So he has. Well, I came alone, Decius, but I didn't come unprepared."

He threw back his cowl and I saw that he was wearing a helmet. Then he dropped his cloak. He had a shield, the small, square *parma* carried by the Thracian gladiators. He also wore a shirt of mail and greaves on both shins. No wonder he had appeared so bulky.

"Your little *caestus* won't be enough to turn the balance in your favor this time, Decius. Pity we don't have an *editor* to give the signal to begin."

I reached to my belt and slipped the *caestus* over my knuckles. "Let Jupiter decide. Next thunderclap."

We waited tensely for a few seconds, then bright lightning flashed so close that the thunder was almost simultaneous with it. We attacked before the sound even began to echo.

Bestia came in with his shield high and well forward. His sword, which was a full-sized legionary *gladius,* he held low, gripping it next to his right hip, its point tilted slightly upward. I flicked my smaller sword toward his eyes to draw the shield up and immediately stabbed low, trying to get his thigh above the greave. He brought the lower edge of the shield down and blocked easily, at the same time driving his blade forward in a powerful, gutting strike. I sucked my belly in and twisted to the right, avoiding his sword by an inch.

An especially bright flash blinded us both for a second,

and I sprang back to get beyond his reach. The rain was beginning to fall in earnest now, and by the light of the next flash I stooped to grab my cloak with my left hand. Fortunately, my *caestus* left my fingers free enough for the maneuver. Bestia came in as I was bent over and I sprang back awkwardly to get away from his slashing blade, but he punched with his shield and caught me a glancing blow on the side of my head.

I dropped to the pavement and kicked out, sweeping his feet from under him. He fell with a clatter and I scrambled to my feet, immediately lunging at him as he surged to his knees and jerked his shield up desperately. I went in over it, trying to get his neck above the mail shirt; but his shield pushed the point aside at the last instant and it caught his upper arm instead, just below the short, iron sleeve.

Meanwhile, his point was coming for my belly again and I swept the blade aside with my cloak, but it bit through the cloth and cut into the back of my forearm. I jumped back, cursing, as he scrambled up and another lightning bolt temporarily blinded us again. I used the reprieve to wiggle the fingers of my left hand and assure myself that the cut hadn't been a crippling one. Bestia was fast and strong and highly trained and well armed, and I was in deep, deep trouble.

At the next flash I swirled my cloak at his face to blind him, but he slashed out and his sword point ripped the cloak for almost its entire length. When I dodged his next cut, my soles slipped slightly on the wet pavement. He came for me again and I threw the shredded cloth into his face and ran a few steps until I was off the pavement and standing firmly on rough stone.

He was right after me and I tried to remember those clever moves I had been taught in the *ludus* years before.

Shield high again, he thrust for my chest. Lacking a shield, it is possible to use the sword defensively, although it is extremely dangerous and only to be employed thus in desperation. I was desperate. Our blades rang together as I knocked his to my left. Immediately I snapped it against his shield, driving it to my right and creating an opening. I drove into it with both hands. My sword caught in his mail shirt and would not penetrate, but my *caestus* cracked against the cheek plate of his helmet and rocked him. He fell back and I was right on top of him. Too late I saw the leg coming up. The decorated bronze of his greave smashed into my face, and I felt the bone in my long, Metellan nose give way with an audible crunch.

I staggered back, lights brighter than the lightning sparkling behind my eyelids. Blood gushed onto the breast of my tunic and I fell, feeling the rugged stone of the Capitol against my back. As he got to his feet Bestia was blinded by another bolt, and I shook my head, trying to clear my vision. When I could see, he was standing over me and his sword was behind his right shoulder. The gladius is designed for stabbing but it cuts exceedingly well and now it was coming down in a skull-splitting stroke.

From blind instinct I threw up my left hand. Better to lose an arm than a head. I felt a shock all the way to my shoulder when the blade connected. It struck the knuckle bar of my *caestus*. The sharp steel of the edge bit into the softer bronze and held there for an instant.

In that instant my sword snaked in below his shield and above the greaves. Then I jerked it back in a draw-cut against the inside of his left thigh. I felt the keen edge scrape bone; and when I pulled it free, it was followed by a great gush of blood from the severed artery. It splashed my face and arms and chest before I could scramble back, getting to my feet while Bestia stood there like a sacrificial ox stunned by the hammer.

Sword and shield fell from his nerveless hands and for the first time I realized that we now stood atop the Tarpeian Rock, only inches from its edge. Nothing can save a man when that artery is cut, and I didn't want Bestia to die that way. I grabbed his arm and turned him to face the edge of the cliff as a lightning flash lit up the Forum far below.

"No honorable death for you, Bestia!" I informed him. "*This* is how we execute traitors!" I placed a boot against his buttocks and pushed. He had enough strength left to scream as he fell.

Wearily, I turned and walked off the rock of execution. I crossed the rain-swept pavement and stopped at the foot of the stair before the temple and I held my arms wide.

"Jupiter, Bringer of Rain!" I shouted. "Jupiter, Best and Greatest, hear me! Have I pleased you? I am polluted with blood and cannot enter your temple, but I stand here awaiting your judgment!"

I waited for a long time, watching the god within the temple, but there was no more lightning, no more thunder. The rain began to fall in earnest. I resheathed my sword and tucked my *caestus* beneath my belt once more.

Slowly I descended the winding road down the face of the Capitoline. Long before I reached the dark Forum, Jupiter's good rain had washed all the blood from me.

These things happened in the year 695 of the city of Rome, the consulship of Marcus Calpurnius Bibulus and Caius Julius Caesar.

GLOSSARY

(Definitions apply to the year 695 of the Republic.)

Acta Diurna   Literally, "daily acts." An account of the doings of the Senate and other news, painted on white boards and posted in the Forum. It was probably instituted by Julius Caesar during his aedileship and became immensely popular, the newspaper of its day.

Arms   Like everything else in Roman society, weapons were strictly regulated by class. The straight, double-edged sword and dagger of the legions were classed as "honorable."

The **Gladius** was a short, broad, double-edged sword borne by Roman soldiers. It was designed primarily for stabbing.

The ***Caestus*** was a boxing glove, made of leather straps and reinforced by bands, plates, or spikes of bronze. The curved, single-edged sword or knife called a **sica** was "infamous." *Sicas* were used in the arena by Thracian gladiators and were carried by street thugs. One ancient writer says that its curved shape made it convenient to carry sheathed beneath the armpit, showing that gangsters and shoulder-holsters go back a long way.

Carrying of arms within the *pomerium* (the ancient city boundary marked out by Romulus) was forbidden, but the law was ignored in troubled times. Slaves were forbidden to carry weapons within the city, but those used as bodyguards could carry staves or clubs. When street fighting or assassination were common, even senators went heavily armed and even Cicero wore armor beneath his toga from time to time.

Shields were not common in the city except as gladiatorial equipment. The large shield *(scutum)* of the legions was unwieldy in Rome's narrow streets but bodyguards might carry the small shield *(parma)* of the light-armed auxiliary troops. These came in handy when the opposition took to throwing rocks and roof tiles.

Balnea   Roman bathhouses were public and were favored meeting places for all classes. Customs differed with time and locale. In some places there were separate bathhouses for men and women. Pompeii had a bathhouse with a dividing wall between men's and women's sides. At some times women used the baths in the mornings, men in the afternoon. At others, mixed bathing was permitted. The *balnea* of the republican era were far more modest than the tremendous structures of the later empire, but some imposing facilities were built during the last years of the Republic.

Basilica   A meeting place of merchants and for the administration of justice.

Campus Martius   A field outside the old city wall, formerly the assembly area and drill field for the army, named after its altar to Mars. It was where the popular assemblies met during the days of the Republic.

Circus The Roman racecourse and the stadium that enclosed it. The original, and always the largest, was the Circus Maximus. A later, smaller circus, the Circus Flaminius, lay outside the walls on the Campus Martius.

Curia The meetinghouse of the Senate, located in the Forum, also applied to a meeting place in general. Hence Curia Hostilia, Curia Pompey, and Curia Julia. By tradition they were prominently located with position to the sky to observe omens.

Eleusinian Mysteries The most famous mystery cult of the ancient world. Their exact form is unknown because initiates were forbidden to discuss them or write about them. The initiation ceremony took several days and seems to have involved fasting, a descent into the underworld, and culminated in some sort of demonstration of life after death. Cicero, a rational and sceptical man, was an initiate and called his experience one of the most profound of his life, so it must have been an impressive ritual.

***Eques* (pl. *equites*)** Formerly, citizens wealthy enough to supply their own horses and fight in the cavalry, they came to hold their status by meeting a property qualification. They formed the moneyed upper-middle class.

Families and Names Roman citizens usually had three names. The given name (**praenomen**) was individual, but there were only about eighteen of them: Marcus, Lucius, etc. Certain praenomens were used only in a single family: Appius was used only by the Claudians, Mamercus only by the Aemilians, and so forth. Only males had praenomens. Daughters were given the feminine form of the father's name: Aemilia for Aemilius, Julia for Julius, Valeria for Valerius, etc.

Next came the **nomen**. This was the name of the clan (**gens**). All members of a gens traced their descent from a common ancestor, whose name they bore: Julius, Furius, Licinius, Junius, Tullius, to name a few. Patrician names always ended in *ius*. Plebeian names often had different endings.

Stirps A subfamily of a gens. The cognomen gave the name of the stirps, i.e., Caius Julius *Caesar*. Caius of the stirps Caesar of gens Julia.

Then came the name of the family branch **(cognomen)**. This name was frequently anatomical: Naso (nose), Aheno-barbus (bronzebeard), Sulla (splotchy), Niger (dark), Rufus (red), Caesar (curly), and many others. Some families did not use cognomens. Mark Antony was just Marcus Antonius, no cognomen.

Other names were honorifics conferred by the Senate for outstanding service or virtue: Germanicus (conqueror of the Germans), Africanus (conqueror of the Africans), Pius (ex-traordinary filial piety).

Freed slaves became citizens and took the family name of their master. Thus the vast majority of Romans named, for instance, Cornelius would not be patricians of that name, but the descendants of that family's freed slaves. There was no stigma attached to slave ancestry.

Adoption was frequent among noble families. An adopted son took the name of his adoptive father and added the genetive form of his former nomen. Thus when Caius Ju-lius Caesar adopted his great-nephew Caius Octavius, the lat-ter became Caius Julius Caesar Octavianus.

All these names were used for formal purposes such as official documents and monuments. In practice, nearly every Roman went by a nickname, usually descriptive and rarely complimentary. Usually it was the Latin equivalent of Gimpy, Humpy, Lefty, Squint-eye, Big Ears, Baldy, or something of the sort. Romans were merciless when it came to physical peculiarities.

Fasces   A bundle of rods bound around with an ax projecting from the middle. They symbolized a Roman magistrate's power of corporal and capital punishment and were carried by the lictors who accompanied the curule magistrates, the *Flamen Dialis,* and the proconsuls and propraetors who governed provinces.

Forum   An open meeting and market area. The premier forum was the **Forum Romanum,** located on the low ground surrounded by the Capitoline, Palatine, and Caelian hills. It was surrounded by the most important temples and public buildings. Roman citizens spent much of their day there. The courts met outdoors in the Forum when the weather was good. When it was paved and devoted solely to public business, the Forum Romanum's market functions were transferred to the **Forum Boarium,** the cattle market, near the Circus Maximus. Small shops and stalls remained along the northern and southern peripheries, however.

Freedman   A manumitted slave. Formal emancipation conferred full rights of citizenship except for the right to hold office. Informal emancipation conferred freedom without voting rights. In the second or at latest third generation, a freedman's descendants became full citizens.

Gracchi, the   In the late second century B.C. the brothers Tiberius and Gaius Gracchus, although members of the nobility, championed the cause of the urban and rural poor. The Senate regarded them as dangerous radicals. Tiberius was killed by a mob and Gaius forced to commit suicide. Eventually, almost all their reforms were adopted by the Senate and they were revered by the plebeians. Their mother, Cornelia, was always referred to as Mother of the Gracchi and became the model for the Roman mother who raised her sons to serve the public good whatever the cost.

Haruspex A member of a college of Etruscan professionals who examined the entrails of sacrificial animals for omens.

Imperium The ancient power of kings to summon and lead armies, to order and forbid and to inflict corporal and capital punishment. Under the Republic, the *imperium* was divided among the consuls and praetors, but they were subject to appeal and intervention by the tribunes in their civil decisions and were answerable for their acts after leaving office. Only a dictator had unlimited *imperium.*

Insula Literally, "island." A detached house or block of flats let out to poor families.

Janitor A slave-doorkeeper, so called for Janus, god of gateways.

Legion They formed the fighting force of the Roman army. Through its soldiers, the Empire was able to control vast stretches of territory and people. They were known for their discipline, training, ability, and military process.

Lictor Bodyguards, usually freedmen, who accompanied magistrates and the *Flamen Dialis,* bearing the fasces. They summoned assemblies, attended public sacrifices, and carried out sentences of punishment.

Ludus (pl. **ludi**). The official public games, races, theatricals, etc. Also training schools for gladiators, although the gladiatorial exhibitions were not ludi.

Mollossian Hound These were enormous dogs renowned in antiquity for their ferocity. Probably some sort of mastiff rather than true hounds, they were originally hunting dogs but were bred to fight. They were used to execute felons in the arena, hunt runaway slaves, and by the army to run down fleeing enemies. What they looked like is unknown but they were universally acknowledged to be terrifying.

Munera Special games, not part of the official calendar, at which gladiators were exhibited. They were originally funeral games and were always dedicated to the dead.

Mundus An opening into the underworld. There were several located around the Mediterranean. They were used for rituals involving the cthonic deities and to convey messages to the dead.

Municipia Towns originally with varying degrees of Roman citizenship. A citizen from a *municipium* was qualified to hold any public office. An example is Cicero, who was not from Rome but from the *municipium* of Arpinum.

Novus Homo Literally, "new man." A man who is the first of his family to hold a curule office in Rome, giving his family the status of nobiles.

October Horse, the Each year, in mid-October, a horse race was held in honor of Mars. The winning horse was sacrificed and beheaded, then the men of two city districts, the Via Sacra and the Subura, fought over the head, each trying to carry it back to their own district, where it would be displayed and bring the district good fortune for the next year. It was a rite so old that the Romans no longer remembered why they did it.

Offices A Tribune was a representative of the plebeians with power to introduce laws and to veto actions of the Senate. Only plebeians could hold the office, which carried no *imperium*. Military tribunes were elected from among the young men of senatorial or equestrian rank to be assistants to generals. Usually it was the first step of a man's political career.

A Roman embarked on a political career had to rise through a regular chain of offices. The lowest elective office was ***quaestor***: bookkeeper and paymaster for the treasury, the grain office, and the provincial governors. These men did the scut work of the Empire.

Next were the **aediles**. They were more or less city managers who saw to the upkeep of public buildings, streets, sewers, markets, and the like. There were two types: the **plebeian aediles**, and the **curule aediles**. The curule aediles could sit in judgment on civil cases involving markets and currency, while the plebeian aediles could only levy fines. Otherwise, their duties were the same. They also put on the public games. The government allowance for these things was laughably small, so they had to pay for them out of their own pockets. It was a horrendously expensive office but it gained the holder popularity like no other, especially if his games were spectacular. Only a popular aedile could hope for election to higher office.

Third was **praetor**, an office with real power. Praetors were judges, but they could command armies and after a year in office they could go out to govern provinces, where real wealth could be won, earned, or stolen. In the late Republic there were eight praetors. Senior was the **praetor urbanus**, who heard civil cases, between citizens of Rome. The **praetor peregrinus** heard cases involving foreigners. The others presided over criminal courts. After leaving office, the ex-praetors became **propraetors** and went to govern propraetorian provinces with full *imperium*.

The highest office was **consul**. Supreme office of power during the Roman Republic. Two were elected each year. For four years they fulfilled the political role of royal authority, bringing all other magistrates into the service of the people and the city of Rome. The office carried full *imperium*. On the expiration of his year in office, the ex-consul was usually assigned a district outside Rome to rule as **proconsul**. As proconsul, he had the same insignia and the same number of lictors. His power was absolute within his province. The most important commands always went to proconsuls.

Censors were elected every five years. It was the capstone to a political career but it did not carry *imperium* and there was no foreign command afterward. Censors conducted the census, purged the senate of unworthy members, and doled out the public contracts.They could forbid certain religious practices or luxuries deemed bad for public morals or generally "un-Roman." There were two censors, and each could overrule the other. They were usually elected from among the ex-consuls, and the censorship was regarded as the capstone of a political career.

Under the Sullan Constitution, the **quaestorship** was the minimum requirement for membership in the Senate. The majority of senators had held that office and never held another. Membership in the Senate was for life unless expelled by the censors.

No Roman official could be prosecuted while in office, but he could be after he stepped down. Malfeasance in office was one of the most common court charges.

The most extraordinary office was **dictator**. In times of emergency, the senate could instruct the consuls to appoint a dictator, who could wield absolute power for six months. Unlike all other officials, a dictator was unaccountable: He could not be prosecuted for his acts in office. The last true dictator was appointed in the third century B.C. The dictatorships of Sulla and Julius Caesar were unconstitutional.

Patrician   The noble class of Rome.

Plebeian   All citizens not of patrician status; the lower classes, also called **plebs.**

Popular Assemblies   There were three: the centuriate assembly (**comitia centuriata**) and the two tribal assemblies: comitia tributa and **consilium plebis, q.v.**

Populares   The party of the common people.

Princeps: **"First Citizen"**   An especially distinguished senator chosen by the censors. His name was the first called on the roll of the Senate and he was first to speak on any issue. Later the title was usurped by Augustus and is the origin of the word "prince."

Priesthoods   In Rome, the priesthoods were offices of state. There were two major classes: **pontifexes** and *flamens*. Pontifexes were members of the highest priestly college of Rome. They had superintendence over all sacred observances, state and private, and over the calendar. Head of their college was the ***pontifex maximus***, a title held to this day by the pope. The *flamens* were the high priests of the state gods: the ***Flamen Martialis*** for Mars, the ***Flamin Quirinalis*** for the deified Romulus, and, highest of all, the ***Flamen Dialis***, high priest of Jupiter. The *Flamen Dialis* celebrated the Ides of each month and could not take part in politics, although he could attend meetings of the Senate, attended by a single lictor. Each had charge of the daily sacrifices wore distinctive headgear,and were surrounded by many ritual taboos.

Another very ancient priesthood was the ***Rex Sacrorum***, "King of Sacrifices." This priest had to be a patrician and had to observe even more taboos than the *Flamen Dialis*. This position was so onerous that it became difficult to find a patrician willing to take it.

Technically, pontifexes and *flamens* did not take part in public business except to solemnize oaths and treaties, give the god's stamp of approval to declarations of war, etc. But since they were all senators anyway, the ban had little meaning. Julius Caesar was *pontifex maximus* while he was out conquering Gaul, even though the *pontifex maximus* wasn't supposed to look upon human blood.

Rostra (sing. rostrum) A monument in the Forum commemorating the sea battle of Antium in 338 B.C., decorated with the rams, *rostra,* of enemy ships. Its base was used as an orator's platform.

Saturnalia Feast of Saturn, December 17–23, a raucous and jubilant occasion when gifts were exchanged, debts were settled, and masters waited on their slaves.

Senate Rome's chief deliberative body. It consisted of three hundred to six hundred men, all of whom had won elective office at least once. It was a leading element in the emergence of the Republic, but later suffered degradation at the hands of Sulla.

Sibylline Books These mysterious books of prophecies were brought to Rome in legendary times and were kept by a college of priests called, in pedantic Roman fashion, the *Quinquedecemviri* (the Fifteen Men). In times of extraordinary calamity the Senate could order a consultation of the Sybilline Books. The prophecies were usually interpreted to mean that the gods wanted a foreign deity brought to Rome. Thus Rome built a temple to Ceres, a goddess of Asia Minor, and others. When the deity was Greek, the rites remained in the Greek rather than the Roman fashion.

Soothsayers The Roman government used two types: First were the **augurs**. These were actual officials who belonged to a college and it was a great honor for a Roman to be adopted into the College of Augurs. They interpreted omens involving heavenly signs: lightning and thunder, the flight and other behavior of birds, etc. There were strict guidelines for this and personal inspiration was not involved. An augur could call a halt to all public business while he watched for omens. The augur wore a special, striped robe called a *toga trabaea* and carried a crook-topped staff called a *lituus,* which survives to this day as a part of the Roman Catholic bishop's regalia.

The second type was the **haruspex** (pl. **haruspices**). These were not officials but professional soothsayers and most were Etruscans. They took omens by examining the livers and other organs of sacrificial animals. Highly educated Romans considered them fraudulent but the plebs insisted on taking the *haruspices* (the term also referred to the omens themselves) before embarking on any important public project.

Official Roman soothsayers did *not* predict the future, a practice that was, in fact, forbidden by law. Omens were taken to determine the will of the gods *at that time*. They had to be taken repeatedly because the gods could always change their minds.

SPQR *Senatus populusque Romanus.* The Senate and people of Rome. The formula embodying the sovereignty of Rome. It was used on official correspondence, documents, and public works.

Tarpeian Rock A cliff beneath the Capitol from which traitors were hurled. It was named for the Roman maiden Tarpeia who, according to legend, betrayed the Capitol to the Sabines.

Temple of Saturn The state treasury was located in a crypt beneath this temple. It was also the repository for military standards.

Temple of Vesta Site of the sacred fire tended by the vestal virgins and dedicated to the goddess of the hearth. Documents, especially wills, were deposited there for safekeeping.

Toga The outer robe of the Roman citizen. It was white for the upper class, darker for the poor and for people in mourning. The **toga praetexta**, bordered with a purple stripe, was worn by *curule* magistrates, by state priests when performing their functions, and by boys prior to manhood. The **toga picta,** purple and embroidered with golden stars, was worn by a general when celebrating a triumph, also by a magistrate when giving public games.

Transtiber   A newer district on the left or western bank of the Tiber. It lay beyond the old city walls.

Triumvir   A member of a triumvirate—a board or college of three men. Most famously, the three-man rule of Caesar, Pompey, and Crassus. Later, the triumvirate of Antonius, Octavian, and Lepidus.

Vigiles   A night watchman. The *vigiles* had the duty of apprehending felons caught committing crimes, but their main duty was as a fire watch. They were unarmed except for staves and carried fire buckets.

Witches   The Romans recognized three types. Most common were *saga,* "wise women" who were simply herbalists and specialists in traditional cures for disease and injury. More ominous were *striga,* true witches ("strega" still means witch in modern Italian). These could cast spells, had the power of the evil eye, could lay curses, and so forth. Most feared were *venefica* "poisoners." Ancient peoples had a supernatural dread of poison and lumped its use together with sorcery rather than pharmacology. The punishments for poisoning were dreadful even by Roman standards. The Romans associated all forms of witchcraft and magic with the Marsians, a neighbor people who spoke the Oscan dialect.